ALSO BY MA...

Memories Live Here

ALTERED PAST

ALTERED PAST

CHERL
BOOK 2

MARC SHEINBAUM

ROUGH
EDGES
PRESS

Altered Past
Paperback Edition
Copyright © 2024 Marc Sheinbaum

Rough Edges Press
An Imprint of Wolfpack Publishing
1707 E. Diana Street
Tampa, FL 33610

roughedgespress.com

Paperback ISBN 978-1-68549-713-2
eBook ISBN 978-1-68549-415-5
LCCN 2024939687

To my mother and father

ALTERED PAST

ALTERED PAST

CHAPTER
ONE

ALINA SIPPED on her cosmo as she anticipated her opportunity. Buford Chambers slurped down another Bluepoint oyster which he chased with his second Macallan on the rocks. Having pegged him in the three-drink-minimum category, Alina was not surprised when he motioned for another round.

"How about you?" he asked her when the waiter arrived. Alina politely shook her head. The devious expression worn by the sixty-four-year-old executive signaled that she needed to stay in full possession of her faculties. Tonight was too important.

"Come on, little lady. Your profile said you liked to party." He pointed at her glass. "You've barely touched yours. I feel like I'm drinking alone."

Alina seductively raised an eyebrow. "Dulls the senses," she whispered.

Chambers smiled. "Well, then, Dina. We can't have any of *that*, can we?"

Alina lifted a shell and slid an oyster into her mouth, keeping her green eyes locked on the man she and her handler had targeted on the sugar daddy website. Chambers would have assumed that the discreet SugarConnections site had sorted through "over two hundred personal attributes, preferences, and desires" to find the perfect "sugar baby" for his needs. But it didn't take long for someone with Alina's skills to hack the basic system underlying this type of website. She had ensured her profile would be matched with the CEO of Aztec Enterprises.

When his third drink arrived, the heavyset Chambers stood and excused himself. "Nature calls."

Good, she thought. This would be easier now that she didn't need to concoct an elaborate distraction while floating her hand over his glass. She checked her watch. It was ten fifteen. She estimated they'd be back at the hotel in about an hour—thirty minutes to eat their main course, another twenty or so to linger over dessert, and then a ten-minute ride to the Waldorf. Chambers had consumed so much alcohol, Alina almost decided to start him out with only a small dose of her narcotic. She could add more back at the hotel if she needed to. But she had learned an important lesson from her first and almost disastrous encounter with the man who had used the code name Tuxedo. It was better to slip these men too much GHB rather than too little.

She removed a vial from her purse and in one nonchalant move, emptied the full contents into Chambers's scotch, keeping a watchful eye for her "date." She gave the drink a quick stir with her finger and returned the empty vial to her bag.

When Chambers returned, instead of remaining on his end of the three-sided booth, he slid over until their legs touched. "That's better," he said. "It felt like we were on opposite ends of the restaurant."

Alina fought the urge to move away. Instead, she leaned into him and said, "I was wondering why you were sitting so far away." She placed her hand on his thigh. "I thought maybe you were afraid of me."

"Me?" he asked, his feigned shock morphing into a

wide grin. "Why should I be afraid?" Then, moving closer, he whispered, "What's going to happen to me?"

She smiled slightly, and Chambers straightened when the waiter arrived with their main courses. Over the next few minutes, she watched him devour his oversized portion of veal parmigiana. Still, he managed to banter between bites.

"I'm on the road all year," he started. "It's important that I can unwind and relax. The stress is incredible."

"I'm sure," she said.

"My wife's a great gal," he said. "It's just…"

She nodded. "You've grown apart."

"Exactly." He smiled. "And I have so much to offer."

She picked at her overcooked scallops, eating slowly so the GHB had time to slice through his bloodstream, while she fed Chambers her well-honed responses: The pressures of running a company must be enormous, and a young woman like her could benefit from his support and guidance as she navigated her nascent career in advertising.

"I think that an…arrangement," she said as Chambers polished off his drink, "could benefit both of us."

Chambers gave her an appreciative look and signaled for the waiter.

"Bring me another scotch," Chambers said.

A potential miscalculation on her part, Alina thought. Another drink and Chambers might not make it back to his hotel room. Sure enough, after polishing off his fourth drink, Chambers rose and seemed to wobble. She stood and slipped her arm through his as he focused his attention on his phone. He managed to steady the device long enough to pay the bill and summon his autonomous car. She tried to hold him firmly as they walked past the maître d'.

"Don't you have a briefcase?" she asked as they stopped for their coats. He wouldn't be her first mark to forget his laptop at the coat check.

"Iz back at the hotel," he slurred as he walked unsteadily into the cold Chicago evening, where his car was already waiting by the curb.

On the ride to the Waldorf, Chambers squinted through half-shut eyelids and garbled his words. The GHB was impacting him too quickly. How was she going to get him into the hotel?

"Buford," Alina said. "Don't sleep yet, honey." She slowly ran her hand up and down his thigh as she whispered into his ear. "Come on, Buford. We have a long night ahead of us."

Chambers's eyes opened wide, and he smiled as the car turned onto a brightly lit street and came to a stop. Alina exited the car and came around to help Chambers from the vehicle. He leaned his two-hundred-plus-pound frame on her as he staggered through the lobby of the Waldorf and rode the elevator to the twenty-third floor. Alina guided him to room 2306, which she helped him unlock with his smartphone. Chambers stumbled past her and made his way into the bathroom, shutting the door behind him. Good, she thought. Let him pass out on the toilet. He wouldn't be the first unconscious man she'd undressed.

Alina placed her purse on the desk and spotted Chambers's computer case on top of the minifridge. When she heard the toilet flush, she decided to wait a few minutes before removing his laptop. He'd be out cold soon enough. But moments later, the bathroom door swung open, and Chambers stood in the doorway.

He was completely naked, and his pale, flabby abdomen draped over his sagging genitals.

Alina swallowed hard.

"Guess I had a little jet lag there for a minute," the CEO said, rubbing the back of his neck. He approached her, extending his arms. "Now, how about we consummate that arrangement?"

Alina's hands shook. How had she misjudged so

badly? Chambers approached and wrapped his arms around her slender frame. He slid his hand down her back and onto her butt, giving her a rough squeeze. She felt him grinding into her. She smelled the alcohol on his breath as he planted his lips on her neck.

"Buford," she said, gently pushing away. "At least offer a girl a drink."

"Great idea," he said. He released her and padded to the minibar. "What'll it be?"

"How about we do a couple of shots," she said. "Tequila for me."

Chambers grinned and bent down to remove several mini-bottles of tequila and scotch while Alina moved as casually as she could toward the desk where she'd left her bag. While Chambers poured their drinks, she snapped open the purse without a sound, locating her contingency vial—the extra dosage she kept in case of such emergencies. She flicked the lid up with her thumb and hid her hand behind her back as she slowly moved to the edge of the bed. Chambers came over with the drinks and placed the glasses on the nightstand. When they sat down, Alina drew him toward her and reached behind him, stretching her arm enough to empty the dose into his scotch. His hands moved up the sides of her breasts as she dropped the now-empty vial behind the nightstand.

"Buford," she protested. "Our drinks."

Chambers smiled and handed her the tequila as he drank his scotch in two long gulps. And then he turned his attention back to Alina, undoing the buttons on the back of her silk blouse before pushing her down on the bed.

Alina's heart was pounding. Every instinct she had developed over the past few months signaled that she should abort. But if this was to be the last of these denigrating assignments, she needed to complete this mission, and in order to do that, she needed the CEO of Aztec Enterprises to be unconscious.

He finished removing her blouse. As he unclipped her

bra, she told herself she needed to hang in there only a little longer. He had enough narcotic in him to put down a horse. He rolled on top of her, pressing onto her slender frame. She positioned her right thigh between his legs, readying her knee for an upward strike, when her mother's words drifted in, seeming to freeze Alina's movements:

These encounters are an unfortunate hazard of the approach. When I find myself in these situations, I try to take myself mentally to a different place. I think about why I am here. I visualize my homeland…Whatever takes my mind away from being present.

Alina squeezed her eyes shut and lowered her leg. And then Chambers was inside of her. Yet she felt nothing, as if she were the one anesthetized. Her mind vacant, she thought of nothing.

Moments later, he was done, and it was as if a light switch went off. Alina felt the full weight of Chambers's two hundred-plus pounds as he collapsed, his head sinking into the pillow beside her.

"Asshole," she said, her brain back in the present again as she slid out from underneath his immobile torso and ran to the bathroom. She took a small hand towel and cleaned herself of his residue. Not wanting to waste this extra "insurance," she carefully wrapped the towel in the ice bucket's plastic bag. She turned to start the shower and noticed a glass mirror sitting on the sink with the remains of a white powder. Alina wiped the mirror with her pinky and licked her finger.

"Cocaine?" she said out loud. At least it explained Chambers's sudden revival. She started the shower, stepped underneath the spray while it was still warming, and began scrubbing herself with a washcloth. When she was done, she turned off the water and reached for a towel, but she stopped, remembering Chambers inside of her. She turned the shower back on, lathered up, and washed again, harder and longer this time, before allowing the spray to pour over every part of her body. She made the water cooler, but her insides were still burning.

She swore that nothing like this would ever happen to her again.

Fifteen minutes later she was toweling herself and standing next to the bed in a hotel bathrobe. She checked on the lump of humanity.

He was out cold.

Alina retrieved Chambers's phone and laptop from his briefcase and brought the devices to the bed.

With all the narcotics in him, she had plenty of time to finish what she had come to do.

CHAPTER
TWO

ONE YEAR EARLIER

"I'M VERY proud of you, kroshka," her father said over lamb shashlik at their favorite St. Petersburg café. The smoky aroma of the grilled meat and onions wafted throughout the empty eatery. Outside, the sky was light blue and there was a comfortable breeze, but her father had insisted they sit inside, away from the outdoor tables crowded with people enjoying the mid-spring day.

"Thanks, Papa," Alina said.

"Are you excited?" her father asked.

"It's overwhelming," she admitted, running her hand over the leatherbound folder sitting on the table between them. Alina wanted to open the cover one more time, to stare at the letters written across the diploma tacked inside, to make sure it was real. That she had in fact officially graduated from Moscow's most prestigious university with a combined bachelor's and master's degree in computer engineering, where she focused on artificial intelligence. With her life set to launch, her father had invited her for a talk, and Alina had prepared herself for another one of the intense conversations they'd shared over the years. She knew all his favorite lines. "You're strong, kroshka" or "You need to push harder, my kroshka." Her father rarely called her Alina, preferring her pet name. While it meant "my little one," the twenty-seven-year-old Alina had long ago grown into her five-foot-seven-inch frame.

The deep lines around Grigory Petrov's eyes and his closely cropped gray beard may have made him look much older than his sixty years, but his intense focus remained. An intensity she knew made him a successful oil executive early in his career, before her mother's death —Alina had been just two years old when her mother succumbed to breast cancer—and then an effective English teacher at the International Academy, the school Alina had attended in St. Petersburg.

But on this beautiful late April day, when other diners were enjoying the warming rays of the sun, her father had selected a table hidden in the dark recesses of the café. She steadied herself, expecting to hear his opinions on each of her four job offers. But she soon realized her father had something else on his mind.

"Life can be overwhelming," he said, casually removing the lamb and vegetables from a skewer. "How many offers do you have now?"

"Three," she said. "Four if you count the start-up in Albania."

He waved his hand and said, "Out of the question."

"I know," she said, smiling. "That's why I said three." Another topic of their many discussions over the past year had been his perception of small Albanian companies. "Too many pockets need to be stuffed to have a chance of success," he had said.

She told him about the companies whose offers she was considering—a Berlin-based satellite company, a telecommunications provider in Prague, and a software business located in Istanbul specializing in artificial intelligence. The pull of AI, and of experiencing life in a dynamic city, placed the Turkish company at the top of her list. Besides, she had no job offers that would keep her in Russia. In fact, all her fellow classmates were leaving the motherland for jobs throughout Europe. She hoped her father would understand what she had to do.

"All fine places to work," he said. "I am sure you will make the right choice." He wiped his mouth, adding, "Once you know everything you need to know."

She braced herself, watching him slowly chew his food.

"All right, Papa. What do I need to know?"

He slid his plate away.

"Do you love your country, Alina?"

She pushed her plate away, too, and met his gaze. "Yes, Papa. You know I do."

But her assurance had never stopped her father from expounding on the many qualities of Mother Russia: the rich culture, the traditions, the landscape—the last being what he always referred to as "the soul of the people." She had heard this sermon throughout her childhood but only recently wondered about her nationalistic father's many contradictions. His penchant for bootlegged American movies; the hours he spent poring over Western news sites; and his decision to take a job—and to educate his only daughter—at a private school in St. Petersburg that catered to the children of Western expats and wealthy Russians.

Her father continued, "It is certainly not perfect. But this is our only homeland." She knew where this was leading—he wanted her to keep searching for a position in Russia. But with an economy severely damaged by ceaseless Western sanctions imposed in response to the Ukrainian operation, her prospects for finding a meaningful—and high-paying—role that would allow her to stay had all but evaporated. Still, her stubborn father was not going to support her moving to Turkey or Germany or any of the places thousands of young, educated Russians were decamping to. Alina slumped in her seat, preparing herself for a lecture. But instead, her father's expression softened and he said, "There is something I need to tell you about your mother."

Alina straightened. She placed her wineglass on the table, attentive as she always became during her father's sporadic recollections of the mother she barely knew. As his gaze locked on hers, he brought his hands to his lips as if in prayer and his shoulders sagged.

"Please understand," he started. "I chose not to share this while you were being educated. I did not want distractions or detours. Until you became strong enough to…understand our history."

"What history?" she asked.

"Please, kroshka. I will tell you. You can form your own conclusion about how everything ended for her."

"Is this about her cancer?" Alina asked.

He reached for her hand.

"Alina, your mother was a hero."

She shook her head, startled by the word. There was a portrait in Alina's mind from the stories her father had shared over the years. Of a mother who had been the first in her family to attend university; a supportive wife who agreed to relocate to Lithuania so her husband could oversee a Russian oil company's interests in Europe; a social and outgoing woman, and a doting mother, who was diagnosed with untreatable breast cancer just a year after Alina was born. Alina recalled all the details her father had been willing to share but had few, if any, memories of her own. Yet her father had never used the word *hero* before.

"I don't understand," she said softly. "How was she a hero?"

"This was a long time ago, kroshka. Our country—

the Soviet Union—was breaking apart. We were all proud Russians, but in the nineties, we became untethered to the world as we knew it. All of us trying to find our way."

Alina pulled her hand away from his and asked, "What does any of this have to do with Mama?"

"Your mother loved her country, too. She saw the future. She believed the West sought to keep us weak."

Alina shrugged. "I know our history, Papa. Many people felt that way back then."

"Including a faction of our own government," he said. "They believed the same as your mother. That America feared a resurgent Russia. That..." Her father stopped as the waiter arrived to clear their plates and ask whether they needed anything else.

"Two black teas," Grigory said.

As the waiter left, her father's eyes turned fierce. "Your mother believed America wanted Russia to fail," he whispered.

Her mother's political views had never been part of the details her father had shared in the past. But now he took a deep breath and continued, as if the floodgates of his consciousness had finally opened and he was relieved to let his memories flow out.

"Your mother was always a woman of action," he said. "They thought she had the perfect personality for this assignment. She—"

"What assignment?" Alina asked.

But her father continued as if he already had his words planned out. "She enjoyed meeting people from all over—it came naturally to her, moving in and out of many different social circles, trying to learn what she could. She knew how to ask the right questions, in just the right way, so people opened up. She learned their habits. Their desires and wishes." He stared at Alina and added, "And their weaknesses."

Alina felt her heartbeat accelerate, but she sat motion-less, disoriented, as she tried to process her father's words against the hazy image she had of her mother. Her father pressed on. "Most of the information she gathered was useless. But some of it was not. She could never be sure, so she passed it all on to her handlers."

"Wait," Alina said. She leaned closer. "Mama gathered information? For handlers?" She stared at her father as she absorbed the meaning of his words. "Are you trying to tell me that Mama was some sort of spy?"

Her father placed his hand on Alina's arm as the waiter arrived with two steaming mugs. After the server left, her father glanced around the still-empty café before saying, "Not really a spy, kroshka. Nothing like your American movies. No, your mother was what we called… a scout. She looked for information. To make sure there were no miscalculations. No wrong interpretations." He sipped on his tea. "You've studied history, kroshka. You know that many conflicts emerge from the smallest of misunderstandings. That's really what we saw as our mission."

"*We?*" Alina repeated, staring at her father. He slowly nodded, and Alina merged what he was admitting with what he had always fed her as the truth. "Was this when we lived in Vilnius?" she asked. "When she was pregnant with me? Before she got sick?"

Her father let out a long, slow breath. After a few moments, he said, "Alina, we never lived in Lithuania. And I never worked for an oil company."

Alina felt as if the walls of the café had started to shift around her. She slid her chair away but held on to the sides of the table, afraid she would fall to the floor.

"That was the story the intelligence service created for our return to Russia," he continued. "I couldn't tell our family and friends where we had really been." He paused before adding, "And what really happened to your mother."

Alina stared at her father, but it was as if she no longer recognized the man sitting across from her.

"Kroshka, your mother and I lived undercover in America for over five years. In Chicago—that is where you were born. Where your mother and I worked for Russian intelligence..." He paused, then added, "At least, until your mother disappeared."

CHAPTER
THREE

FIVE THOUSAND MILES and nine time zones away, Lucas Foley checked his watch. It was ten minutes past four in the morning. "Where is he?" Lucas asked as he stared out the windshield of the FBI's unmarked cargo van. He peered down the dark and deserted road leading to the single entrance to the scrapyard, piles of pancaked cars stacked on either side.

"Dunno, man," DeMarcus Miller said, his voice shaking. Lucas looked at the informant sitting beside him in the passenger seat. While perspiration was beading on Miller's forehead, his teeth were chattering. He had been busted transporting a kilo of cocaine up I-57 and, facing twenty years to life, had quickly decided to cooperate with the FBI.

Lucas reached over and grabbed the pencil-thin gangbanger by the arm. "You gotta calm down."

"Gonna die, man," Miller said. "Fuckers'll kill me."

"You're not gonna die, DeMarcus," Lucas said. "This is a business transaction. As soon as we confirm these guys brought the coke, my team will move in. Our boys in witness protection are already working up your new ID cards." But Lucas was also trying to steady his own racing heartbeat as he anxiously awaited his informant's contacts from the notorious Rojas Cartel.

Miller pulled a flask from his jacket and unscrewed the top. He took two quick gulps before Lucas snatched it away.

"Come on," Lucas said. "I don't need you passing out on me."

Miller looked like he was about to argue the point when a pair of headlights appeared through the early-morning fog.

"Game time," Lucas said as he straightened in his seat. He touched the communication device hidden in his ear and said, "You guys are in listening mode only. Wait for my signal."

"Copy that." The response came back in his ear.

Lucas looked at Miller, who was still sweating profusely. "I promise, DeMarcus. I'm not gonna let anything happen to you."

Miller nodded rapidly as the glare from the approaching vehicle grew brighter. A dark SUV came to a stop several feet away. Lucas rolled down his window, keeping his right hand wrapped around the Glock hidden beneath his thigh. The doors of the SUV opened, but the high beams made it difficult to see anything more than emerging shadows. As the two silhouettes moved through the cold Chicago night, Lucas saw they were both burly, dark-skinned men wearing business suits and ties. The one on the left had a bushy beard beneath a bald head; the other was clean-shaven and wearing a Chicago Bears ski hat.

They both carried semiautomatic rifles.

"Shit," Lucas whispered.

The men surveyed the area around the van before the bald man stepped forward and pointed his weapon at Lucas.

"Get the fuck outta the car!" he shouted.

"Stay in the van," a voice instructed through Lucas's earpiece. "We're moving in."

"Negative," Lucas whispered, his heart pounding. "Hold your position." His hand was shaking as he lowered his window. He had to de-escalate. "Gentlemen," he shouted firmly. "Do we really need the guns?"

"I said get da fuck out!" the bald man shouted. "'Less ya wanna bleed where ya sit."

Lucas took a deep breath then called out, "That's fine. You can kill us and take our money. But you'll have to explain to your bosses why you screwed up an opportunity for ten times what I'm carrying. I'll let you decide." Lucas had positioned himself as a man named Luke with the potential to be a major distributor of the cartel's product —a real estate investor with loads of Daddy's cash and warehouses perfect for processing and distributing cocaine. "I've got other options," he added.

"Nobody's robbin' nobody," a voice called out from the direction of the SUV.

Lucas watched as a tall, slim figure approached the gun-toting men from behind. The man was bundled up in an overcoat. On his feet, a pair of red high-top basketball shoes. Lucas's jaw dropped as the man moved toward the van and his facial features came into focus. Lucas had spent days studying video footage and intelligence reports on the entire Rojas Cartel leadership structure. While the man's long face was partially hidden behind a short, boxed beard, there was little doubt Lucas's operation had brought out one of the cartel's rising captains.

Barely loud enough for his earpiece to pick up his voice, he whispered, "I think Mateo Lozano is here."

CHAPTER
FOUR

AFTER LEAVING THE CAFÉ, Alina and her father walked into the Summer Garden toward the palace of Peter the Great. They stood in front of the Carp Pond, and Alina stared into the water, looking for the namesake fish. The surface was calm, but Alina's mind and heartbeat were racing, her memories wrecked as she absorbed the shock of her father's lies. About her own place of birth. About her parents' secret life as spies or scouts or whatever they called themselves. And about her mother's "disappearance." After all these years being told her mother had died of cancer, was it possible the mother she'd never known was still alive? In America? Alina pulled her coat collar around her neck to block the cold air, but she couldn't stop shaking from the anger surging through her.

What else had been a lie? Why had her father kept all this from her? Why choose this moment to reveal the truth, after all these years? Thousands of questions were crisscrossing through her jumbled thoughts, struggling to get organized. So she did what she always did when she felt overwhelmed—she summoned the analytic part of her brain, a gift her father claimed Alina inherited from her long-lost mother. A practice that steadied Alina, calmed her in times of stress and brought her into focus. And she was desperate for that focus to help her now.

She placed her hands on her hips and faced her father. "I need you to start at the beginning."

He closed his eyes and nodded.

"Did you really meet when you were students? Or was that a story, too?"

"That part is true," her father said. "But we didn't meet until our final year at Peoples' Friendship University. And not the way I've always told you." Grigory pushed his hands deeper into his coat pockets, his eyes seemingly transfixed on the pond. "Your mother and I were young and idealistic back then. I was studying economics. She was at the Tourism Institute. But we didn't know each other." He faced Alina. "Not until the Foreign Intelligence Service, the SVR, recruited us. I learned they'd had their eye on me since I had been part of the Communist youth. They knew I was a patriot. They were targeting economists who could help them infiltrate Western companies."

"And what did they want with my mother?" Alina asked.

"Your mother?" He smiled. "They saw a beautiful, smart woman who was at ease with foreigners. That's why she studied hospitality. She knew there would be opportunities as our country opened up to the world."

Alina drew in a deep breath and slowly exhaled. At least that part hadn't been a complete lie. He had always said her mother planned to work in tourism.

"Let's walk," he said, and she followed him down a garden path toward the palace as he recalled their unconventional introduction. "When the intelligence service presented their proposition, I was the one who felt the call of duty. Your mother saw adventure, at least at the beginning. It wasn't until later that she became the true ideologue."

They stopped as two young women pushed strollers up from behind. Her father waited for them to pass before continuing. "The intelligence director liked our comple-ment of skills, so we were assembled as a team."

Assembled? Her parents were *assembled* into a "spy team" —not college students introduced by a mutual friend, as she'd always been told, but thrown together, courtesy of Russia's intelligence service? "Did you even like each other?" she asked her father.

"Our rapport improved over time," he said. "The training program lasted almost three years. Your mother was ready to deploy well before I was. I struggled with my English. Of course, your mother's was perfect. Not a trace of an accent." His eyes locked on Alina's, and he added, "Almost as perfect as yours."

Alina barely registered the allusion to her own language skills. Most of her classmates at the International Academy had mastered fluent, unaccented English.

"For a while," her father said, "our leaders discussed pairing her with a different partner and sending her off to the US. They might have if the program had another man at the ready. That's how excited they were to see what your mother could do in the field."

They approached a large fountain and stood with a group of Chinese tourists watching streams of water shoot into the air. When the crowd dispersed, her father spoke again. "Your mother convinced them to keep us together. She said we had come too far, and she didn't want to put in the work with an alternate. But I thought…" He turned away, but not before Alina noticed something she had never seen before from her stoic father. There was moisture forming in the corners of his eyes. "I thought there was something building between us. Some-thing true. And that we would be more than just… partners."

Over the years, Alina's father had shown scant emotion when telling stories of her mother, rarely delving beyond his benign recollections—recollections Alina now understood were nothing more than a ruse. But the more he unwound his lies, the more his emotional barrier seemed to fall away. Perhaps that was why, as they resumed their stroll, Alina felt her own anger starting to evaporate, along with the tension that made every step she took so unsteady. After proceeding several paces in silence, she asked, "When did you finally go to America?"

"We deployed to Canada in 1994 for an initial transition period. That's where we took on our new identity. It is where your mother and I became Harold and Diane Backus."

"Backus?"

"We had people on the ground in Toronto. The real Harold and Diane died in a car accident. They had immigrated from Lithuania as teenagers. Our team accessed their records, renewed their Canadian driver's licenses and passports with our photos. The Canadian government never ties public records back to death certificates. At least, they didn't back then." He shrugged before adding, "It seems Canadians simply live on."

Alina crinkled her nose as if the fetid scent of dug up gravesites had wafted over the garden. The sensation subsided as they resumed their walk toward the Summer Palace.

"We drove to America later that year," he continued. "Our handlers secured a part-time teaching position for me at the University of Chicago. In economics, of course. At first, I was worried my accent would draw attention. But people accepted the story of my Lithuanian upbringing. Westerners do not have an ear for accents. Within a year, I was offered an adjunct professor position, my ticket to social functions where I could get to know important people." He let out a slight laugh and shook his head. "But I never was a very good scout. I did my best to gather whatever I could. None of it turned out to be very useful."

"And what did my mother do in Chicago?"

"She applied for an entry position at a famous hotel—the Drake—very popular with diplomats and traveling businessmen. With her beauty, her personality, the hotel's young general manager couldn't wait for her to start." A crowd was gathering by the palace in the distance, so he motioned for Alina to stop and join him at one of the benches lining the walkway.

"She started working in the hotel's back office," he said after they sat. "But she talked her way into a job at the concierge desk—a perfect place to meet important visitors." He looked at Alina, his eyes watery again, and added, "Many looking for company."

Alina felt her body shudder as he went on. "Your mother would also join me at university conferences. She was amazing at working a room. I'd point out the professors I knew who were consulting with American corporations, and, well, she knew how to…attract their attention."

"How exactly did she do that?"

He looked toward the palace. "We rarely shared specifics of our tactics, kroshka."

"I thought you were partners!"

Her father seemed to be searching for the right words. Finally, he took a deep breath. His eyes now dry, he said, "Kroshka, some things were just better left unsaid."

CHAPTER
FIVE

IT HAD TAKEN six months of smaller-sized transactions before DeMarcus Miller's street contacts had been willing to connect "Luke" with their Rojas Cartel source. Besides vouching for the "rich white boy," Miller had spread the word that Luke had built a network of high-end dealers from Detroit to Minneapolis and was well positioned to keep product flowing to wealthy clientele.

It seemed tonight Mateo Enrique Lozano had come to personally oversee the delivery of seventy kilos of cocaine. And, perhaps, to size up his potential new partner. Moles within the Rojas Cartel described Lozano as a rising and ruthless star, charged with opening new distribution channels in the Midwest.

Lucas tightened his grip on the Glock. The tall man walked to within ten feet of the van and stopped. "My men need to make sure neither of you is armed," he said.

"Well, we have no weapons," Lucas said. "And we're not coming out when there are guns pointed at our heads."

The man Lucas was certain was Lozano snapped his fingers. His associates in the suits lowered their rifles. Lucas exhaled slowly and slipped the Glock from beneath his thigh and into a hidden compartment between the seat and the center console. He wiped his sweaty palms on his slacks and opened the door.

"Let's go," he said to Miller as he stepped out.

"We're fucked," Miller whispered.

"Just follow the plan," Lucas urged, and Miller finally opened the door. The bald man slowly came forward and patted Lucas down without noticing the listening device hidden in his ear, while the man in the Bears cap frisked Miller. Finding no weapons, the men stepped back, and Lozano approached.

"Forgive my associates," Lozano said. "I pay these men to worry about my safety."

"Yeah, well, I don't need the Scarface routine," Lucas said as he brushed off the lapel of the Canali blazer he'd borrowed from the FBI's property room. "Do you have the product?"

Lozano pulled out a gold cigarette case and said, "My friend. You are in a rush?" He clicked the case open, revealing a mirrored interior that held a white powdery substance. The bald man handed his boss a credit card, which Lozano used to create two neat lines. "Pleasure before business, no?"

The man in the ski hat held out a dollar bill rolled up to form a small straw. Lozano snorted a line and held the mirror toward Lucas. But Lucas had never tried any type of drug, not even marijuana. He wasn't about to start tonight. He waved Lozano's offer away. "Allergies," he said.

Lozano's eyes narrowed. "My product is pure."

But as Lucas tapped his heart and said, "Please do not be insulted," Miller stepped forward, reached for the makeshift straw, and quickly snorted a line. Lucas restrained himself from smacking his drug-addicted informant as Miller cleared his nostrils and said, "It's good, man."

"I'm glad you are pleased," Lozano said as he closed

the cigarette case and turned to Lucas. "May I ask to see my money?"

Lucas motioned for Lozano to follow him toward the rear of the Ford van as the bodyguards and Miller followed. Lucas opened the cargo door, reached in, and slid two Samsonite suitcases to the ground. He kneeled down and unzipped them both, revealing packets of US currency. Lucas held one packet up for inspection, but Lozano bent down and picked up a different stack.

"They're all the same," Lucas said, surprised at how calm his voice sounded given how rapidly his heart was racing. "One-hundred-dollar bills bundled in five-thou-sand-dollar packets."

"I have never been the trusting type," Lozano said as he randomly inspected the packets. After flipping through several, he tossed the money back into the suitcase.

"I'm an honest businessman," Lucas said. He closed each of the Samsonite bags and held them by the handles. "Now, where is my product?"

Lozano motioned him toward the SUV, and they all walked into the bright headlights. The bald man lifted the hatch, revealing three stacks of Nike shoeboxes piled to the roofline. Lucas set the suitcases on the ground and flipped the lid off one of the boxes. Inside was a pair of running shoes, plastic bags containing a white powder peeking out from beneath the tongue of each. Lucas handed the box to Miller, who stuck a finger into one of the plastic bags and then rubbed the powder on his gums. He licked his teeth and said, "It's real."

"Okay," Lucas said, and continued crisply with the words, "Let's make the transfer."

Bright lights flooded the junkyard.

"FBI! Drop your weapons and get down on the ground! Face down!"

Lozano and his men slowly dropped their guns and lowered themselves to the dirt. Following the plan to maintain their deception, Lucas and Miller did the same.

But as the footsteps of the half-dozen arresting agents filled the yard, Lucas heard the engine of Lozano's SUV roar to life. He turned his head and saw the driver's side door of the SUV fly open, bullets erupting from a semiautomatic in the hands of a gunman who had been hiding inside. The FBI assault team returned fire.

"Get back! Get back!" Lucas heard an agent scream. With his body pressed to the ground, he watched Lozano's bodyguards rise, weapons back in their hands, and begin firing in all directions.

"Stay down, DeMarcus!" Lucas shouted as the sound of bullets pinging off crushed metal reverberated across the scrapyard. He tried to crawl toward Miller but was stopped by a barrage of gunfire. He felt a sharp pain in his lower back. Lucas used his arms to cover his head but could still see Lozano moving toward the SUV, shielded by his two bodyguards. The Rojas Cartel captain had a Samsonite suitcase containing the FBI's cash in each hand. As Lozano threw the bags into the back seat and climbed in, Lucas felt a hot fire tearing through his right leg. The SUV tore out, the sound of tires kicking dirt into the air echoing across the yard.

Lucas heard an agent say, "Shit! They took the money!" A sedan sped past where Lucas was lying, sirens blaring. Lucas touched his thigh and felt wetness.

"Is DeMarcus okay?" he asked weakly as members of the FBI arrest team converged.

"Take it easy, Agent Foley," another agent said. "We've got you."

Lucas heard scissors cutting at fabric and felt scorching pain as pressure was applied to his wounds. Just before losing consciousness, Lucas turned his head.

He saw the bloodied and lifeless face of DeMarcus Miller.

CHAPTER
SIX

THEY RODE in silence during the taxi ride to her father's flat. The traffic was particularly heavy, even for a Saturday, with midafternoon shoppers packing both sides of Nevsky Prospekt. Alina stared at the bustling crowds. She had been part of this swarm of shoppers hundreds of times in her life; she was familiar with every inch of the neighborhood, the merchants to avoid and where to get the best deals. Yet now, looking at the passing throngs, the street signs, the shops, little seemed familiar, as if the past few hours had unrooted her from everything she knew.

Later, sitting in the apartment where Alina had grown up, she stared at the fading photographs of her mother hanging on the wall above the kitchen table. Pictures of her parents' wedding day, on a boat cruising through a canal, and of a family hike through the woods, her mother carrying Alina as an infant in her backpack.

"Was that really in the Black Forest?" Alina asked.

Her father set down two empty cups with tea bags and lowered into the chair beside her. "What's that?"

Alina nodded toward the photo. "You always said that was us on vacation in Germany."

He shook his head. "It's actually in America. It's called Wisconsin."

"Wisconsin," Alina repeated. Each new revelation no longer made her feel as if needles were stabbing her insides. She was unsure whether this was a sign of acceptance or whether she was just numb. She would know for sure when her father answered her next question.

"Why did you bother having me?" she asked. "Didn't I just get in the way of your...missions?"

"The Directorate pushed for us to have a family, Alina. No one would suspect a nice young family of working for the Russian government."

"So that's why you had me?" Her voice cracked. "I was part of your cover story?"

"Alina, the why does not matter. Your mother and I cared for you deeply."

"Cared for me?" she said, a tear now rolling down her cheek. "How could you have cared for me? I was just a prop in your little theater."

"You were our daughter, kroshka."

"Is my name even Alina?"

Her father stared at his hands a few moments before answering, "Here, you are Alina. In America, we named you Julie."

"Julie?" Alina scrunched up her sleeve to dab at the corner of her eye.

"I know it's upsetting to hear this. To know the reason why we had you—but this changes nothing. You must know. We both loved you a great deal. We—"

"Your marriage was a lie!" she spat. "Your life together was a lie. Our family was a—"

"Our family was not a lie!" he shouted. He took her by the shoulders and lowered his voice, saying forcefully, "*You* were not a lie!"

Alina shook free as she stood up and moved to the window. She stared out at pedestrians on the street as she tried to steady her breathing. This was the same window she'd sat by countless times growing up, watching children walk home hand in hand with their young mothers. As she watched the passersby below, she remembered her father's comment from earlier, about her mother getting to know important visitors at the hotel.

Men looking for company, he'd said.

The teakettle started whistling.

"I don't want any more tea," she snapped. "Are you telling me she slept with those men?"

"Alina!" he shouted. He went to the stove and turned off the burner.

"Did she?"

"I explained this. I never pushed to find out."

"I don't believe you!"

"It is true, Alina. I always felt if she had to come right out and admit it, we would destroy whatever bonds we had."

Alina felt the bile rise in her throat. Her father's jaw jutted out as he continued, but now in a distinctly monotone voice. "I do know that she did what she had to do. All of us did. If it gave her an advantage with her target, if it led to secrets that would help our country, I know she did not hesitate."

Alina dabbed at the corners of her eyes.

"I know this is hard to hear, kroshka. But these were simply transactions."

There was another question that was about to escape Alina's lips, a question she dared not ask. Maybe the man she had called her father for the past twenty-five years would not even know the true answer. Perhaps there was only one person who knew for certain. So that question would need to wait. Instead, she asked, "Do you think one of these—*transactions*—had anything to do with her disappearance?"

He glanced at the photos above the table and grimaced. "The day she didn't come home…she often stayed out late. Sometimes until the early-morning hours. But when she wasn't in her bed the next morning, I called the hotel, thinking she had gone straight back to work.

But she wasn't there. I signaled our handler, thinking maybe they had her on another assignment, but he said he knew nothing. I know the SVR reached out to our undercover contacts to see if she'd been arrested or even secretly renditioned to another country. But if they knew anything, nobody was talking. It was as if she had disappeared into the wind."

"Did they look at the men she had been in contact with?"

"If they did, they shared little with me. They insisted you and I should return to Russia. I wanted to search on my own, but if your mother was captured or killed by the Americans, the SVR worried I would be next." He paused before adding, "They worried *you* might be next."

"Me?"

He brought the teakettle from the stove and filled his mug. After returning the kettle, he motioned for Alina to sit with him again.

"Having a family was *not* just a cover story. All scouts were expected to develop their children. A future generation of scouts, but actually *born* in America. As American citizens. Going on to work in the corridors of power in business, politics, and technology. Even though we were coming back to Russia, I thought the SVR hadn't given up on that future for you."

"But they did give that up, didn't they? We came back to Russia. I was raised here. How am I like those others?"

"You still have your American identity, your American birth certificate. And…your passport." Her father took Alina's hands in his. "I saw to your continued Western education here in Russia. I got the job as a teacher at the international school so you could attend and no one would question the presence of a Russian child with little means. A school where you would be exposed to Western culture, the best in science and math. To me, this was not a hardship. I knew I was giving you the best education. And preparing you in case—"

Alina pulled her hand away. "Preparing me for *what*? Has my entire life been part of a master plan?"

Her father reached for her, but she slid her chair back. He stood and approached her, cupping her chin in his hand. "I knew that someday I would tell you the truth about your mother. So yes. I did everything I could to prepare you. In case you decided...in case you decided you needed to find out for yourself what happened to your mother."

Alina needed to get away from her father, away from the apartment containing memories of a life she thought she knew, where she had planned for the future. But as her eyes again found the pictures of her mother on the wall, Alina wondered whether that life—that future—had already evaporated before her eyes. She stared at the image from the long-ago hiking trip, of a smiling, two-year-old Alina wrapped in her mother's warm embrace. While the color in the decades-old pictures was fading, her mother's green eyes were sparkling. Her eyes were alive.

How could Alina go on with her life without knowing the truth?

As Alina continued to focus on the Wisconsin photo, a new image seemed to enter her mind. An image of an older version of the woman staring back. Graying hair, crow's-feet around her vivid eyes. The face a little fuller but still very beautiful. Her mother might have been killed all those years ago. But what if she was still alive? What if she was rotting away in an American prison?

"Where would I even start?" Alina said softly.

"There is a man I have stayed in touch with, kroshka. Alexi Romanoff was our handler when we were in America. He is still employed by our government. He has always claimed ignorance, but perhaps he would be more open with you."

She turned and asked, "Why would he tell me if he hasn't told you all these years?"

"You now have…assets, kroshka. Education. Language. Technical skills. All assets I have helped you develop, giving you capabilities to offer in return."

She looked at her father and said, "Tell me where I can find this man."

CHAPTER
SEVEN

"AGENT FOLEY!" said a muffled voice, sirens wailing in the background. "Stay with me, Agent Foley!"

Lucas tried to open his eyes, but the glare from a bright light forced them closed. He was lying on his back, his entire body racked with pain as the speeding ambulance jostled him from side to side. He tried again and managed to half open one eye, through which he saw the serious expression of the young female EMT placing a needle in his arm. He could barely hear her words: "Thirty-three-year-old white male...gunshot wounds... upper right leg and abdomen..."

Lucas wanted to reach for his stomach, but his arms wouldn't respond. The vehicle and the sirens came to a stop, and the ambulance doors burst open. Lucas felt himself being lowered, the sudden motion sending more pain through his torso and leg.

"It's okay, Agent Foley. We just have to get you inside."

The movement became smoother but the clarity of voices around him continued to come in and out: "Femur shattered...severed blood vessel...prep for surgery..."

Lucas tried to speak, but his mouth and nose were now covered by an oxygen mask. Through blurred vision he could see two men in scrubs wheeling him down a corridor and then through some doors into what was presumably an operating room. A doctor plunged a needle into Lucas's IV line, and almost instantly Lucas felt himself drifting off. While his eyes were now shut, he was awake long enough to hear the urgent directive:

"We have to move fast to have any chance of saving his leg."

CHAPTER
EIGHT

THE BLACK ELECTRIC Range Rover was waiting at the side entrance of Moscow's Leningradsky train station. The driver, a short, stocky man dressed in a black suit a few sizes too small, held the rear door open without introducing himself. For the next forty-five minutes, Alina stared out the car window, watching the landscape of decaying factories and warehouses pass by. Since she had left her father's apartment the previous week, she felt as if a small fire were smoldering in her chest. Not learning her mother's fate might keep these embers lit for the rest of her life. She had come to Moscow to learn more from the man who had choreographed every part of her family's lives.

Including Alina's own very existence.

The SUV exited the highway and pulled into a dilapidated service station. The driver stopped next to an abandoned pump. He exited the vehicle stiffly, as if his movements were confined by his jacket, and opened the rear door. Alina felt a chill from the unusually cold but cloudless day.

The driver handed her a slip of paper. "You will need to walk from here."

Alina glanced at the address written on the paper,

then at the broken sidewalk surrounding the station. "What?" she asked. "Aren't you taking me there?"

He pointed to the paper in Alina's hand. "You should get going."

Alina reached for her handbag.

"And you are to leave your phone," he said.

"But I need my—"

"It is safe," he said. "I will bring it to you for your return."

Alina looked at the address on the slip of paper, 160 Dorozhny, and looked around, searching for some sign pointing her toward what she assumed was Romanoff's government office. The street signs told her she was on the corner of Polvo Street and Azov Lane. She flipped over the paper and saw a hand-drawn street map, a red marker highlighting a walking route that twisted through several city blocks.

"How will I call you when I'm ready?"

The driver stood stone-faced and said, "Someone will bring you here."

She looked back and forth from the signs overhead to the map in her hands, trying to get her bearings. Was this some kind of crazy spy test to see whether she could read a rudimentary map? Part of her wanted to end this charade and take the train back to St. Petersburg. But she had come this far.

Noting the sun above the soot-covered apartment blocks across the way, Alina handed the driver her phone, grabbed her bag, and headed north up Polvo Street. She followed the crude sketch, nervously glancing over her shoulder as she made her way through mostly abandoned streets. She came upon a group of men loitering by a gated storefront, but they barely noticed her as she hurried past. Alina buttoned her jacket and pulled up the collar to ward off the early-morning chill, glad she had worn her blue pantsuit instead of a skirt and blouse.

Finally turning right on Dorozhny, she double-checked the address of what she still expected to be some type of government office. The crooked stencil on the corner liquor store read 132, so she knew she was close, even though she saw nothing on the road resembling an office building. She passed a fruit and vegetable market at 146, an internet café at 152, and a phone store at 156. Finally arriving in front of 160, she again checked the slip of paper.

Alina was standing in front of a sign that read AQUARIUM.

She peeked into the window and confirmed 160 Dorozhny was a musty tropical fish store. She was about to turn around and retrace her steps, return to the service station. But she thought she should at least go inside and ask. Perhaps there was a north and south Dorozhny? Or, she thought, chuckling to herself as she remembered those James Bond movies she used to watch with her Western friends at the international school, maybe there was a secret passageway from the fish store to Romanoff's office.

Alina walked in and peered down a dimly lit aisle lined with fish tanks on both sides, the bubbling filters and warm, humid air making her feel as if she had suddenly entered a cauldron. An older woman wearing a faded housedress was on a ladder behind the counter, placing fish food on the shelves.

"Excuse me," Alina said.

"Yes," the woman replied without looking over.

"I think I'm lost. I'm looking for an office building with the same address as yours."

The woman climbed another rung to reach an upper shelf and said, "Check the back of the store."

"I'm not sure if you understood me," Alina said. "Do you know if there are government offices around here?"

"Check the back," the woman repeated, continuing to stock the upper shelf.

Alina shook her head and walked up the aisle.

Reaching the rear, she tried to open a door but it was locked. Glancing around the shop she saw nothing but fish tanks. She started lifting the lids, clicking on the lights in several tanks containing dark catfish and colorless guppies, thinking that if there were a secret passageway, some type of switch would activate it. But nothing happened. She turned up the next aisle to head back to the front of the store and started to squeeze past an older heavyset man in a blue smock.

"You look lost," he said as he scrubbed the inside of a tank.

"There's been a mistake," Alina replied, moving past him.

"Maybe I can help?"

Alina thought he was a bit old to be working in a pet shop. The white whiskers lining his chin were the only hairs visible on his otherwise shaved head. She rolled her eyes. "Do you know of any government office buildings in the area?"

"We are a fish store, my dear," he said. "Would you like to buy some fish?"

"Maybe next time," Alina said, turning again toward the front as the woman from behind the counter appeared.

"Everyone has reported in," the woman said. "She hasn't been followed. Scanning signals from the drones were all green. No tracking devices have been detected."

"That is good," the man said. He stared at Alina's face, then broke into a broad smile, revealing a wide gap between his front teeth. "My goodness, Alina. You look exactly like your mother."

"Wait," Alina said. "*You* are—"

"Alexi Igorevich Romanoff," he nodded. "I apologize for our little subterfuge," he added as he escorted Alina back to the rear of the store. "I have wanted to meet you for a long time."

"Why did you make me walk here?" she asked.

"We do not like calling attention to ourselves with fancy cars pulling up in front. And we needed you on foot to make sure nobody was following or tracking you."

Romanoff placed his right hand along the frame of the locked door. Alina heard a lock snap open, and the door slid to the side.

"Where are we going?" Alina asked.

Romanoff held his hand up and said, "Please. You will see."

Following him down a short corridor, Alina heard the electric hum of an arriving elevator. She pulled her jacket around her tightly, feeling a flow of cool air as if they were approaching an open refrigerator.

"We keep it chilled for our computers," Romanoff explained as they entered the elevator. After descending for a few moments they came to a stop, and the doors opened into a large office. Every item had been meticulously placed. A dark mahogany bookcase lined the wall to her right. On her left hung several enlarged and elaborately framed photographs of Romanoff in fishing gear, standing atop a frozen lake, rod in one hand and holding bunches of what looked like perch and pike in the other. Two leather sofas positioned in the center of the room sat atop a red Persian rug. On the far side was an antique desk stationed in front of a large glass wall.

Alina flinched at the sound of the elevator doors closing behind her.

"Please, have a seat," Romanoff said as he hung his smock on a coat rack and motioned her toward the sofa. But instead of sitting, Alina was drawn to the glass wall behind the desk. She moved close enough to observe a warehouse-sized sublevel buzzing with activity, the room packed with row upon row of workstations. Even from this distance, Alina could tell each workstation was stocked with state-of-the-art computer equipment. She thought there had to be several hundred people working in the cavernous space.

"What is all of this?"

Romanoff stood beside her and puffed out his chest. "This is the home of our new Russian heroes."

"And they all come to work through the fish store?" she asked.

Romanoff laughed, his high-pitched cackle surprising Alina. "We have several entrances; I can assure you. It makes things easier to close one off if it's accidentally discovered. But you can imagine, there is no easy way to enter this facility. The KGB made sure of that when they built this bunker during the Cold War."

Alina's mouth went dry at the mention of the Soviet-era security agency. She swallowed and pointed at the glass. "What are they all doing?"

He waved his arm in front of the partition. "They are all technologists, Alina. Skilled and trained, like you. But none share...*your* history."

"Did you recruit them from universities?" she asked. "The way my mother and father were recruited?"

Romanoff's expression didn't change with the mention of her parents. "Most, but not all. Some we discovered while they perfected their craft. Disorganized hackers breaking into companies and governments for sport or petty theft." Now Romanoff grinned. "On-the-job training, I guess you would call it. We monitored their activities, of course, making sure they weren't directing their energies at...well, the wrong targets."

"So, after you...discovered them," she said, choosing her words carefully, "they immediately came to work for you?"

Romanoff shrugged. "When the alternative was several years in prison?"

He was nothing if not direct, she thought. Hopefully he would be as forthcoming about her mother.

"They were very excited to join our cause," he continued. He motioned again for her to sit on one of the sofas, and he joined her on the one opposite. Two ashtrays, a humidor, and a piece of paper sat on the coffee table. Romanoff opened the humidor and chose a cigar. Then he put on a pair of bifocals and picked up the paper.

"I've followed your progress for many years," he said as he ran his eyes across the paper.

"Your academic performance is quite impressive."

"Thank you," she said flatly.

"You must be very happy with all the job opportunities in front of you," he said, fingering the cigar in his hand.

"It is exciting," she said.

"You must feel like...what's that expression?" He looked up. "Oh yes, that the world is your oyster."

"You are very kind."

Romanoff was now grinning. "Perhaps our little enterprise could figure into your equation."

He wasn't wasting any time trying to reel her in, as if he were reeling in a pike on one of his ice fishing expeditions. She didn't want to refuse him too quickly. Not until she could get him talking about her mother. But something told her the best way to engage would be to show an interest in his cause. Lead him to believe she was open to his overtures. She would take it slowly. Besides, she actually was curious to learn exactly what was going on down in that hidden warehouse.

"Maybe you could tell me more about your...operation," she said.

Romanoff abruptly stood and walked to the elevator. Alina worried she had again said something offensive, but he motioned for her and said, "We can discuss more after my lieutenant provides you with a tour."

CHAPTER NINE

ALINA FOLLOWED several steps behind Dmitri Fedorov as they made their way across the elevated metal footbridge. She gripped the handrail tightly, trying not to peer down at the stacks of computer servers positioned at least three stories below. When Alina finally caught up with Romanoff's tall and fit operations leader, he asked, "What do you think of our server farm?"

Alina inhaled and managed to say, "Extraordinary."

"This gives us enormous processing power," Fedorov said. He held open the door they had reached and smiled. "And it always impresses our recruits."

Alina wanted to remind Romanoff's young right-hand man that she wasn't his recruit, but at the moment her main thought was to get off the footbridge. She felt her body relax as soon as Fedorov led her into the cavernous room she had observed from Romanoff's office. Despite the vast assemblage of workstations and programmers, the room was eerily quiet. She surveyed the expansive space, taking in the tall, soundproof walls surrounding them. The sole window was the one where Romanoff now stood, hands behind his back, peering down at her from behind the glass.

She cleared her throat and asked Fedorov, "How many people work here?"

"Over five hundred. We had two hundred more in a satellite facility, but with funding sources drying up, we have learned how to become more efficient."

"Five hundred coders is still a lot," she said. It wasn't difficult to sound impressed.

Fedorov escorted Alina to the first cluster of workstations. "Everyone here is organized into specific missions." He introduced Vera, a well-dressed woman with closely cropped black hair who was manning what appeared to be the supervisor's desk. A small handwritten sign read MINISTRY OF PROPAGANDA.

"A little levity by the team," Fedorov said with a small smile. "Vera runs our disinformation campaigns. Her team members have become experts in infiltrating the emails of foreign governments, searching for damaging information. Her team also scours the Western internet, extracting what some would call 'interesting points of view.' Which we amplify using our digital megaphone."

Vera nodded and said, "Citizens of our adversaries have no idea what is real and what is not."

Alina suppressed the impulse to snicker. Like most Russians, she knew all too well about disinformation campaigns within her own country. At least she and her classmates at university had learned how to ignore "facts" disseminated by state-controlled media.

Fedorov pointed toward an adjacent cluster of workstations, where the seats were empty. "Years ago, the team that sat there wrote chatbots to deliver discordant messages, launching them on fake social media accounts. Today we use our own generative artificial intelligence system to automate the entire process."

"Wait." Alina turned to Fedorov, her eyes wide. "*We* have generative AI?" At university she had attended demonstrations of America's generative AI system—

witnessed how it fabricated astonishingly humanlike content. She didn't know Russia had its own application.

He nodded. "Vera's team simply suggests the topic and the appropriate…point of view. Artificial intelligence generates and launches 'output' faster than our enemies can identify and remove it. We've taken this capability well beyond simple social media posts. Today, AI fabricates newspaper articles, books, essays, even editorials. Anything we can use to distort public opinion, in whichever language we choose around the world."

Fedorov escorted her by the arm to the next workstation group. A disheveled, gray-bearded man was adjusting one of his two large monitors. "Ah, Stepan," Fedorov said. "Bring up POTUS. I want to show our guest."

Stepan ran his hands across his keyboard. In an instant, a video appeared on the screen on the right; Alina recognized the president of the United States.

"Hello, my fellow Americans," the president said. "It has come to my attention that there are elements within our government that are conspiring to take down my administration."

Alina's body shuddered with shock.

"They have been gathering members of regional militias across the country and plan to attack several of our domestic military bases. I am calling on all able-bodied Americans to join with me in defending our country. Defending our *democracy*. I—"

"That's enough, Stepan," Fedorov said. "You can turn it off."

"This is incredible," Alina said, her heart racing as she thought of the implications of a coup within the American government. "When did this happen?"

Fedorov touched her arm again and smiled. "It is not real, Alina. It is what we call a Deep Fake. Perfect digital imitations created from our vast library of video and audio recordings."

Alina let out a slow exhale. "It's…so real," she said

with her hand on her chest. "Was this actually shown in America?"

Fedorov shook his head. "But we ran a test in a small village using a version of the Ukrainian president during the early days of our conflict. Residents did as he asked and laid down their weapons. But we have held back from attempting anything in America. Let's just say it is in our AI arsenal."

Alina leaned on Stepan's desk, feeling slightly unsteady as she imagined the chaos such a devastating tool might unleash. She had learned about these deep learning algorithms that made the fake appear real, but none of the prototypes they'd reviewed at university were remotely as convincing as Fedorov's demonstration.

They walked and stopped in front of a severe-looking man named Pavel. The sign on his workstation read SNEAK PREVIEW.

"Things get even more exciting over here," Fedorov said. "Pavel flexes many of our 'cyber muscles,' showcasing our latest arsenal."

Alina was afraid to take in any more, but Fedorov stood back and started projecting his voice, clearly wanting Pavel and his team to hear him extolling their accomplishments.

"We might scramble the systems of a government agency. Flood a financial system with 'denial of service' traffic to slow ATM networks. Rearrange railway signals." He leaned in toward Alina and whispered, "Nothing gets the citizenry more agitated than when the trains stop running."

He stood back and resumed speaking aloud. Alina couldn't tell whether Pavel's team was even listening, as not a single one of them had looked away from their screens. "This is how we send a strong message to our adversaries—demonstrating our capabilities, but not enough to risk drawing return fire." Alina felt as if a vise were pressing in on her head as she imagined the catastrophic response America might unleash against her own country—against her own people. When Fedorov led her away, she managed to ask, "Do the Americans know this is...*us*?"

"Of course they do, Alina. You see, while we never penetrate directly from Russian cyberspace, we do purposely leave faint fingerprints in order to send a message. The Americans understand this is only a small fraction of the damage we could inflict."

Mutually assured destruction in the cyber age, Alina thought.

Fedorov led Alina toward a young woman wearing eyeglasses and a sleeveless white blouse. Alina stared at the red tattoo of a cherry the woman had on the side of her neck.

"Kira, would you bring up one of our subjects."

The woman pressed a few keys, and her computer screen started filling with sentences.

Hey Bob. Thanks very much for dinner last night. I'm glad we got together and straightened out the last few deal points. I'll speak to our attorneys later today and start drawing up the contracts. My client in Beijing will be very pleased with the final terms...

"I don't understand," Alina said.

"Kira here is testing our latest stealth keylogger," Fedorov said. "It's impossible to detect."

"A keylogger?"

"A malware tool that captures and transmits keystrokes. Once planted on a target's computer, we learn every secret created from that keyboard. Kira's module re-creates emails, memos—even formatted presentations." Fedorov smiled and added, "As you see, translated into perfect Russian, of course."

"Fascinating." Alina's head was spinning. Why was Fedorov being so open about this entire operation? About Romanoff's supposedly secret operation? Had Fedorov been told she was already part of his cyber army? The chill Alina had felt since entering the lab had yet to fade. *This* couldn't be the reason she had studied technology at the finest university in Russia, no matter what information Romanoff had to offer about her mother. Alina had great passion about the endless possibilities of AI. But what Fedorov and Romanoff had created was a perversion, a brand of artificial intelligence designed to start a war.

She told Fedorov that she was ready to head back upstairs.

"We are almost done," he said. "Alexi Igorevich wants you to see one more area."

Alina took a deep breath as they proceeded around the corner and entered a corridor with several doors on each side. Fedorov opened the one with a sign posted on the right:

AI SCOUTS.

They entered a conference room, revealing eight men and two women, each wearing headsets and keying onto their laptops. Schematic diagrams were posted on the far walls.

"Every analyst in here is an AI expert," Fedorov said. "They build and manage our AI scouts—high-speed search engines, really. Programs we plant inside the government systems of our adversaries, where AI can probe and identify people who meet a certain...profile."

"What kind of profile?" Alina asked.

"It depends what we are looking for. As you know, AI is extremely versatile, as long as we have sufficient data with which to train the system. Today, this team is building AI scouts which will search for foreign candidates to be recruited as counterintelligence assets."

Alina looked over the shoulder of an analyst who was rapidly keying what appeared to be lines of Python code, one of the many programming languages Alina was familiar with.

Fedorov walked to the far end of the room. "Mikhail

here manages data loads," he said when he stopped next to an analyst. "The Kremlin provided us with the complete profile of every American and European who secretly spied for our country in the past one hundred years. The successes and the failures. As you know, AI must learn from both. Mikhail loads their upbringing, education, career progression. Family life and lineage. Articles they may have authored. Publicly available interviews. Everything we know about them."

Fedorov shifted over to the next analyst. "Yuri's team uses that treasure trove of knowledge to build and train AI scouts, using inference engines to derive what we call 'look-alikes.' Western citizens who have the exact attributes of our former assets that would make them perfect spies." Fedorov patted Yuri on the back before proceeding to a wavy-haired brunette working closer to where Alina stood. "And Mila manages our suite of hacking routines— she is quite effective at inserting these scouts into the personnel systems of government agencies." He grinned and added, "AI scouts are the perfect way to rummage through files to find what—or, I should say, who—we are looking for."

CHAPTER
TEN

THE FIRST THING Lucas noticed was the odor, a distinctive fusion of antiseptic chemicals and bodily fluids.

A smell unique to hospitals.

Through the beeps and pings chiming from the monitors above his head, Lucas heard the sound of rhythmic snoring.

He opened his eyes and saw his father sitting in a chair by the window, a Northwestern University Medical Center logo displayed on the wall to his left. Alec Foley's round, ashen face was tilted back, his mouth open. Lucas tried to shift in the hospital bed but felt a knifelike pain cut through his back. He squeezed his eyes shut until the pain eased.

And then the memories started flooding in.

The drug bust gone bad. The gunman hiding in the SUV. The gun battle at the junkyard. The drug captain, Mateo Lozano, escaping. DeMarcus Miller's lifeless body. The searing pain in Lucas's own right leg.

His recollections of being shot were hazy, as was the ride in the ambulance. But some overheard words starting playing in the back of his mind: *We have to move fast to have any chance of saving his leg.*

Lucas looked toward the bottom of his hospital bed.

He didn't recognize the swollen toes of the elevated right foot protruding from underneath the covers. But if there was a right foot, that meant his right leg was still intact. Lucas tried to signal his brain to move his toes, but the foot wouldn't respond. He felt a sudden chill and reached for the call button hanging on the bed's guardrail. Moments later, a petite nurse of no more than twenty-four came in.

"Oh, Mr. Foley," she said. "You're awake. I'll let Dr. Lloyd know."

"Just a second," Lucas said. "What's going—" but the nurse was already out the door.

His father's head jerked forward. "Heeey," Alec Foley said, clearing his throat. "You're awake."

Lucas smiled wanly.

His father moved to Lucas' side and held his hand. "You scared the shit out of me."

"It wasn't my intention."

"How you feelin'?"

"Like I got hit by a truck," Lucas said. "How long have you been sitting here?"

"I don't know. You've been in and out for a few days."

"Days?"

"What's the difference?" He squeezed Lucas's hand tighter. "A fellow agent goes down, I'm there to pick him up."

His father always liked to refer to Lucas as a "fellow agent." But the truth was, their time at the bureau hadn't overlapped. In fact, it had been a decade since Alec Foley had retired as one of the most decorated undercover agents in FBI history, having infiltrated the mafia, international gunrunning organizations, and human trafficking rings, which had led to the arrest and incarceration of a wide range of miscreants.

"Did they get Lozano?" Lucas asked. He knew his father still maintained close contacts at the bureau.

His father shook his head. "I hear there's a dragnet across five states. No sign of him yet."

Lucas said, "Dad, you probably haven't slept in days. Go home and get some rest."

"I'll leave in a bit," his father said.

Lucas heard a knock and turned to see a young man in a doctor's coat entering the room.

"Mr. Foley? I'm Dr. Lloyd, the orthopedic surgeon."

"You look like you're fresh out of school," Alec said.

Dr. Lloyd smiled and asked Lucas how the leg felt.

"You tell me, Doc," Lucas said. "I can't move my toes."

"What?" his father said.

Dr. Lloyd placed his tablet on the side table and said, "Let's take a look." He slowly pulled the blankets away. Lucas's right leg was wrapped in bandages like a mummy, elevated on a pile of pillows. The doctor moved to the foot of the bed and took a pen from his coat pocket. As he ran it along Lucas's toes, he asked, "Any sensation?"

"A little," Lucas said. But he barely felt the pen.

"It will take time for feeling to return. The bullet fractured your femur and damaged blood vessels and tissue. I had to insert a metal rod and plates for stability. Dr. Cartwright's vascular team did most of the heavy lifting."

"Jeez," Lucas whispered.

"Look, you're facing months of pretty intense physical therapy, but you should regain full mobility."

"How many months?" Alec asked.

"At least six. Maybe a full year." He turned to Lucas. "Until then, you'll have to rely on a cane."

Lucas stared at his immobilized leg as his father said, "Dr. Lloyd, my son is a field agent for the FBI. He can't be hobbling around on a cane for a year."

"Dad!"

"Look," Dr. Lloyd's expression became stern as he addressed Lucas. "You're actually quite lucky to be alive.

The slug that entered your back passed completely through without striking a single vital organ."

Lucas shivered, remembering the intense pain when he had tried to shift in bed. He had no recollection of being shot in the back.

"We need to keep you here for a few days to monitor for infection," the doctor continued as he picked up his tablet and walked to the door. "I'll have the social worker start looking into rehab centers."

"Rehab centers?" Lucas whispered.

Dr. Lloyd stopped and turned back toward Lucas. "I'm sorry, Agent Foley. I can see your disappointment. But at least for the next year, you'll need to find a different way to chase after the bad guys."

CHAPTER
ELEVEN

ALINA FOUND Romanoff still standing by his glass observation post, staring down at his creation. With his back turned, he asked, "What do you think of our cyber forces?"

"They're impressive," she replied. Her voice sounded calm, but her insides were churning. Working in that cyber war room would not be her life.

He nodded several times, seeming to acknowledge the compliment. "The next battles will be fought in the digital universe, Alina. Using artificial intelligence." He turned to face her and added, "Your specialty, if I'm not mistaken."

Alina steeled herself for the pressure she felt was coming. She knew she should simply leave. Walk back to the service station, where hopefully the driver was waiting for her. Away from this former KGB bunker. She would not be part of Romanoff's war machine. She was ready to accept the position in Istanbul and start the life she had planned before her father's revelations. But first, she had to find out what Romanoff knew about her mother's disappearance. So, for now, she needed to engage. She nodded toward the glass and said, "Dmitri Vladimirovich seems to know everything going on down there."

"It is his business to know everything." Romanoff moved to his bar and opened a bottle of scotch. "Drink?"

"Why not." It might settle her nerves.

Romanoff smiled as he poured. He brought her a glass and motioned for her to sit. She took three quick sips as she lowered onto the sofa. The calm she hoped for didn't have time to arrive before Romanoff sat beside her and got right to the point.

"I understand you have many fine offers," he started. He pointed at his viewing window again. "But your country could use your talents here."

"But…I have different…career plans."

He gave a quick laugh. "What plans could be more important than working for Mother Russia?" He took a large gulp and added, "After all, your father invested tremendously in your upbringing. It is time to give something back, is it not?" He placed his glass on the coffee table, next to the still unlit cigar. "You will have plenty of time for your"—he waved his hand dismissively—"pursuits. Sometime in the future."

She took another sip. "I never pictured myself working for the government."

"Not many do," he said. "Certainly your parents didn't. Yet they were patriots. And they did what needed to be done."

She took a deep breath and said, "My father told me everything."

"I'm sure it came as a shock," Romanoff said. "It always does when the children of our agents learn the truth."

"Was my mother good at what she did?"

He leaned toward her and said, "Your mother was one of our best."

Alina shifted back, finished her scotch in two long gulps, and placed the empty glass on the table. "Do you know what happened to her?"

Romanoff cleared his throat. "As I said, your mother was a very good agent. Extremely intelligent. Very engaging. Very effective. She could improvise better than anyone I ever worked with. She knew how to get Americans to…relax. She used all her assets to get her targets to let their guard down. Especially her beauty. She—"

"You mean sex?" Alina interrupted.

Romanoff leaned back. He seemed startled by her bluntness.

"Did she have sex as part of her…*mission*?" Alina asked.

Romanoff stared at the empty glass in front of her. When he spoke, his words came out firmly. "In those days…it was a different world. *Sex*, as you call it, was used very…strategically. But only in the right hands." He paused and looked up at Alina. "Skilled hands."

"Of people like my mother?"

Alina waited. She still hoped to hear some type of denial. But after a few moments, Romanoff's eyebrows furrowed, and he asked, "Is this why you came here today, Alina? To find out if your mother used sex as an agent?"

"I came to find out what happened to her," she replied. "When she disappeared." Alina crossed her legs and leaned back. "My father told me she didn't die of cancer as I'd been told."

Romanoff looked away, seemingly in deep thought. Alina sensed that everything this man did—and said—came after careful consideration. Finally, he turned back and said, "We were never able to confirm anything about what happened to her. Internally, our leaders believe she was captured. Interrogated." He shook his head without looking at her. "And that she most likely did not survive."

"Most likely?" Alina repeated. "You're not sure?"

Romanoff took a last sip of scotch and reached for her glass.

"None for me," she said.

He walked to the bar, poured a splash into his glass and returned to the sofa. "We pressed the Americans for information. We offered to trade for her, just as we had done with Anna Kushchenko, Vladimir Guryev, and many other undercover operatives. But as other trades took place, the Americans always denied having any knowledge of Valeriya Petrova or Diane Backus." He swallowed a quick gulp and said, "If she *was* killed, it was an interrogation gone wrong. Followed by a cover-up for their carelessness."

Alina stood and said, "So you *do* think she is dead."

Romanoff shook his head. "Actually, I do not."

Alina felt her legs wobble. "What?"

"We do not normally kill each other's spies. I have no facts. Everyone in the SVR said I was a fool. But personally, I always suspected she went underground."

Alina couldn't move. It was as if her feet were cemented in place. "Underground?" she asked. "Why do you think that?"

"I think our assets within America would have confirmed if she had been captured or killed. And there was no evidence that anything she had knowledge of was revealed. It was like everything she knew disappeared with her."

Alina let his words sink in.

"The only possibility left is that she assumed a new identity," he continued. "Built a different life."

"Why?" Alina asked. "Why would she do that?"

"Your mother was very committed to our cause, Alina. Perhaps the most dedicated agent I've ever seen. But she was not pleased with the directives coming from home. Telling her to have children to reinforce the illusion of the average American family."

Alina's felt her neck tighten. So her mother *had* been directed to have children. Directed to have *her*.

"She worried that having children would force her to

cut back on operations," Romanoff said. "I never thought that was the right approach with such a high-caliber agent. She was restless. Dangerously so at times, but she wanted to do more, not less. If not with us, then…"

"Hold on," Alina managed to say, trying to stay focused on her inquiry. "You think she's…spying for someone else?"

"It is simply a theory, Alina. There were many willing to pay handsomely for someone with your mother's skills." He shrugged and added, "But as I said, I have no evidence."

Alina's entire body felt numb as she dropped back onto the sofa. Was that all her mother was, Alina thought. A "high-caliber agent for hire," too restless to raise her own daughter? Was Alina simply a prop in her mother's life of deception, discarded when the Russian operative was ready to move on to the highest bidder? For Alina's entire life, she had accepted her father's story—that her mother was dead. And she could accept that now. But if her mother was actually alive, something inside Alina's core told her that the mother she barely knew would not have abandoned her. At least not voluntarily.

She had to find out the truth.

"If you are right," she said firmly, "that means my mother is alive."

Romanoff shook his head. "It has been almost twenty-five years. I know this is painful. But the best thing is for you to put this behind you. If you want to be true to your mother's legacy, the best thing you can do is put your skills to work for us. Walk down her path. I am sure this is what she would have wanted for you."

As Alina stared at Romanoff, she felt certain of one thing. She had no idea what she would do when she got to America, but she could not go on with her life without knowing her mother's fate.

Especially if she was alive.

"Alexi Igorevich, do you have family?"

"Yes. A brother, Ilya," he replied. "We worked together in the old KGB. He's now a businessman, of all things. Why?"

"If he was in trouble, would you help him?"

"Ilya has seen his share." He smiled briefly. "In fact, I do help him all I can."

"Well, this is *my* family." Her voice was shaky. "I want you to send me to America. To see if I can find out what happened to her."

Romanoff sat completely still. Motionless. But Alina thought she detected a slight smile at the corner of his mouth. He slowly leaned forward and picked up the cigar. "Do you mind?" he asked.

Alina shook her head.

But Romanoff didn't raise the lighter as he said, "You are wasting your time."

"Maybe," she said. But she knew she had no choice. And she needed his help. She had no idea where she would start. She knew no one in America or this city of Chicago, where her parents had lived.

Alina leaned toward Romanoff, and said, "Help me, and I will help you."

He cleared his throat. "We only send agents abroad after years of training."

Alina put her hand on his arm. "There must be something I could do for you without years of training. I already understand Western culture. I speak perfect English." She nodded toward the window. "And I know as much AI as anyone you have down here."

Romanoff glanced at the hand resting on his arm. Once again, he seemed to be contemplating Alina's words. He slowly rose and walked back to the observation window. He continued to twirl the unlit cigar between his fingers as he looked down at his creation, as if digesting her decision not to join his team of hackers.

Alina stood and walked to the elevator. If Romanoff

wouldn't help her, Alina would figure out how to get to America on her own.

"Alina Grigoryevna."

She stopped and turned to face him.

"There actually might be something you can do."

CHAPTER
TWELVE

ALEXI ROMANOFF TOOK a long drag on his Cohiba and peered at his computer screen, watching Alina Petrova walk down Azov Lane and enter the black SUV waiting at the service station. His stealth surveillance drones had monitored her every step from when she had exited the fish store fifteen minutes earlier. Romanoff slowly blew out the smoke and leaned back from his desk.

She was exactly what he needed to put his exit strategy in motion.

Over the years, he had done everything the SVR had asked of him. But they wanted more. They always wanted more. He had long ago resigned himself to the fact that *his* call would never come.

"It's not your time," the head of Russia's Foreign Intelligence Service, Igor Grosky, had told him repeatedly when explaining why someone else had been selected for a senior position.

How could it still not be his time? After everything he had accomplished and built.

He had worked his way up through the security services during the early part of his career, first at the KGB, and then, after the fall of the Soviet Union, in its successor, the Foreign Intelligence Service—the SVR. He had stewarded the scouts program through years of success. He oversaw every detail of building their fabricated life stories, their "legends." And having personally experienced the long-term effects of being alone in a foreign land, he was the one who'd insisted Russian scouts be paired as married couples, engineered to remain in place for long durations, potentially decades. And he was the one who insisted they have children, raise them as local citizens in their adopted homeland—develop and educate them to assume their rightful place as future operatives.

It wasn't his fault when Valeriya Petrova disappeared. It wasn't his blunder—or hers—when several scouts were discovered and arrested in the United States. A Kremlin investigation concluded that the identities of those scouts had been revealed by a mole in Moscow. The Kremlin knew he wasn't to blame. Yet his stature and career were never the same. And when it was time to name a new worldwide head of the undercover unit, his superiors had passed him by, naming his rival, Igor Peltz.

Instead of a leadership position, Romanoff had been handed a new task.

"I'm looking for someone to start a technical unit—a troublemaking unit," Grosky had explained. "Off the grid. Officially, we will know nothing of your activities. If you are discovered, we will say you are nothing to us. Simply a disgruntled former official. A renegade. You cannot so much as send me an email. But this is a way for you to be noticed by the Kremlin."

So, with little technical background, Romanoff had grabbed hold of the opportunity and launched into his new endeavor with vigor.

"We'll funnel some money to you through third parties," Grosky had promised. "But you will need to develop alternative funding sources." When Moscow's start-up funding turned out to be too meager to hire more than a small team of hackers, Romanoff set out to build a war chest for grander schemes. Ransomware was his preferred and very lucrative method of attack. His team kept its demands relatively small at first, finding small European companies to be easy targets. Almost all were willing to pay a "fee" to decrypt their customer files. Once funds were transferred, his team always made sure to fully release any locked-up data. After all, it was important to build a reputation as a credible negotiator.

As Romanoff's team grew larger, he'd converted this abandoned KGB bunker into an underground tech center, with state-of-the-art servers and communications gear. Adding the loyal Fedorov—a rising star at Yandex, Russia's largest technology company—was the final touch. Fedorov molded the assortment of hackers and aspiring AI coders into a team with the skills and confidence to go after US entities. And all along, Romanoff was assured that the Kremlin was appreciative of his achievements.

But now, all these years later, Romanoff had given up the idea of joining the leadership ranks of the SVR. If the Kremlin still blamed him for the collapse of the American program over twenty years ago, there was little more he could do. His window of opportunity for advancement had closed. And despite Fedorov's boast of his team's successes, corporate cyber defenses had become practically impenetrable, especially in America. It was virtually impossible to remotely place ransomware anymore. Romanoff had known that the day was approaching when ransomware installations and other cyberattacks would need to take place behind enemy lines —from *within* the corporations themselves.

Romanoff stood from the desk and walked to his observation window. He gazed down at the horde of coders below and took another puff from his cigar. Spending time with the beautiful daughter of his long-lost agent brought back vivid memories. SVR leadership had been so elusive all those years ago whenever he asked about Valeriya Petrova, refusing his request to organize his own search. He had never been able to discover what his bosses were hiding. He had never been able to provide answers to Grigory Petrov, who always hinted that his daughter, Alina, would one day seek the truth. And as expected, here she was, Valeriya Petrova's beautiful and Western-educated daughter, offering her...*skills*, in return for his assistance.

Romanoff had been patiently preparing.

He and Fedorov had already designed a shortened and intensive training program for a new asset, more than sufficient for the hacking scheme Romanoff had envisioned for the past five years. A highly trusted member of Fedorov's team had already mastered the inner workings of the websites connecting rich lonely men with willing young women. Romanoff had prepared several false identities these dating websites would verify as authentic—thanks to Fedorov's team—giving a sense of security to these American businessmen. The plan, which he and Fedorov would keep secret from their superiors in the SVR, was ready to be executed.

He had simply been waiting for someone like Alina to arrive.

And Romanoff knew he possessed the perfect incentive to ensure Alina would carry on with what she might find to be a distasteful assignment. He would slowly provide her with pieces of his extensive documentation on Valeriya Petrova's time in America, information he had poured through countless times over the decades. While he'd discovered little of consequence in these files, the sheer volume would be enough to keep his new agent flailing around in endless pursuit of a ghost. His documents would satisfy her desire for information while she helped him build enough personal wealth to more than comfortably retire off the Amalfi Coast—and elude the reach of a Russian security apparatus that might take exception to Romanoff lining his pockets with an "off-the grid" ransomware operation. If Alina was ever discovered by either the Americans or his own intelligence services, Romanoff would simply deny any knowledge of her activities.

Romanoff placed his cigar down and removed the back of his humidor, revealing a small communications device enabled with Fedorov's "home-grown" encryption system. It was a device he used on the rarest of occasions. His index finger slowly typed out a message to his lead operative in America:

> **Ready to commence Operation Sugar.**

He was not going to spend the rest of his life in this dungeon after all.

CHAPTER
THIRTEEN

SIX MONTHS LATER...

THROUGH THE RUMBLE of the decelerating engines, Alina could barely discern the announcement as the plane descended below fifteen thousand feet.

"Ladies and gentlemen, we are making our final approach to O'Hare airport in Chicago."

She did not move or open her eyes until she felt a hand on her shoulder, followed by a firm command. "Ma'am, we need your seat to be in the upright position."

Alina squinted, her vision blurred, as she fumbled for the button on her aisle seat and snapped herself forward. She glanced at the teenagers who had been seated beside her for the eight-hour flight from Heathrow. She had hoped to catch a few hours of sleep on this last leg of her week-long journey, but the bantering and giggling American girls had kept her awake most of the way. Her head felt heavy with exhaustion. Alina reached into her handbag and checked on her compact travel kit. She would wait until they had landed and deplaned to close herself in a bathroom stall and apply the medicated lubricant drops to her bloodshot eyes, followed by a light touch of mascara.

The adrenaline rush from the excitement of leaving Moscow seven days earlier had made sleep all but impossible during Alina's circuitous journey through Belarus, Latvia, and Poland—she presented fabricated passports at each border crossing. But three days of crowded trains, dilapidated buses and cheap hotels had left her bone-tired. She slept the entire four-hour flight from Krakow to London where she was met by two of Romanoff's men. There, they'd spent four days in a suburban safe house, walking her through her "transition package." In addition to new personal provisions—fashionable but sensible European-style clothing, Swiss-branded makeup and toiletries—the package included a refurbished smartphone and a laptop filled with innocuous files: contacts, emails, and family photos, all doctored, of course, to portray the engaging life of a University of Edinburgh graduate student in artificial intelligence. Most important, the package contained her new documents. Not as Julie Backus. Her father had kept her original passport up to date, but Romanoff said using that name could prove risky. So Alina would become an entirely different person, one with no ties to Harold or Diane Backus. Alina would enter the US as Brianna Danis, a dual American and Latvian citizen, bearing passports from both countries, along with a driver's license issued by Scotland.

But the rapid four-day stopover in England hadn't been sufficient time for Alina to clear her head or to personally familiarize herself with Edinburgh or Latvia, the country Brianna supposedly migrated to from America when she was just two years old. Alina had argued with Romanoff for more time in Riga to allow her to match what she learned about the "country of her childhood" with the physical setting, but he had deemed it too risky.

"Eastern Europe is overflowing with agents from all sides," he had warned.

So the four days outside of London had to suffice,

after which Alina had taken a train to Heathrow for her final flight. She'd spent her transatlantic journey in a deep haze, unable to sleep until about an hour before hearing the United Airlines flight attendant's welcome message. But now, as the plane touched down late in the afternoon, Alina could feel the rush of adrenaline coursing through her veins, her heart thumping so hard she found it difficult to breathe.

"Ladies and gentlemen," the flight attendant announced, "welcome to Chicago."

You've made it, she said to herself. She was in America.

Where her search for her mother could begin.

She told herself to stay cool as the plane taxied to the gate. She stood with the other passengers and reached into the overhead storage bin for her roller bag. A hand reached up and brought it down for her.

"Oh, thank you, sir." Alina turned and smiled.

The well-groomed gentleman nodded. His dark hair was graying at the temples. Alina thought he was forty, maybe forty-five. He wore a white open-collared shirt and an eager expression. Alina rolled her bag down the aisle. Was that the type of man Brianna would encounter on Romanoff's assignment? Alina had convinced herself over the past six months that her task would be simple. After all, a good portion of her training had focused on the pharmaceuticals that would ensure each encounter was quick and uneventful. She'd also perfected Fedorov's simplified computer hacking techniques, sufficient for any contingencies that might arise.

Signing up for Romanoff's scheme was a small price to pay in return for his establishing her in Chicago—and for furnishing the files he claimed to possess on Valeriya Petrova's time as an undercover scout in America.

CHAPTER
FOURTEEN

"COME ON!" Theo Barkley urged. "Gimme ten more!"

Lucas inhaled deeply and pressed his palms against the mat. Lying on his back, he slowly raised his battered right leg off the floor before lowering it back down.

"That's one," Lucas's physical therapist counted out. Lucas took several breaths before duplicating the movement. By the time the muscular Barkley called out, "And that's ten!" Lucas was exhausted. Barkley touched Lucas's shoulder and said, "Great work today, man. Meet me on the table and I'll get some ice for that leg."

As Lucas pushed himself into a sitting position, a familiar voice asked, "You need some assistance?" Lucas looked up at the outstretched hand of Supervisory Special Agent Hank Ramsey.

"Thanks, boss," Lucas said as he grabbed hold of the meaty hand and pulled himself up. Lucas balanced on his left leg and hopped over to the wall to retrieve his cane. He leaned on the wooden handle as he maneuvered to the trainer's table, the sounds of exertion from other patients echoing off the walls of the physical therapy facility.

"You seem to be getting around better," said the fifty-year-old head of Chicago's undercover operations. Ramsey was husky, with a receding gray hairline.

Lucas rolled his eyes as he sprawled onto the table. Months of agonizing and exhausting physical therapy had increased his mobility, while Percocet alleviated the pain. But doctors said he was still months away from being cleared for the demands of undercover fieldwork. They also said that even after ditching the cane, Lucas might never lose his noticeable limp.

"What brings you?" Lucas asked as Barkley returned with an ice blanket in which he wrapped Lucas's aching thigh.

"You still looking for something to do?" Ramsey asked.

Lucas leaned up on his elbow. He was itching to go after the Rojas drug traffickers who had maimed him and killed his informant. But as if reading Lucas's mind, Ramsey held his hand up and said, "It's not for my undercover unit, Lucas. I've been asked to deploy one of my agents to the cybercrime team that's trying to infiltrate online hacking groups. They want their engineers to learn from an undercover agent."

Lucas dropped back onto the table and asked, "What do I know about cybercrime?"

"It doesn't matter, Lucas. They've got plenty of technical knowledge. But they know nothing about the art of deception. This might be a good way to ease you back in."

"My undercover knowledge is from the streets, Hank. Those cyber guys work behind computers."

Ramsey shrugged. "The top brass thinks we're all interchangeable, Lucas. To them, it's just law enforcement. Besides, before long, every crime will be cyber." Lucas rolled his eyes, but Ramsey pushed ahead. "Think of this as an opportunity to broaden your network, burnish your credentials for when promotion time comes around." Lucas saw Ramsey glancing at Lucas's leg. "And let's face it. This is about all you can handle right now."

"My leg is getting there," Lucas said unconvincingly.

"Look," Ramsey said. "This was the director's idea. He really wants to see this happen. I can tell him you're not ready, but that still leaves you on the sidelines."

Lucas inhaled and blew the air out slowly. "How long do they need me for?"

"Four or five months."

Lucas shook his head. He sat up and pulled the ice blanket off his leg. "Five months is a long time, Hank."

"But you'll be working again, Lucas. Isn't that what you wanted?"

Lucas silently rubbed at his throbbing leg and thought about Ramsey's proposal as he surveyed the rehabilitation center. Lucas had gotten to know several of the injured cops and FBI agents working out at the facility, everyone fighting their way back to active duty. Lucas reached for his cane and carefully lowered himself off the table.

"What do you say?" Ramsey asked.

Lucas forced a tight smile then said, "Whatever you need, boss."

Cybercriminals operated on a different playing field than undercover field agents, but at least Lucas would be back in the game.

CHAPTER
FIFTEEN

ALINA'S HANDLER had a calm voice with a hint of a French accent. His brown hair was clipped in the back and sides but full on top. From the lines surrounding his eyes in the rearview mirror of the Toyota Landcruiser, she thought Charles Gagnon to be in his early forties. Alina closed her eyes, slowly inhaled, and let out a long, deep breath, allowing the tension and adrenaline to release from her entire body. When she awoke, Gagnon was navigating up a wide boulevard alive with activity. Shoppers in heavy coats and bulky hats emitted clouds of condensation as they hurried along in the frigid, morning air.

"Where are we?"

"This is their downtown district," the Frenchman said. "They refer to it as the Magnificent Mile. You will become familiar with this area soon enough."

She glanced out the other side and watched several driverless cars moving in the opposite direction. She knew of this technology but had never seen it in practice in her own country.

"Amazing," Alina whispered.

"What's that?" Gagnon peered at her in the rearview mirror.

"Americans trust their technology to operate their cars."

He ran his hands along the sides of the steering wheel. "I prefer to be in control." He stopped at a red traffic light, and Alina watched as a sea of pedestrians crossed in front of them. She examined the faces in the bustling crowd, giving closer scrutiny to older women.

Women around the same age her mother would be today.

When the crowd cleared, Alina spotted a police officer standing on the corner. He looked over, and their eyes met. For some unexplained reason, she couldn't look away, and neither did the policeman. Her heart started racing. When the light changed, the policeman turned his attention to the hordes crossing from the opposite direction. She let out a slight laugh.

"What's funny?" Gagnon asked.

"Nothing."

Alina sat back. A few minutes later a hotel came into view on her right. The building, which stretched for an entire city block, looked vaguely familiar. As their car stopped at the traffic light, Alina turned to see a small black-and-gold plaque embedded in the corner limestone: THE DRAKE HOTEL.

She talked her way into a job at the concierge desk, her father had told her. *A perfect place to meet important visitors.*

Alina couldn't catch her breath. She had researched the hotel, examined online photographs. And here it was —the Drake Hotel—the place her mother had worked before she disappeared.

The light changed, and they started to move again. "Wait," Alina said, looking at Gagnon in the rearview mirror. "Go back."

"You will have plenty of time to explore," Gagnon said as he maneuvered onto some type of highway. "We should get to your apartment."

"Please," she pleaded. "I need to see the inside of that hotel. Just for a few minutes. I promise not to be long."

Gagnon's silent glance alternated between the road ahead and her reflection. His mouth twitched as he pulled off the first exit and circled back to the southbound lane. He drove past the hotel entrance and pulled around the corner before parking near a fire hydrant.

"There are several stores in the lower lobby," Gagnon said. "You should appear to be window-shopping."

"You know the hotel?" she asked.

Gagnon nodded. "The main lobby is up the stairs. Do not be long."

Alina exited the car and proceeded around the corner. As she approached the hotel, she was awed by the size and brilliance of the overhanging marquee, the building's classic architecture a sharp contrast to the surrounding structures. Alina pushed through the gold revolving doors and browsed inside a small flower shop. After a few minutes, she walked up the blue-carpeted steps into the hotel's main lobby. She stood under two large crystal chandeliers that hung from the ceiling. She closed her eyes, waiting for some type of sensation, some feeling or sign that her mother had been here.

She felt a tap on the shoulder, and she turned to see a bellhop wearing a brown coat with gold trim. "Welcome to the Drake, ma'am. Do you need help with your bags?"

"Um...I was just taking a look around. I've heard so much about this hotel."

The bellhop motioned with his hand. "Of course. Please. It's quite impressive."

"Thank you," Alina said.

She strolled slowly toward the shops, but her eyes kept darting back to the main lobby, studying the faces working behind the wood-paneled front desk. As she made her way past the restaurant, she glanced to her right. An attractive, professionally attired middle-aged woman with wavy gray hair was sitting behind a large oak desk, to her side a display of pamphlets emblazoned with titles like *The Art Institute* and *The Adler Planetarium*. The woman was speaking to a young couple bundled up in heavy overcoats. Alina moved around to get a clearer look at the desk placard: CONCIERGE.

Alina felt her mouth go dry. She knew she should keep moving toward the exit, where Gagnon was waiting.

"I know you'll have a wonderful time," Alina heard the concierge say. The couple took a stack of pamphlets before strolling away. Alina turned and started for the steps when she heard a voice call out.

"Hello. Can I help you?"

Alina stopped. The gray-haired woman came out from behind her concierge desk, smiling with an outstretched hand. "You looked like you were patiently waiting to see me." She took Alina's hand.

"Oh," Alina said. She tried to pull her hand back, but the woman's grip was firm. "No. I'm fine. I was just…" Alina waved at the chandeliers with her other hand. "I was just admiring the chandeliers."

"Ah," the concierge said while looking up. Her lapel tag indicated her name was Ella Schmidt. "The crystal is truly magnificent, for sure." The firmness with which Schmidt held her hand made Alina's pulse quicken. Did Schmidt work at the Drake all those years ago? "May I help you select some sightseeing excursions? Perhaps a show?"

"Please," Alina said, finally pulling her hand away, "I have to go." She turned and raced down the steps and out the exit, walking briskly through the frigid air to rejoin Gagnon.

"Was that helpful?" Gagnon asked when she returned to the back seat.

Alina shrugged her shoulders and tightened her seat belt until it restrained her so much she could barely breathe.

CHAPTER
SIXTEEN

GAGNON PARKED in front of a low, brick-faced apartment building. He carried Alina's bag up three stories to apartment 3B and opened his phone, entering a three-digit code that instantly unlocked the door.

The apartment was plain and simple. Heavy brown curtains were drawn, making it feel more like midnight than eleven a.m. The small sitting area contained an olive-green couch surrounded by matching black end tables. The kitchenette, with a small eating counter and two chairs, was tight but clean.

Gagnon opened the refrigerator, revealing fully stocked shelves. "Hungry?"

"Famished," she said, joining him in the kitchen.

Gagnon made her a sandwich of wheat bread, mayonnaise, cucumber, and Havarti cheese. "Not quite the Russian tea sandwich you are used to," he said. "My men said they couldn't find any kielbasa."

Alina took three fast bites and washed the food down with a glass of water from the sink. "It's wonderful," she said. She carried the sandwich into the living room and walked to the window, separating the curtains to glance out into the bright sunshine.

"This neighborhood will suit your needs," Gagnon said as joined her by the window. "People move in and out all the time, which is very good. Your arrival should not be noticed. There are only three other apartments on your floor. All occupants have been thoroughly vetted."

"Why is it so dark in here?"

"My team closed the curtains while they worked. Once I am gone you may do as you like. Come. Let me show you the back."

She followed him down a short hallway, stopping to peek into the small bathroom before entering the first bedroom, which contained a twin bed, a white dresser, and a small closet.

"I'm afraid there's not much room back here," Gagnon said.

"You've obviously never lived in St. Petersburg," she said. "It will be fine."

He led her down the hallway to the other bedroom and handed her a key. She unlocked the room and flipped on the light, revealing a large, wide metal desk. On top of it sat a closed laptop connected to a six-inch, black cylinder. Alina placed her hand on top of the laptop and asked, "Is Fedorov's hacking software installed?"

Gagnon nodded. He flipped open the laptop and ran his hands over the keys. He stopped and pointed to an icon at the bottom of the screen. "You and I will communicate using this encrypted application." He then opened the bottom right-hand drawer, revealing several small boxes. "These contain burner phones to use on each mission. Do not use them to text me unless it's an emergency. We should stick with the laptop's secure system." Gagnon closed the drawer and his hands returned to the keys on the laptop. The screen filled with a long list of female names.

"Let me have your Brianna Danis passport and credentials," Gagnon said. "Now that you've made it through American security, you'll be using a different set of false identities. Driver's licenses for each are in the top drawer." Gagnon closed the laptop and pointed at the black cylinder. "And this storage device contains Romanoff's gift."

Alina tilted her head.

"Documents Romanoff has retained for over twenty-five years," Gagnon explained. "Each with information about a certain agent you might be looking for. Over five hundred files have been loaded."

Alina sank into the chair. She ran her fingers along the top of the cylinder as her entire body tingled. Five hundred files! Each containing information about her mother.

"Each has been temporarily encrypted," Gagnon said.

Alina looked up at him. "Where is the decryption key?"

Her handler looked away. "First, Romanoff would like to see some results."

"What?" she shouted, her fingernails digging into the palms of her clenched fists.

"Shhhh." He put an index finger to his lips. "I do not make the rules. He fears you will focus solely on your search." He paused and leaned on the metal desk. "Given your insistence on stopping at the Drake, I cannot argue the point."

Alina took in a long breath and exhaled slowly. What other surprises would Romanoff and Gagnon reveal now that she was here?

"Once you have delivered on an infiltration," Gagnon said, "and the first ransom payment is made, he will begin unlocking files."

Maybe she could crack into the encrypted files on her own. She surveyed the desk again. To the left of the laptop was a small box labeled USB FLASH DRIVES, and a yellow notepad with what looked like website names.

SugarConnections.com, NoComplications.com, and SeekingCompanion.com were at the top of the long list that ran down the page. And alongside the pad, a tray holding several vials filled with a clear liquid.

Gagnon said, "I think you will find everything you need to get started."

CHAPTER
SEVENTEEN

ALINA STOOD on the corner of Grand Avenue and North Clarke Street and eyed the crowd milling in front of Jezelle's Tavern, trying to muster the courage to enter. She pulled her heavy coat more tightly around her but felt her insides shaking on this cold Chicago evening. Despite all her mental preparations, she still wasn't sure whether she was prepared to dive into what she had learned was referred to as "the Sugar Bowl." She thought back to that day Romanoff had come to her with his proposition.

"I am *not* going to be a prostitute!" she had stated firmly.

"This is not prostitution," he'd countered. "We have investigated this world thoroughly, Alina. We believe it is a perfect way to gain access. These particular websites are frequented by wealthy, successful American businessmen. Many in senior positions in the type of companies we are after. These men are vulnerable. Some divorced, some estranged, others...well, let's say they suffer from a type of wanderlust. This makes them easy targets. Men seeking...companionship. They believe they are helping a young woman. Financially, of course, but also with a type of mentorship. But you will never see them again after your first date. As long as you are effective at dangling an…implied agreement. They will let their guard down."

"Just like my mother," Alina whispered to herself as she crossed the street and entered the crowded Chicago bar. The music was loud. To Alina, this whole city was loud. She glanced around at the patrons, many of whom seemed to be around her own age. Alina thought this a strange place to be meeting the forty-year-old executive at an import company she and Gagnon had found on SweetNothings.com. She slid past a cluster of men wearing sports jerseys—Gagnon had spent hours grilling her on the difference between a Cub and a Bear and a Blackhawk and a Bull—and found her way to the rear dining area. She looked around, searching for a man matching the description he'd posted in the website's messaging app:

```
I'll be wearing a blue blazer,
pink tie. Jet-black hair and
dark goatee. You can't
miss me.
```

He went by the name Tuxedo and listed his occupation as a "senior executive in a midsize firm." Even though he was one of the few that declined to post a picture of himself, Alina and Gagnon had agreed that Tuxedo's position made him as good a first mark as any. But when Alina scanned the dining area, she saw a young couple deep in their burgers and beer and a mother trying to control her toddler while a baby in a highchair threw pretzels on the sawdust-covered floor. In the back left corner, a bald man wearing a jean jacket and sunglasses was sipping on his cocktail. No sign of anyone resembling Tuxedo's description. Alina sat at a table off to the right and ordered a glass of wine.

"Could you do me a favor?" she asked the waiter. "I'm supposed to meet a friend here. I think he'll be wearing a blue sports jacket. Can you just send him back my way?"

"Sure thing." But as soon as the waiter turned away, the bald man in the jean jacket approached Alina and removed his sunglasses.

"Excuse me," he said. "I couldn't help but overhear. Any chance you're Nina?"

Alina was about to shake her head when she stopped. "Wait. You're—"

"Tuxedo," he said, sliding out the chair opposite her. The olive-skinned man was broad shouldered, his head and face completely shaven. "I know," he said. "I apologize for the deception." She thought she detected a Spanish accent. "I'm always a little cautious on the first meeting," he said, before adding without a trace of irony, "I can't tell you how many people aren't honest with their profiles."

Alina held herself back from laughing out loud as his eyes wandered from her face down to the cleavage she allowed to peek out from her low-cut light blue blouse.

"You certainly were one of the honest ones," he said with a mischievous smile. "Your photo doesn't do you justice."

Her picture and physical description, other than the flowing red wig, had actually been the one genuine part of the profile posted on the website. Gagnon had taken several full-length photos of her to be matched with each of her false identities—multiple personas using wigs, makeup, and various styles of attire he had assembled. As Nina Gladway, wearing simple jeans and several dime-store necklaces, she was a shapely, twenty-five-year-old data analyst. Nina was physically active, citing her love of running and ice skating. She also posted she loved "talking tech" and that she was "looking for the company of a mature man who enjoys good wine and a fine meal."

Tuxedo's bio seemed to make him a perfect target for Romanoff's scheme—"a successful corporate executive seeking companionship during frequent trips to Chicago." But the man who now said his real name was Henry

Garcia also admitted he was only part owner of his family's small import business.

Small import business? Alina pursed her lips but otherwise hid the fury she felt inside, mostly at herself. She should have searched the internet to verify Tuxedo's background, verified Tuxedo's profile before making the connection.

"I don't want to beat around the bush," Garcia continued. He must have sensed Alina's fading interest. "I've tried being honest on those sites, but I find the toughest part is getting someone to meet me. But here's my truth." He paused before continuing. "Our business is small, but I make a great deal of money." Garcia glanced around as if looking to see who was watching. He leaned across the table and lowered his voice. "I'm just looking for someone worthwhile to share it with."

Alina studied the untruthful but eager man across from her. Although she had most likely burned through the Nina Gladway persona without anything to show for it, perhaps she could salvage the evening by doing a test run. See how much GHB it took to incapacitate this diminutive but broad-shouldered man. And while Garcia's family enterprise didn't match Romanoff's target —"only significant enterprises will pay hefty ransom to decrypt their systems"—Alina could still try out her hacking technique to see how easily she could penetrate Garcia's computer defenses and inject the malware.

She felt for the vial in the pocket of her jeans, put on her best suggestive smile, and asked, "What hotel do you like to use when you're in town?"

———

TWO HOURS LATER, after devouring his salad and marinated chicken breast, Garcia leaned back in his chair, his eyelids starting to droop. She had slipped half the contents of her vial into his second martini while he was momentarily distracted by a soccer match on the TV screen.

"It's called GHB," Fedorov had explained during her limited training with the substance. "It's a type of sedative."

"You want me to drug people?" she asked. "I'm liable to kill someone."

"You won't. Start out with half dosages. Slightly more for larger men. Gauge the impact before increasing. As long as you bring on the effects before you arrive at the hotel."

Given her date's stature, Alina had decided to start with a little more than half a vial. Garcia's speech was slurred by the time the waiter cleared their plates. He mumbled something about going back to his place while using his smartphone to pay for dinner and request a car. Minutes later, Alina put on her coat, draped her arm around his waist, and slowly escorted him to the curb and the waiting, driverless sedan.

"I'm sorry, Nina," Garcia said softly. "I can usually... hold my liquor."

"Don't worry," she said, helping him into the car. "Maybe you're just dehydrated. We'll get some water into you back at the hotel."

The sedan pulled away, and Garcia rested his head on her shoulder. As the car approached the downtown area, it suddenly turned right and entered the southbound lane of I-55.

"Where are we going?" she asked, watching the lights of Michigan Avenue disappear through the rear window. "I thought you said your hotel was north of downtown."

Garcia opened his eyes and gently waved her question away. "It's all good." He leaned back and closed his eyes again. Alina pulled at the sleeve of his jacket. "Didn't you say you were staying at the Omni Hotel?"

Garcia cleared his voice. "I enjoy...the Omni. I've stayed...many times. But now..." He smiled. "I'm... renting home. Hotels...tedious." He grabbed her arm and pulled her closer, whispering, "and I love to cook."

Alina sat back. The car was moving too fast for her to get out. Five minutes later, they merged with traffic onto another roadway. When they passed a sign for Englewood, the sedan finally slowed and veered off the next exit. They stopped at a red light in front of a twenty-four-hour bodega. Garcia was snoring now, his eyes closed. The streets were quiet. Based on Fedorov's directive, she had thought Garcia would need another dose of the GHB to ensure his full incapacitation. But maybe Fedorov was wrong. She looked at Garcia and shook her head. She had learned enough for one day. She would get out here and call a car service from the bodega. She pulled on the handle, but the door was locked and wouldn't open.

"Where ya goin', Nina?" Garcia mumbled as the car started moving again. His eyes remained shut.

"Uh, nowhere," she said. Garcia turned his head away and was sleeping again. She would try again at the next traffic light. But five blocks later the sedan pulled over and stopped in front of a single-story brick house. This time, the car doors unlocked, and Garcia's eyes popped open. He looked around and slurred, "Thiz is it." He pushed the car door open as Alina did the same on the opposite side. The street was dark and deserted.

"Come," he directed as he staggered to the front entrance. Now that she was here, she figured she might as well stick with her original plan to test her malware-planting technique. Garcia opened the door, flicked on the lights, and stumbled into the front room.

"Take yer coat off," he said as he wobbled down the hallway. "I'll...be right back." When Alina heard the bedsprings squeak, she knew for certain she had given Garcia more than enough sedative. She walked into a large, well-kept living room and searched for his computer. A dark blue sofa and matching chairs sat atop a cream-colored area rug. Next to the sofa rested a two-foot-tall bronze version of America's Statue of Liberty, right arm and miniature torch extended toward the ceiling. Alina moved to the adjoining dining room, which contained a white table and chairs, but no computer. She tossed her coat on a chair before moving to the office at the back of the house. She opened every cabinet and drawer. Still no computer. As Alina crept down the hallway where Garcia had disappeared, she could hear him snoring. She peeked in to see him lying on the bed, flat on his back, arms and legs splayed out. She inched in and started opening dresser drawers. She opened his closet and found clothing and a small, empty gym bag. She opened the drawers on his nightstand. Nothing. Garcia either hid his computer well, or he was the only man in America without one.

Alina dropped to the floor and searched underneath the bed. She found a medium-sized duffel bag and pulled it toward her. She got up on her knees and unzipped the bag.

And then she let out an audible gasp.

Before her was a mountain of money. Neat packets of American currency. Alina removed the elastic band that held one of the packets together and counted the one-hundred-dollar bills. The single packet contained five thousand dollars. The bag had to contain forty or fifty packets of similar size. Why would an executive in a small family import business have so much cash?

Unless Garcia had a side hustle, she thought.

She zipped the bag closed and pushed it back beneath the bed. What a waste of time, she thought. She grabbed her coat, walked to the front door, and pulled out her phone to call for a taxi service that accepted cash. Gagnon had instructed her never to leave a digital trail using the rideshare apps.

But then she stopped, and her thoughts returned to

the duffel underneath Garcia's bed. Hundreds of thousands of American dollars inside. Garcia had bragged that he had a lot of money. He wouldn't even realize if she made a small withdrawal, money she could stash away as a contingency fund, in case Gagnon and Romanoff sprang any more surprises. She still fumed every time she thought about Romanoff's encrypting the files he had on her mother until she'd delivered a ransomware attack.

Alina returned to Garcia's bedroom. His eyes were still closed, but he was no longer snoring. She went to his closet and grabbed the empty gym bag. She walked to the bed, knelt, and pulled the duffel out from underneath. Once again, she unzipped the bag and exposed the endless packets of bills. Alina stuffed eight packets into the gym bag before closing the duffel and returning it to Garcia's hiding place. She came up on her knees facing the bed.

Garcia's eyes were open, looking straight at her.

"What are you doing?" he murmured.

She grabbed her coat and the gym bag and jumped to her feet, but Garcia reached out and grabbed her arm. She twisted away as his leg swept off the bed and landed a blow to her ribcage. Alina doubled over and fell to the ground, trying to catch her breath. She heard a thump as Garcia rolled off the bed onto the floor. Alina was gasping for air but rose onto her hands and knees. She crawled into the hallway, dragging the gym bag with her, but felt a hand latch on to her ankle. She kicked to free herself as she was finally able to suck in some air. She crawled into the living room and made it past the sofa, the front door only a few feet away. She tried to stand, but Garcia tackled her to the ground.

"No one steals from me," he snarled. She kicked at him, but he tightened his grasp and started dragging her backward. Alina's nails dug into the area rug, and she watched in horror as she slid by the sofa and toward the bedroom. She was now eye to eye with the miniature

Statue of Liberty. As he dragged her back, she reached out and grabbed hold of the statue's arm.

And with a strength Alina hadn't known she possessed, she swung Lady Liberty up in the air and behind her, whipping the heavy object down as hard as she could.

CHAPTER EIGHTEEN

WHEN ALINA OPENED her eyes the next morning, sunlight peeked in through the drawn curtains. Her left arm and shoulder felt sore. She rolled over and winced from the dull ache in her rib cage as memories from the previous evening came flooding back. Garcia's kick to her stomach. Her wielding the heavy statue to free herself from his grip. Her run through the frigid streets before ducking into an abandoned service station to call for a taxi.

She used the laptop to send an encrypted message to Gagnon as soon as she arrived at her apartment.

```
Misfire. Tuxedo not who he
said. No laptop.
```

She omitted that she had stolen money from her potential sugar daddy. Nor did she include details about their physical struggle or hitting Garcia with the statue to release his grip on her. Gagnon—or Romanoff—might abort her entire mission if they knew the risks she had taken in stealing Garcia's cash. She would keep these details to herself, confident the man who called himself Tuxedo would have no idea who Alina was or how to find her. Before she went to bed, Alina had deleted all traces of Nina Gladway from SweetNothings.com.

Alina climbed gingerly out of bed. On the floor in front of her closet lay her discarded clothes and eight bundles of hundred-dollar bills, fifty bills in each packet. She had counted them all before collapsing into her bed the night before.

Forty thousand American dollars.

A good contingency fund indeed, more than enough to get her back to Russia on her own, if needed. After last night, she was more mindful of how things could go wrong and about the fact that she wasn't the only one masquerading out there on the sugar daddy circuit. And despite Gagnon's assurances, he couldn't protect her during these assignments.

She was on her own.

Alina looked at her laptop, wanting to see whether Gagnon had responded. She had two encrypted messages. She unlocked the first, from her handler:

> Need to improve candidate
> screening.

She let out a short laugh, tempting to text back, "Thanks for stating the obvious." Instead, she scrolled down to the next message, assuming she would find additional admonishment. But the next message was from AR. Alexi Romanoff.

> Despite failure, decryption
> key for file one attached.
> Consider it inspiration.

Alina's body shook. She quickly used the code to decrypt the first of the files locked on the storage cylinder. It took less than ten seconds for a document about her mother to transfer to the laptop and appear on the screen. It was a memo addressed to Alexi Romanoff, dated

January 12, 1997. And when Alina read the name at the top, her heart started pounding in her chest.

The author was her mother, Valeriya Petrova.

Date: January 12, 1997
To: Alexi Romanoff
From: Valeriya Petrova
Subject: Thoughts on intelligence-gathering operation

As you requested, I am providing my thoughts in order to modify and improve training and psychological preparedness.

Alina took a deep breath and exhaled as she slowly scrolled down to read on:

As we have discussed on many occasions, if our scouts are to have long and productive assignments, my approach for obtaining intelligence should be used sparingly. Moving through multiple targets in this manner is a stressful and high-risk endeavor. While perhaps not your primary concern, it also has the potential to leave long-lasting psychological scars on scouts. It is only for those scouts strong enough to compartmentalize the physical and emotional toll from their own sense of self, to remember that this is not who they are. It is a means to an end. A sacrifice for the good of our nation, no different than soldiers putting themselves in the line of fire for their country. And just as war veterans pass down their knowledge to the next generation, I am presenting my brief guidance in order to maximize the effectiveness of "future operatives" who enter this arena.

Alina stared at the words *future operatives*, which had been set off in quotes. Had her mother expected her own daughter to someday read these words? Here in America?

Background
   As you know, our existing training for deployment overseas is informed by over seventy years of intelligence-gathering techniques. It is important to continue with the current indoctrination

regime, as all must learn these important skills, which are crucial for our success. That is not to say each scout will not gravitate toward the tools they are most comfortable with or that they find most effective. I myself tried several practices over the course of my time in America. Success came after a period of trial and error.

Alina thought of her misstep with Tuxedo the previous evening. How long would her own trial and error period last?

Targets to Avoid

Younger men—which I generally classify as below the age of forty—who have many female options before them and are therefore more difficult to manipulate.

In addition, younger men tend to be single, which will render them more difficult to compromise, a step often necessary if we are to recruit them. Or, at the very least, to keep them quiet if they discover our involvement.

Perhaps most important, the risk vs. reward equation is not in balance, as younger men have yet to achieve the status to have much to offer. While certainly more natural for our younger scouts, these targets should be avoided.

Alina felt a bead of sweat forming on the back of her neck. This was her mother's playbook—her approach for targeting the men for her brand of espionage.

I have come to a similar conclusion about older targets in their late fifties and beyond. I found older men more suspicious of an approach by a young female. They tend to repel an attractive woman in her late twenties or early thirties. I believe older men believe younger woman are after something—usually money. The existence of this suspicion does not present a platform conducive to my approach. In addition, many in this age category are either divorced or separated, which, again, could make them more difficult to compromise: They have nothing left to lose.

The Ideal Target

This leaves us with the category where I have achieved optimal success. If a scout is to get close to a target—close enough to gain his or her trust, to create an environment where they let their guard down, to escalate to an effective compromising position— married men between the age of forty and fifty-five are the most productive marks. They are at their peak value, having achieved high-level positions with access to critical information. As such, this group also tends to have the most to lose. In fact, this targeted age group is likely to have teenage or young adult children, increasing the leverage points.

Planting the Bait

If a scout is attractive (which of course, they MUST be), many targets will actually take the lead on a seduction. Initial positioning is important. An approaching scout must place him or herself in a situation to be noticed by the target, which is why scouts need to secure the most optimal profession in the target country. In my case, the concierge desk at the hotel has been extremely advantageous. But an encounter may occur at a cocktail party. Or it may require tailing a target until he has moved to a more opportune locale. A shopping mall. A grocery store.

Or a sugar daddy dating site, Alina thought. She wondered whether they existed back in the late nineties.

In some cases, it may require obtaining a temporary job at an establishment frequented by the mark. Whatever the location, a scout must position him or herself where it is easy to make subtle eye contact, without being too aggressive or obvious. Just enough to show the mark that he's been noticed. Ambitious men—men who have power—love to be noticed. Once scouts develop some experience with this maneuver, they will find that most of these men will approach on their own.

Sinking the Hook

Scouts should exhibit some vulnerability during early interac-

tions—complain about difficulties with a career, a boss, a broken marriage. They should develop compelling backstories, so believable they feel the emotion inside when they recite it. Once they've made the connection, they will learn to spool the story out over the course of their interactions. It is critical that it is woven in such a way that the target believes he can help, that he can take the scout under his wing. This will be apparent when he starts trying to impress the scout with how important he is, with who he knows, and what information he possesses.

For the next hour, Alina continued to read through her mother's memo, the words a continuous stream of guidelines on the art of seduction for purposes of fulfilling a mission. Her mother's tried-and-true formula for success as an undercover agent. But when Alina read the last few paragraphs, her body started to quake:

The most effective way to bring in the target is with the allure of a sexual encounter. At times, this can escalate into the act itself.

It was true. Her mother *had* had sex with these men.

While this can and should be avoided, these encounters are an unfortunate hazard. When I find myself in these situations, I try to take myself mentally to a different place. I think about why I am here. I visualize my homeland. My family. I visualize a favorite setting. The ocean, the small garden I tend at home. Whatever takes my mind away from being present.

Alina pushed back from the desk and walked shakily to the kitchen, then to the living room window, trying to calm her thoughts. She parted the curtains and stared into the dark, deserted street. How could this have been who her mother was? And these words—this guidebook was so…clinical. So cold. The guidance to show vulnerability, to let a target take you under his wing, and to focus on married men. And how sex was a "hazard of the approach." Were these directions meant for her? Did her mother know Alina would be here in America a quarter century later? Is that why this was the first file Romanoff had decided to unlock? Alina tightened the curtains and returned to the back room. She sat, folded her hands gently on the desktop, and rested her forehead on top of them.

Of course her mother's words showed no emotion, Alina thought. How else could anyone carry out these missions, which Alina now understood from her experience with Garcia, could be extremely dangerous? You would need to steel yourself. You would need to ward off any qualms. These words might not have put Alina any closer to learning her mother's fate, but still, for some unexplained reason, Alina actually felt...comforted. As if her mother were alive in these pages. Alina was no longer alone.

She had her mother's guiding hand.

But she needed to learn more. There were hundreds of locked files on the external drive. She had tried several times to break the encryption code, without success. Now she would do whatever it took to unlock the files about her mother as quickly as possible.

She sat up and opened a new window on her laptop.

She had a lot of work to do.

CHAPTER
NINETEEN

SPECIAL AGENT LUCAS FOLEY pulled up to the Southside Urgent Care clinic on Ashland and gingerly stepped out of his car. The clinic was surrounded by yellow police tape, and a crowd of onlookers had gathered behind the barricades. Lucas leaned heavily on his cane for support as he made his way through the crowd and ducked under the tape, showing his badge to the officer at the entrance.

Once inside, he followed the trail of blood to room 7, where a forensics team was processing the corpse. The victim, a Hispanic male with a medium build, was lying on the table with a large wound on the left side of his skull. Blood had pooled around his head, and his eyes were open and staring blankly at the ceiling.

"What do we know?" Lucas asked, turning to the forensic investigator who was dusting the room for fingerprints.

"Blunt trauma to the cranium," the investigator replied. "Looks like he was hit with something heavy."

Lucas leaned over and examined the deep and jagged wound. He rubbed at the dull ache that started running down the side of his own battered leg.

"Where's the doc that was on duty when the victim was brought in?" Lucas asked.

"In the back. I think a couple of FBI guys are talking to him now."

Lucas was slowly making his way down the hallway when a door to exam room 10 opened. Supervisory Special Agent Hank Ramsey came out. "Oh, Lucas. Good, you're here."

Ramsey pulled Lucas into the examination room and closed the door.

"Thanks for calling me in on this, Hank."

"Well, you're the only person at the bureau that had eyeballs on Lozano and his men. Besides, I figured the cyber guys would let you off for good behavior."

"I don't recognize him," Lucas said. "The dead guy back there. He doesn't look like either of Lozano's body-guards from the junkyard."

"Are you sure?"

"Hard to forget the guys that almost killed you," Lucas said.

"Is it possible the guy in there was the gunman in the SUV?"

Lucas shrugged. "I never got a good look that night. Why do you think it could be him?"

"Do you remember the name Guillermo Garcia?"

"The Rojas hitman?" Lucas remembered the profile he had studied months earlier. Garcia had served three years at Mexico's Altiplano maximum-security prison before he mysteriously escaped.

"Yeah. He liked to use the name Henry. We sent fingerprints from the corpse to Mexican police, and they made the match."

"Do we know who bashed in his head?"

Ramsey shrugged. "Maybe he finally went after the wrong people. Maybe he was trying to position himself for a bigger role within the cartel."

Lucas had spent enough time studying the Rojas

Cartel to know Ramsey could be right. Informants reported the cartel had an ample supply of field soldiers vying to move up the chain of command.

"We might learn more about how he died after the autopsy and toxicology tests," Ramsey said.

"How did Garcia make it here to the clinic?"

"The doctor on duty said two burly Hispanic males carried him in."

"The bodyguards from the junkyard," Lucas said.

"We think so."

"Can we speak to the doc?"

"Already finished with him." Ramsey retrieved a pad from his breast pocket and read from his notes. "Burly guys rang the overnight buzzer around two a.m. and carried the victim in. Injured man wasn't breathing and had already lost a lot of blood. Doc told the men that he needed to call for an ambulance—injured man needed to get to a hospital—but one of the big guys flashed a gun and said, 'No ambulance. No cops.' Doc says he did what he could, but condition was too severe. He asked the goons how the injury occurred, but all they said was something about a 'date gone bad.'"

"A date?"

Ramsey shrugged. "I assume 'date' means another narcotics transaction. Anyway, doc said he was afraid of what these guys would do if the victim died, so he kept working for close to an hour. But when it was pretty obvious Garcia was gone, the guy with the gun dropped a packet of hundred-dollar bills on the table and told the doc to get their friend a proper burial." Ramsey closed the pad and looked at Lucas. "The packet had five thousand dollars, Lucas. We're checking the serial numbers."

"You think it's our money from the junkyard?" Lucas asked.

"We'll know soon enough."

"How about security cameras?" Lucas asked.

"None here," Ramsey said. "Community doesn't like to be filmed coming in for medical help."

Lucas gripped the handle of his cane. "Well, if Lozano's bodyguards are still in Chicago, maybe Lozano is too." Lucas moved closer to Ramsey.

"I know what you're thinking, Lucas." Ramsey shifted. "But you're not medically cleared for undercover work."

"Come on, Hank," Lucas pleaded. "I'm ready."

Ramsey shook his head. "And you're also knee deep with the cybercrimes task force."

Lucas was helping the cyber team develop a rapid deployment group, capable of setting up within forty-eight hours of a reported incident. "I'm nothing more than an adviser over there."

"I gotta go, Lucas." He walked to the door and stopped. "Listen. The bureau is paying you the same whether you're dodging bullets or advising computer geeks. If I were you, I'd enjoy the desk work while it lasts."

CHAPTER
TWENTY

ALINA UNDRESSED AND TOOK A LONG, hot shower while her software churned through the sugar daddy websites. The extensive hacking skills she had learned during Fedorov's months-long training program were more than enough to get around the sites' meager protections. While many assured clients of "the highest level of privacy and security," it was obvious these dating companies invested little on security protocols. They were as protected as an unlocked car with the key in the ignition. Alina had coded a program to compare the profiles of potential targets on multiple sites to publicly available information on the Web, along with a slew of industry and professional networking sites.

She put on an oversized T-shirt and dried her hair. By the time she returned to check her screen, her software had discovered a great deal about the twenty-two sugar daddy websites and the profiles listed on them. Many of the sites, such as SweetTooth.com and SugarFix.com, were littered with liars and scam artists. Like Tuxedo. So much for their extensive vetting processes, Alina thought.

Several, like Chugar.com, featured legitimate businessmen but attracted a largely international crowd.

Gagnon had told her not to do anything that might attract the attention of European and Asian police.

Then there were the diligent companies, like Discreet-Agreements.com, which promised extensive background checks—"fully inspecting against multiple databases, including DMVs, criminal records, US federal sanctions lists, and the national credit bureaus."

Alina checked the accuracy of her code one last time and glanced at the clock. It was four a.m. and the caffeine from the four cups of coffee had worn off. It was time to call it a night.

When she awoke at eleven fifteen, she padded over to her workstation and initiated the code. The results were ready within minutes, organized into several folders.

She clicked through the profiles and accompanying photos in the first folder, which she had dubbed JOKERS—their false identities caused her to chuckle. There was the film producer who posted that he would "put his dates in movies"—turns out he owned several car dealerships around Chicago. There was the forty-year-old sports agent who posed with pictures of his Lamborghini. In reality, he owned thirty pretzel franchises around the Midwest. A sixty-year-old who pitched himself as a globe-trotting wine importer owned a mannequin manufacturing plant outside Naperville.

Alina dragged the Jokers file into her trash bin.

She moved her hand over to the folder marked THE ACCOMPLISHED. Alina's software had verified that these were, in fact, a group of well-paid professionals, all listing their legitimate credentials. Lawyers, doctors, architects, even some musicians. Not her target audience, but she saved the folder on her drive. They might come in handy later.

She smiled as she opened the third folder, the one she had labeled HIDDEN GEMS. The men in this grouping had much in common. Each held senior positions in sizable corporations—the kind of companies that had the resources to pay meaningful ransom, and the kind of companies that liked to make problems disappear. These sugar daddy prospects were in their late forties and early fifties—the sweet spot, according to her mother's guide-book. A stage in life where their great success made them feel powerful. Where they would be prone to letting their guard down.

Men who felt as if they could do anything they wanted.

But Alina's code had flagged an interesting subset. While each of these executives listed themselves as single or divorced, Alina's search prioritized ten who were still legally married.

And at the very top of her prioritized Hidden Gems was the name, James McKinsey.

CHAPTER
TWENTY-ONE

ALINA WALKED through the lobby of the John Hancock Center past an inebriated group of men, their ID cards swaying from neck straps as they stumbled toward the exit. As she went by, one of them said something in her direction, but she kept moving toward the elevators as a loud roar of laughter echoed off the walls. She wrapped her coat more tightly around herself, thinking these were the type that would someday populate her Jokers file.

Alina took the elevator to the ninety-sixth-floor Signature Lounge and ducked into the ladies' room. She removed the new coat she'd bought at Bloomingdales and straightened the short black dress she had selected to accentuate her features.

This time, Alina planned to land her target.

She opened her small handbag and checked that she had the three vials of liquid. Gagnon had convinced her to bring extra as a precaution. She freshened her lipstick, moved a stray brown hair from her wig into place, and gave herself an imperceptible nod of encouragement.

As Alina entered the lounge, the warm sound of soft jazz floated over the hushed conversations of the important-looking patrons. She scanned the glass-enclosed room, looking for her mark, but her eyes were distracted by the expansive view of the surrounding city. The night was clear, and the skyline was stunning. Alina was about to move closer to the windows to get a better look when she heard, "Welcome, miss. May I help you?" The dark-suited maître d' was standing by her side.

"Oh...I'm supposed to meet a friend. His name is James McKinsey."

"Yes, Mr. McKinsey is here. May I take your coat?"

He took Alina's coat and guided her toward the back corner where McKinsey was sitting. Lean and handsome, in his early fifties, he had a full head of dark hair, slightly gray at the temples. The man exuded an air of confidence as he chatted with a waiter.

McKinsey glanced up as they approached his table, his face hesitant at first. Yet, as it became apparent who the maître d' was escorting, his eyes seemed to sparkle with anticipation. He stood as she approached.

"Deirdre?" he asked, extending a hand.

"James?"

"It's Jim," he said. They shook as the maître d' left them. "Oh, your hands are freezing," McKinsey said with a smile as he motioned her to join him. "I thought you'd be used to this cold based on where you came from." Alina had posted on the sugar daddy site that Deirdre had recently moved from Vancouver.

"I'm sorry," she said, looking away as she sat across from him. "I guess I'm a little nervous."

McKinsey arched his eyebrows. "First timer?"

Alina gave a slight smile and nodded. Having digested her mother's instructions, she knew it was best to position herself as a vulnerable rookie. "How about you?" she asked.

"I've been on a few dates," he replied, and he looked down at his fingers brushing at the white tablecloth. But Alina already knew the answer. According to the sites she'd tapped into, the CEO of IB Corporation had at least three active relationships in other parts of the country. He looked around and waved. "Let's get you something to drink." Moments later, the waiter took her order of a gin and tonic.

"How long have you been in Chicago?" he asked.

"Just a few weeks. I'm still trying to find my way around the city." Alina certainly had that in common with Deirdre.

"It's a fairly easy town once you get the hang of it," McKinsey said.

"Do you live here?"

"I'm out in the suburbs, but I stay in town often enough. I usually grab a room at the Drake."

Alina bit her lower lip but kept her gaze on McKinsey as he sipped his drink.

"You have unbelievable eyes," he said.

"I got them from my mother," she said, wincing inside as soon as the words left her mouth. She had read through her mother's material at least a dozen times to get ready for this evening. But as the waiter brought her drink, Alina worried that mentioning her mother, who would be around the same age as McKinsey, was a careless error. *Do not bring up anything that draws attention to the age difference*, her mother's memo had instructed. *Just let him admire the bait.*

Alina leaned back and slightly arched her back as McKinsey raised his glass. "To beginnings."

They drank as she casually shared Deirdre's fabricated background living a sheltered life in Walnut Grove, a small suburb of Vancouver. "A real hockey town," she said, looking at McKinsey over the rim of her cocktail.

"I played hockey in high school," he said.

She wanted to say, "I know you did, Jim," but instead she smiled and said, "So did I," which was the truth. She was actually a decent right winger in the St. Petersburg junior league.

"I shouldn't be surprised," he said with an eager grin. "You look very fit. Do you still play?"

"Not really," she said. "But plenty of girls from my hometown do." She leaned in and whispered, as if she were about to share a big secret. "All that skating and hitting, my body just couldn't take it. I guess I'm just too soft."

McKinsey cleared his throat.

They continued with their banter and cocktails for the next half hour. He leaned in to his obviously well-honed charm to portray himself as an important man. Someone who enjoyed having fun but rarely had the time.

Of course, he failed to mention anything about his wife, Lenora. Alina had found out all about their marriage of twenty years on several social media websites. McKinsey just continued to describe his life as a lonely business executive. Trips to London and Paris at least once a month. Hong Kong and Sydney four times a year.

"It must be so exciting," Alina gushed. "So glamorous."

McKinsey stared at his glass, seemingly lost in thought. "Paris is not so bad. I usually take the red-eye over on Sunday night. I get to my hotel room for a quick breakfast and a shower. And then I'm off behind closed doors in meetings the rest of the day. Then there are the client dinners, before I'm off to the next city to do it all over again."

"Don't you ever see the sights?" she asked, hoping she looked sufficiently interested.

He shook his head. "At least I can tell you the best hotels to stay in."

She couldn't believe he was actually looking for sympathy from *her*. She thought she'd better play along. She reached across the table and touched his hand. "You should learn how to relax," she said.

"Is that right?" McKinsey's eyes locked on Alina's. He smiled and asked, "What do *you* do to relax?"

"Well," she said as she pulled her hand back and raised her glass. "This is a good start." She took several sips, trying to calm her nerves. McKinsey took another sip, and his expression turned serious.

"Tell me," he said, "what brought you to Chicago?"

"I was ready for a change." Then, feeding the line she had crafted for him, she added, "And I wanted to find a job with a start-up company. I hear there are many possibilities in Chicago."

McKinsey looked off, seeming to contemplate his response before downing the rest of his scotch in one gulp. "Would you like to get some dinner? I know a nice little French bistro not too far."

Alina smiled, her first genuine reaction of the evening. She loved French food.

———

AS THEY STARTED on their second bottle of pinot noir and were halfway through their duck à l'orange, McKinsey looked closely at Alina. "You know, I like that this is your first time."

Alina silently dabbed at her mouth.

"There's a professional circuit of sugar babies out there, going from one guy to the next."

"I didn't know that," she said.

"And you know, Deirdre, I know a lot of people funding start-up companies. They're all looking for talent." He leaned in closer and added, "I think I could really be helpful."

She smiled broadly. "That would be wonderful, Jim."

McKinsey slid his plate to the side. He leaned back and steepled his fingers. "This seems as good a time as any to discuss a possible arrangement."

She felt a jolt in her chest. It was happening. McKinsey continued with the air of the confident CEO, businesslike. About to enter a negotiation.

"I come into the city at least once a month," he said. "Sometimes for a few days. I hate going out for those business dinners. They bore the hell out of me." He motioned to Alina. "I'd much rather spend my evenings in the company of an attractive, intelligent person like you." She smiled softly as he continued. "This could work out very well for both of us. You're a young person trying to make your way. I've coached people throughout my career. I could help you get established. Guide you."

"Like a mentor?" Alina smiled, but her heart was pounding.

McKinsey lightly slapped the table. "Exactly. Like a mentor. And if we don't find something for you here, there are plenty of other great cities where I can set you up." He waved his hands around the bistro. "And I know all the great restaurants in every city." He folded his arms and leaned them on the table. "It seems like we have a lot in common, right?"

"Hockey," she said.

He laughed. "Yes. Hockey, and French food, too, right?"

"This was an excellent choice."

"So"—he raised his glass—"we have a deal?"

"Deal." She forced herself to maintain her smile. The evening had gone well, but the vials were still sitting in her handbag. McKinsey hadn't taken his eyes off her the entire evening. And he'd never left the table to use the bathroom. Alina felt a bead of sweat dripping down her spine. She raised her glass to meet his, hoping to toast their new arrangement, share a good-night kiss, and come back prepared on their second encounter. But as they clinked glasses, she learned that McKinsey had other plans.

"Now that we have entered this new arrangement," he said. "Should we celebrate with a drink back at my hotel?"

CHAPTER
TWENTY-TWO

WHEN ALINA OPENED HER EYES, a ray of light was peeking through the drawn curtains. She rolled onto her side and pulled the comforter over her head. All she wanted was more sleep, even though sleep was all she had done for the past four days since her encounter with McKinsey. She had barely left the bedroom, other than to pick up groceries at the corner market. She had shut out the world, trying to forget about where she was and who she was working for.

Trying to forget what she had done.

Every few hours she'd checked her laptop to see whether Gagnon had sent a message. Other than the encrypted text he'd transmitted the morning after her encounter with McKinsey, her handler had maintained his silence. At least Alina knew from that text that the malware she had planted on IB Corp.'s system was active. She assumed Gagnon would have told her if he'd heard that the narcotics had inflicted any lasting damage on McKinsey. Still, she was shaken by the experience, worried she'd been sloppy, that she'd left behind clues that would lead IB Corp. back to this apartment.

Yet everything seemed to have gone well that night. She'd slipped the GHB into McKinsey's cocktail while he was distracted by a text message at the Drake's bar. Then she stalled with meaningless conversation, allowing ample time for the narcotic to take effect. McKinsey was slurring his words by the time Alina escorted him to his room, and he had been completely under the drug's influence by the time she undressed him. He was fast asleep when she opened his laptop and then pulled back his eyelid to perform the retinal scan that authenticated his system credentials. She keyed in the security code IBC sent back to his phone. Alina then inserted her flash drive and initiated the ransomware installation. McKinsey was still sleeping soundly when Alina removed her own garments and lay down beside him. She used her phone to take several photos of her naked body next to his before texting him the most incriminating shots, along with a warning note, to ensure the married man's silence. As soon as she returned to her apartment, Alina sent the encrypted text message to Gagnon:

One incoming.

Yes, everything had gone according to plan. All she could do now was wait to hear from Gagnon.

She padded to her bathroom and looked in the mirror. It was obvious the mixture of adrenaline and fear had taken a physical toll. Alina's normally bright green eyes were bloodshot, her lips dry and cracked, and her shiny blond hair looked matted and dull. It was time to pull herself together. She heard a brief ping coming from the bedroom. She held her breath as she walked to check her laptop.

GAGNON:
Payment received!

The air cleared from Alina's lungs. Had IB Corp.— James McKinsey's company—really paid Romanoff a one-million-dollar ransom? The malware she had planted contained instructions on how to transmit digital currency to an untraceable crypto wallet. She wondered whether Fedorov had now sent IB Corp. the decryption key to release the files the malware had locked. And how long before Gagnon expected her to move on to the next name on her Hidden Gems list.

In any case, the next action belonged to Romanoff and her handler.

Romanoff will unlock the next set of files after a successful mission, Gagnon had assured her. Files from the scout known as Diane Backus. Now that Alina had delivered, she expected Romanoff to do the same.

The news of a successful payment roused Alina from her stupor. She took a long, hot shower, dried her hair, and placed it in a bun. She donned a gray jogging suit, a baseball cap, and sunglasses. She needed some fresh air. Maybe she'd find a café to have lunch nearby. Even if she would dine alone. Again.

She was at the front door about to head out when she heard another ping coming from her laptop. She walked to the bedroom and opened the new message.

```
Decryption key attached for
next files.
```

ALINA'S right hand was shaking as it hovered over the laptop's keyboard. Her life had been turned upside down by her father and Romanoff and all their revelations. She had agreed to do these…things—things she would never have imagined doing—in order to be sitting here today, in a position to learn the truth about her mother. Yet Alina still wasn't sure she was prepared for what she might find.

Nevertheless, she inhaled and moved the new decryption key onto the storage device. Over the next few minutes, thirty documents—hundreds of pages—were unlocked and transferred onto her laptop.

While four hundred and seventy files remained encrypted.

Alina opened the first file.

The first page displayed the name and the beginning of some type of biography. The name at the top was Foster Dingle:

Professor Dingle conducts and directs research at the University of Chicago. The university describes his work as "aiming to address some of the most intractable natural resource challenges facing the human race." He has published eighty-seven peer-reviewed articles in leading scientific journals. He has penned ten highly classified documents on desalinization and water resource solutions that are high on my target list.

Alina skimmed through several pages containing dry accounts of the professor's work. She came upon a section describing his family life. The forty-two-year-old Dingle was married. His wife of twenty-years, Patricia, was a homemaker who raised their twelve-year-old son, Darren, and eight-year-old daughter, Maura. Nothing remarkable here. But as Alina read down, one sentence caught her attention.

Most promising, he has a predilection for expensive cigars, marijuana, and trips to underground clubs in Greenwich Village while in New York for speaking engagements.

Alina leaned back. This abstract of Dingle's professional and personal life was, in fact, some type of malevolent dossier. Information her mother had gathered to understand his weaknesses.

Alina scrolled through the rest of the file and found similar backgrounds and notes on the personal lives of three different executives employed at American military contractors and a senior political operative in the Democratic Party. She scanned through similar information on an undersecretary of defense and a professor of astrophysics at the University of Chicago.

How deeply had her mother infiltrated the lives of these people? Did any of them know her fate?

She advanced to the next file, and her screen filled with a black-and-white photograph. Alina squinted to make out the hazy image of her young, smiling mother, smartly attired and waving. She was standing on the steps in front of a placard that read THE DRAKE HOTEL. Clicking ahead, she found a color photo, the image clear and crisp, as if it had been taken only a few days ago. Alina's strikingly beautiful mother, blond hair flowing to the top of her strapless red satin gown. At her side, an equally attractive young man in a black tuxedo and bow tie. Alina studied the man's strong jaw and dark complexion. Alina was certain this was not a picture of her father. But who was he? Alina's eyes shifted back to her elegant mother standing in front of a ballroom full of revelers. So tall and poised, a smile that exuded a warmth even in these twenty-five-year-old pictures.

Alina opened the next file. Maybe she would come back to these photographs later.

As she scrolled through, she discovered words, sentences, even whole sections blacked out—redacted to such an extent that it rendered them incomprehensible. Other files were filled with schematic diagrams, including one labeled GUIDED MISSILE SYSTEMS FROM 1996, the name Raytheon in bold at the top. Another outlined a description of 1997 NATO maneuvers in eastern European countries. She skimmed ahead to a file that contained invoices of US military equipment sold to foreign governments and policy briefings prepared for the year 2000s presidential election. Another file contained a CIA analysis of internal politics within the new Russia. Alina laughed when she read the 1998 memo predicting Boris Yeltsin "would hold on to lead Russia for another ten years."

Were these the spoils of her mother's missions?

Three hours later, her eyes were still running across the pages, but her mind had become too numb to process anything meaningfully. Reading further would only add to her growing sense of helplessness. She had no idea what she was looking for. Any clues buried within might be purposely vague.

How would she ever understand the meaning embedded in this information? Hundreds if not thousands of documents were locked in the remaining files. She couldn't decipher this on her own. She was not an investigator. She had no idea how to cull clues that might be planted throughout these files. She was only a computer engineer, an artificial intelligence engineer. She knew how to build AI models. Models that learned from—

The memories from her tour of Dmitri Fedorov's lab came flooding back, jolting Alina from her seat. *AI is extremely versatile, as long as we have sufficient data with which to train the system,* Fedorov had said. *AI scouts are the perfect way to rummage through files to find what—or, I should say, who—we are looking for.*

Of course Alina's brain couldn't interpret all these documents on her own. She was not an investigator.

But with a little help, she might be able to build one.

CHAPTER
TWENTY-THREE

ROMANOFF POURED HIS FINEST COGNAC, and he and Fedorov raised their tulip glasses.

"Za uspeh!" Romanoff said.

The men drank to their success, then both audibly exhaled, appreciating the French brandy. Fedorov extended his glass again and said, "And here's to Alina!"

Romanoff smiled and took another sip. The McKinsey success had certainly proved that Alina had learned important lessons. Romanoff felt confident that additional ransom payments would soon follow. Which was why he had decrypted some of the files on Valeriya Petrova. A small reward for Alina's early success. He had hundreds still encrypted, more than enough to keep Alina highly motivated to continue.

Fedorov said, "I felt certain IB Corporation would try to negotiate or disable my malware before parting ways with one million US dollars' worth of cryptocurrency."

"One million is a rounding error for a company of that size." Romanoff placed his hand on Fedorov's shoulder. "And your encryption malware is not easily defeated." He took another sip and said, "Have you learned anything from the keylogger you included?"

"Nothing of value, Alexi Igorevich. We had a very short window to transmit McKinsey's keystrokes before his IT team wiped his laptop clean."

Romanoff was not surprised. His lieutenant had insisted on hiding the tool for capturing keystrokes inside Alina's malware, hoping valuable secrets would be disclosed by CEOs distracted by a ransomware crisis. But Romanoff knew that many Russian leaders tended to write short, cryptic notes, impossible to decipher on their own. He had expected nothing different from American executives.

"We will continue to monitor future transmissions," Fedorov promised. "I am confident something useful will be disclosed."

Romanoff grinned. "Let us not take our eyes off the larger prize, Dmitri Vladimirovich. After all, twenty percent of IB Corporation's million-dollar payment has already been converted to euros and is earning interest in your personal Swiss bank account. Just think of how it will feel when Alina brings you ten or twenty times that amount."

Fedorov took another sip of the Cognac, and then his face broke into a wide smile.

CHAPTER
TWENTY-FOUR

ALINA OPENED her computer's operating system and checked on the processing power of the device Gagnon had provided and confirmed that it should have enough capacity to create the tool she envisioned—an artificial intelligence program built using Valeriya Petrova's voluminous documents. AI that would search through government databases to learn the fate of Diane Backus.

Alina would build her own AI scout.

She recalled a very similar project that she had peer-reviewed during her graduate studies. Several of her class-mates had interned with a professor who was constructing an AI system, allegedly to help locate missing children. After the professor abruptly resigned to take a senior position at the Kremlin, the students discovered that the program he left behind had probed university files for the sole purpose of predicting—or *inferring*, in AI speak—who might become anti-government dissidents. Alina had paid very close attention during the peer review debrief. She remembered enough about the design that she thought she could attempt a similar approach. Just as Fedorov's cyber team had used the history of counterintelligence assets to find new recruits, Alina's AI would analyze and interpret the disparate documents about her mother, organizing the results into common data sets—common bases of knowledge that she would use to train her system. Still, she knew she might need help building the inference engine that would extrapolate a possible set of outcomes —in effect, infer what might have happened to her mother. She dismissed the idea of sending Fedorov her more technical questions, as she doubted their periodic encrypted-message exchange could replicate the iterative process she'd thrived on throughout graduate school. Far better to have a local adviser—someone who wouldn't be suspicious of her numerous inquiries, a subject matter expert eager to impart knowledge. Besides, she didn't want Romanoff to know what she planned to build, lest he think she was distracted from his mission.

She had an idea. With the McKinsey success, she knew Gagnon would expect her to go after her next sugar daddy targets. But his sporadic assignments would leave Alina with plenty of time during the day.

She entered her query for "top AI professors" in the Chicago area. Most of the names displayed in the results were associated with the University of Chicago and Northwestern University, but Alina knew she couldn't just walk onto a college campus and enroll. She needed a school where she could get started right away. And a place she could pay for with the cash she had pilfered from Tuxedo.

Alina scrolled down and clicked on the URL of Horizons, an AI coding school "where experienced coders learn skills that will land them high-paying jobs."

A quick review revealed that several of the instructors had impressive résumés. Two had worked in Silicon Valley, one at a successful start-up in Texas. Alina saw the coding school's location was just a few blocks from her apartment.

Perfect. She had nothing to lose by trying.

She accessed the false identities stored on her computer's C drive, and her eyes ran down the list of names. Ana Dafoe was as good as any. She marked the name as used, to avoid posting it on future sugar baby profiles.

Tomorrow, Ana Dafoe would enroll in the Horizons Programming Boot Camp.

CHAPTER
TWENTY-FIVE

ALINA'S former classmates in Russia had always spoken about America's superior AI capabilities, so she worried that the learning curve at the programming school might be steep. But on the very first day of class, Horizons' energetic founder, Ben Colias, assured his new cohort that he had developed a "surefire method for all levels" of artificial intelligence education.

"I guarantee that each of you will launch into a successful AI career," Colias insisted. He was so confident of the future success of his method, he even offered the class a chance to invest in his venture to open Horizons boot camps all over the country. Alina overheard a few students conferring about investing in Colias's boot camp once they landed their own, lucrative jobs.

During the first two weeks, Alina spent her mornings at home designing and coding a prototype of the AI scout program that would perform a high-speed search for her mother. In the afternoons, Alina attended hour-long lectures, mostly given by a stout woman named Dawn Cornell. Alina kept to herself, sitting in the back to stay separate from her twenty-six classmates. Cornell was knowledgeable but avoided the more technical areas of AI. Then, at the beginning of the third week, the class was turned over to a tall Texan named Logan Greig, who announced the commencement of projects and teamwork.

"That's why we call it a boot camp, people," Greig said with his hands on his hips. "The rest of your time with Horizons will all be hand-to-hand engagement."

Greig said he'd spent twenty years working for a Silicon Valley company called AI Solutions and cashed in his stock options when the company went public. Horizons was offering him an opportunity to open a new location in his hometown of Dallas. But first he wanted "experience with the curriculum here at the mother ship." Alina sat closer to the front of the room during Greig's detailed and analytically focused lectures. As he answered every question the class threw his way, Alina believed she'd found the expert she was looking for.

For her initial project, Ana Dafoe was grouped with a quiet and petite Vietnamese woman named Phuong and a shy Indian man named Ashwini. Their assignment was to use a natural language processor to create a bot that recited a summary of the American Revolution. She tensed up when Phuong and Ashwini suggested that Ana, as the American in the group, would be the best one to present what they'd created. Fortunately, while Greig moved around and checked on the various teams, he never made his way to Alina's group.

By the middle of her second month at Horizons, as the prototype for her AI scout started taking shape, Greig assigned projects that pushed into more technical aspects of building an inference engine. This was Alina's opening to probe the instructor. After all, the AI scout she was building to analyze the files about her mother was based on this exact technique, a technique that could search through millions of data points and infer what might have happened—infer who the Russian agent might have become if she had stayed in America for the past twenty-five years.

And whether she was alive or dead.

Between building her program and these afternoon Horizons classes, Alina was back in her element. Building intelligent systems—*this* was what she was meant to do.

She peppered Greig with questions, all positioned to help her latest team assignment to query fictitious patient databases and deduce medical outcomes. She played the overeager student, anxious to learn as much as she could. And Greig was more than willing to impart his knowledge, even when it was obvious her questions had nothing to do with the team project.

"You know, Ana. You will go far in life with such an inquisitive mind," Greig told her on more than one occasion.

Over those same early weeks and months at Horizons, the confidence and focus Alina brought during the day to both her studies and the AI scout program seemed to translate to her evening sugar daddy assignments. She still had her share of fumbles, like the digital music producer from Nashville who passed out on the ride from the Chicago Chop House to his hotel. She abandoned him in the driverless car at a red light two blocks from the hotel. But for the most part, she became pretty good at timing the GHB so her dates stayed conscious but were on their way to dreamland well before becoming too aggressive. Her first success after McKinsey was with the general counsel of a biotech company. Although she had to practically carry him from the Ritz-Carlton's elevator to his room on the seventh floor, she was able to install the ransomware on his computer without a hitch. Subsequent efforts were more like the date with the real estate developer from Glencoe. His collapse coincided perfectly with their arrival at his room at the Peninsula. She hadn't so much as kicked off her shoes.

Each time she had planted the ransomware, the companies had paid for the decryption key that unlocked their systems. And after every confirmed transfer of funds,

Romanoff released another batch of his files on her mother, which Alina immediately uploaded to train her vastly improved AI scout. Each newly unlocked file brought Alina one step closer to the truth. Just as Fedorov's team had used AI to infiltrate government personnel systems to identify recruits for foreign assets, and just as the Russian professor had used AI to probe university files for anti-government dissidents, Alina's scout was almost ready to probe America's vast internet-connected infrastructure to look for her mother.

Yet as the calendar changed to March, there were still hundreds of files that she still didn't have access to. If only she could come up with a way to accelerate their release. If only she could develop a plan to deliver Romanoff an even bigger ransom payment—a payment so large that he would willingly liberate what remained encrypted on the storage device in her apartment. There had to be a method that was far less denigrating and risky than posing as a sugar baby. But it took a calculating mind like Romanoff's to conceive of these devious schemes. Alina's engineering brain just didn't operate in that manner. And she didn't think it ever could.

But that was before she met Donny Brodsky.

CHAPTER
TWENTY-SIX

LUCAS WAS FINISHING up another morning session with his physical therapist when his cell phone vibrated.

"Lucas. Where are you?" Hank Ramsey asked. "The cyber team's been looking for you. They're meeting on the Sudex case later this morning." Sudex was a ring of hackers siphoning off millions from bank accounts across the country. Lucas had been assisting a small team of undercover cyber agents trying to infiltrate Sudex's network, without much success. Turned out undercover work in cyberspace was just as challenging as chasing drug lords through junkyards. "They're meeting as soon as O'Connell gets in."

"Shit," Lucas whispered. The head of the Chicago bureau had a habit of calling pop-up meetings on cases that were on the radar of the higher-ups in DC. It seemed elected officials didn't appreciate when their constituents' bank accounts were cleaned out by cyberattacks.

"Didn't we just brief him last week?" Lucas asked, leaning against a table. "Why again?"

"I don't know, Lucas. I don't ask a lot of questions when the bureau chief tells me he wants something.

That's what happens to you when you get within three years of retirement. You learn to just do what they ask."

That much was true, Lucas thought. Ramsey had recently confided that he planned to take the early retirement package as soon as he was eligible, which would be soon. Lucas still thought he had a chance at getting Ramsey's job. But only if he could find his way back into undercover operations.

"Let me get showered," Lucas said. "I'll be there."

"Listen, Lucas. We can talk about this later. But the cyber team asked if you would stay on and take the lead on one of their cases. They'll partner you with a junior IT agent to do all the grunt work."

Lucas took a long, deep breath and rubbed at his temple. "I can't stay on cyber, Hank. Maybe I can't go undercover yet. But there's plenty I can do to help you get the cartel."

"Lucas. Listen to me. This new case will be much better given your...situation. Your leg is not back to full strength. This is a solid case, Lucas. A whistleblower reported a ransomware attack."

"Ransomware?" Lucas repeated, feeling his undercover career slipping further away.

"The whistleblower claims his company's CEO was involved."

"I'll come in and we can talk about this." But it was clear from his boss's response that the decision had already been made.

"The company is called IB Corp.," Ramsey said. "They're a private company out in Evanston. Semiconductors. I think they're a big supplier to the autonomous car companies."

There was nothing more to say to his boss. "Send me the case file."

CHAPTER
TWENTY-SEVEN

DONNY BRODSKY STOOD out from the millennials trying to improve their AI skills. He was considerably older—Alina thought he looked closer in age to her sugar daddy targets, but not nearly as polished. He had an ample midsection, a receding gray hairline, and a scraggly mustache. She noticed him ogling at her during one of the happy hours she started attending with her fellow students. Alina faked her way through a bar-side discussion with the inebriated students about the state of the job market while Donny hung back just outside their circle. The following day, she and Donny were paired with two other students to work on Logan Greig's latest project. Donny approached her in Horizon's small kitchen near the coffee machine.

"You know," he said, "I couldn't help but overhear you at McGee's last night. I agree with what you were saying. About us all helping each other with job contacts." Moments later, he added, "I know some very powerful people."

Alina stopped and stirred her coffee. The words *powerful people* had gotten her attention.

"Really?" she said.

"Sure, er…like my brothers. That's right. My brothers. They're both big shots. They both have very big jobs."

"That's very interesting," she said, leaning against the counter.

Donny cleared his throat. "Yeah—one was a very senior AI guy at the Defense Department. Now he's in Silicon Valley. He's in a very big position at Sway, Inc. They're always hiring."

"Wow. He's at Sway?" Even Alina knew that Sway was one of the largest technology firms in the world. "Are the two of you close?"

"Of course. Very close. With my other brother, too. He's an investment banker. He works on deals with huge companies all the time. Tons of contacts for job leads."

Alina didn't know much about investment bankers other than that they made a lot of money. She wondered whether these brothers might present the opportunity she was looking for: to deliver larger ransom payments.

Donny said he had joined the class in the middle of this semester, meaning he'd missed the founder's presentation on his desired countrywide expansion. That gave her an idea.

———

THAT NIGHT, Alina looked at Donny Brodsky's profiles on various social media sites, which corroborated that he was, in fact, connected to a Josh and a Louis Brodsky. And it did not take her long to confirm their positions as senior executives, well-placed in financially significant enterprises. Louis Brodsky was in her sweet spot—a forty-five-year-old married man with one daughter. The older Josh was single. But for what Alina had in mind, age and marital status would not really matter.

These might be very good targets, indeed.

She used her own Horizons log-in credentials to get behind the school's layers of security and easily located

Ben Colias's business plan for expanding his boot camp program across America. She copied and modified a version, placing Ana Dafoe's name prominently on the cover page. She embedded Fedorov's malware in the altered document, but not before boosting the ransom demand. Five million dollars from each brother should be enough to get Romanoff's attention. She downloaded her newly merged creation onto a fresh memory stick.

Over the next few days, she and Donny carried on their conversations around the coffee machine where Alina shared pieces of Ana Dafoe's concocted history. Perhaps she was being careless, but she knew Donny Brodsky was more interested in getting laid than performing a background check.

That evening, she suggested that a few members of her project team, including Donny, continue their work session at Gibson's Bar and Steakhouse. The other team members peeled off after two drinks, leaving Donny and Alina alone in a corner booth. After the waiter brought them their third vodka martinis, Alina slid over to Donny's side.

"I'm glad they left," she said. "They weren't helping much."

"I'm not sure I am either," Donny said. "You've got this stuff down cold. I mean, you could *teach* this class. What are you doing here?"

"You're perceptive," she said, laughing before taking another sip. "Let's just say it's an investment of my time."

Donny leaned back. "What kind of investment?"

"Well." She removed the swizzle stick and picked off an olive with her teeth. "I'm doing reconnaissance. Seeing what I'm up against." She leaned in closer and whispered, "And lining up some partners."

"What kind of partners?" he asked, his voice cracking.

"Well," she said, "I know a lot about technology. I'm not seeing anything in this class that would be so difficult to teach. I'm already a pretty good trainer…"

"You're a *great* trainer," Donny gushed.

Alina giggled, then changed her expression into a pout. "But I don't know much about raising money to start my own business."

Donny took three quick sips of his drink, then said, "What are we talking about here? I mean, what kind of business?"

Alina sat up straight, donning a businesslike expression. "I want to open up my own programming boot camp. Only AI languages. Java, Python, C. These Horizons guys are doing a terrible job. My students would come out so much better prepared and qualified than anyone finishing our classes here."

Donny stirred his martini.

"I've put a plan together," she continued. "But I need investors to get it off the ground." Alina sipped her martini, then asked, "Do you think your brothers would be interested?"

"My brothers?"

"Yes," she said. "I need funding to get it off the ground. Do you think they would invest?"

"I don't know, Ana," he said. "I guess if they thought they were investing in *me*, that would be one thing. But…"

Alina smiled, pleased at how deep the hook was sinking in. "Well, I do need someone with good business sense. I don't really know much about running a business. But I do know technology."

"Well, Ana," he said, "it just so happens that I have run and sold several companies, so I know a little bit about what it takes to manage a successful business."

"Really?" Alina said. But Donny wasn't the brother she was after.

"I'm just doing these programming gigs until I find my next big idea," Donny explained. "Something I can sink my teeth into."

"That's all so impressive." She slid closer. It was time.

"Do you think you could help me?" Alina removed the thumb drive from her purse and slid it over to him.

"Would you and your brothers look at my business plan?"

He stared at the small memory stick. After a few moments he said he thought they would. But his tone sounded unsure. Hesitant. Maybe she needed to apply some of her recently developed skills after all. Alina moved closer and placed her hand on his knee. She slowly slid it up his thigh.

Donny opened his mouth but could only manage to say, "Maybe we…"

"Yes?" she asked.

He tried again. "Maybe…we should go…look at it together."

She had several spare vials of GHB in her purse, but they wouldn't be necessary. At least not tonight. Alina finished her drink and pushed the glass away. With her hand still resting on his thigh, she said, "I think we'll have to see what you can bring to the partnership first."

Alina was excited as she exited Gibson's and walked north on Rush Street. She imagined Romanoff's reaction when millions in ransom payments started flowing in from her new scheme. He would be so impressed; she was sure he'd release every one of the files on her mother.

Alina just needed Donny's brothers to open up the email they got from him with her business plan attached.

CHAPTER
TWENTY-EIGHT

TRAFFIC EASED up as the driverless car turned off Lakeshore Drive onto North Sheridan Road. Lucas looked up from the briefing materials he had been staring at for the past hour as the car made its way to the headquarters of IB Corp. in the town of Evanston, just north of Chicago.

"Interesting company."

Lucas looked to his right, at the source of the matter-of-fact voice.

"Yeah, for sure," he responded to the junior agent sitting beside him.

He had almost forgotten that Agent Sarah Fernandez, fresh out of cybercrime training at the FBI Academy, was in the car with him. Petite and olive-skinned, Fernandez had her dark hair pulled up into a tight bun. While her file listed her as twenty-seven years of age, she looked as if she were still in high school.

Lucas wasn't really in the frame of mind for small talk. He was still pissed about being assigned to another cyber case, even though he decided to follow the advice his father had given him countless times over the years: "Sometimes you have to just suck it up and do as you're told. If not, trust me, the bureau will use it against you."

"Space satellites," Fernandez continued as she scrolled through her tablet. "Cars. Drones. Gaming. Their chips are everywhere." She continued to rattle off various facts and figures that Lucas's distracted mind wasn't absorbing. He hoped he had picked up enough of the salient details to plow through this first meeting. What he did know was that the company was slated to go public in the next few weeks—not the best time for a scandal involving the CEO.

When Fernandez finally stopped talking, Lucas quickly skimmed through a copy of IBC's internal analysis from three months ago. The company hadn't reported the ransomware attack to the authorities until the whistleblower filed a report with the FBI. The conclusion of IBC's security team: "No evidence of any of the normal hacking techniques or external infiltrations." Instead, the ransomware had been launched internally, from the computer of the company's founder and CEO, James McKinsey.

He closed the folder and stared out the window as the car turned past a sign that read WELCOME TO IBC and proceeded down a long driveway before stopping in front of a glass office tower. Lucas carefully got out and did his best to keep up with the fast-walking Fernandez as she led the way into the atrium lobby. After they had shown their credentials at the security desk, Lucas said, "Take it easy, Agent Fernandez. I'm working with one good wheel."

"Sorry," she said. "Guess I'm a little excited."

A security guard escorted them past endless cubicles filled with young, casually clad employees, heads down, working on whatever people do at offices like this. The guard deposited them in a conference room. A long, rectangular-shaped table stretched from one end of the room to the other and was surrounded by over a dozen leather-backed chairs.

"Help yourself to coffee," said McKinsey's blond-haired assistant as she pointed to the tall stainless-steel container sitting atop a service cart. "I'll let Mr. McKinsey know you're here."

Coffee was a good idea, Lucas thought. Anything to jolt him into focus. He saw Fernandez eyeing the second shelf of the cart, which held two trays overflowing with assorted muffins and bagels.

"How many people are we expecting?" she said, waving toward the trays.

"Who knows?" Lucas poured himself a cup of coffee and used his cane to make his way over to an eight-foot-tall glass cabinet. He took a sip and looked over the display of the company's achievements. Multiple awards and citations for excellence, rapid growth, and contributions to local causes. Photos of company executives, he assumed, shaking hands with dignitaries and some of Chicago's most popular professional athletes. Other pictures of the same executives holding trophies at pro-am golf tournaments. All validations of their fat cat existences.

"What's taking him so long?" Fernandez asked as she took a seat at the conference table.

"Be patient. I'm sure he'll be here soon." He turned to see Fernandez pulling items from her bag and placing them neatly in front of her. A tablet. A notepad. Two pens. Her phone. "You look prepared," he said. She looked up and nodded. Lucas let out a slight laugh. He remembered when he was on his first assignment and interrogated a suspect. He had been so nervous, he hyperventilated and had to leave the room to catch his breath.

"I'll handle the main interview, Agent Fernandez," Lucas said.

She smiled. "Whatever you need, Agent Foley."

Moments later, the door opened, and the CEO entered. James McKinsey was tall and slender, his hair unnaturally dark, other than the slight graying at the temples, given his reported age of fifty-seven. Without shaking hands or otherwise greeting the agents, his expression was severe as he leaned back against a side credenza. A *JM* monogram was visible on the cuffs of his tailored blue shirt.

McKinsey folded his arms and said, "I did nothing wrong here."

"No one is saying you did, Ji—" Lucas stopped and looked at McKinsey. "Oh, I'm sorry, sir. Is it all right if we call you Jim?"

McKinsey waved his hand dismissively and stared out the window.

Lucas took a seat next to Fernandez and asked, "So how do you think the malware got on your computer?"

"I've told everyone the same thing," he said. "I have no idea how it happened."

Lucas glanced at the copy of IBC's internal report displayed on his laptop. "Well, it looks like your own IT team found the malware entered the corporate network from your computer back in December."

"I read the report," McKinsey said.

"On a…Monday night, December third." Lucas leaned back. "Your team must be good. They even know the time: ten thirty-four p.m. Central. Was your computer in your possession on that day?"

"It rarely leaves my side."

"Were you out of town?" Lucas asked.

"Not exactly."

"So you were home."

McKinsey shook his head again. "I had an evening speaking engagement." He paused before adding, "At the McCormick Place."

"And you didn't go home afterward?"

McKinsey studied a vase of fake flowers on the conference table, seeming to not hear the question.

"Jim, do you think you were speaking to your audience at that time?" Lucas asked. "Maybe someone had access to your laptop while you were at the podium?"

McKinsey's gaze shifted to look out the conference

room window. "I really don't remember much about that evening."

The CEO had had plenty of time to jog his memory since the breach was discovered.

"Is it possible you were at dinner when the breach happened?" Lucas asked.

McKinsey turned to face him. "I've got a lot on my mind, Agent Foley. I can't remember where I was every minute."

Lucas nodded and scribbled some notes, as if McKinsey had said something really insightful.

"We should get receipts from your assistant," Agent Fernandez said.

"Excuse me?" McKinsey said.

Lucas looked over at the junior agent.

"Well, she would have your schedule from that evening," Fernandez continued firmly. "And restaurant receipts are usually time-stamped. At least that could help pinpoint whoever you and your laptop were with for dinner, and what time."

Lucas fought back the urge to smile as he watched McKinsey's face redden. It appeared that Fernandez wasn't too nervous to join in after all. Lucas leaned forward and said, "Ah, that's right. It was December. So, if you went out to dinner, you probably used the coat check. You would have left your briefcase there, too. It's possible that's when someone was able to plant the malware."

McKinsey walked to the conference table and slumped into a chair on the opposite side of the two agents. "There wasn't a group dinner that night. After my speech, I just went back to the hotel."

"Which hotel?" Fernandez asked.

"The Drake. On Michigan Ave."

"Nice," Lucas said. "And you went right to sleep?"

McKinsey shrugged.

Lucas scribbled a note to have Fernandez check the

Drake security cameras, then asked, "Do you remember if you used your laptop at the hotel?"

"I don't know. Maybe."

Lucas exchanged glances with Fernandez. When he looked back at McKinsey, the CEO's expression had turned firm again.

"Agent Foley, you're asking me to remember what I did three months ago at an exact time of day. I was in my hotel room. I don't remember using my laptop that night. If I did, it would have been to check emails. I told my IT guys that's probably how the malware came through my laptop."

"Your IT security team checked that out," Fernandez said. "The malware did not come through an infected email."

McKinsey raised both palms and said, "Well, that's all I can tell you."

Lucas scribbled "Order forensics on McKinsey laptop." Maybe IBC's team had missed something. "Did you go to the office the next morning?" he asked.

McKinsey rubbed his chin. "No. I left for Japan."

"That's got to be a long flight."

McKinsey stood. "Just another day, Agent Foley. In fact," he looked at his watch, "I have another meeting to get to right now."

Lucas reviewed his notes and checked the time. They had enough follow-up tasks for now. They were sure to have more ammunition once Fernandez had the FBI's cybercrimes lab analyze the laptop and malware forensics. He would also have her scour through the Drake's security tapes. He flipped his laptop closed and was about to stand when Fernandez said, "We should have the FBI lab have a look at your personal devices, Mr. McKinsey."

The CEO stiffened as Fernandez continued. "Home computer. Cell phone. You never know how far the bad guys are willing to go." Fernandez looked over at Lucas. "And Agent Foley, you also mentioned that we should get copies of Mr. McKinsey's credit card statements. Bank and brokerage accounts. To make sure the hackers didn't do any personal damage. Right?"

McKinsey sank back into the chair. Where was Fernandez going with this? Surely she'd learned in FBI 101 that without a warrant, they had no right to examine McKinsey's personal devices and records. But from the way McKinsey was chewing on his lower lip, the CEO was clearly visualizing a proctology exam on his activities. Lucas would follow along, see where her tactic might lead them.

"Ah, that's right, Agent Fernandez," Lucas said. "Thanks for reminding me. It will be important to verify. In case, Jim, you forgot something along the way." Lucas paused and grinned. "After all, you've got a lot on your mind."

They started to pack their briefcases as McKinsey sat frozen. When they stood to leave, the CEO shook his head and rolled his chair closer to the conference table. He started rubbing a smudge on the wood table, studying it closely. Without looking up he said, "Agent Foley, can I speak to you in private?"

Lucas looked over at Fernandez, who was now gripping the back of the leather chair she had recently vacated. He had no idea why McKinsey wanted Fernandez to leave the room, but the CEO clearly had something more to share. When Lucas nodded toward the door, Fernandez grabbed her bag and said curtly, "I'll wait outside." Lucas would deal with the residual damage on the ride downtown.

After Fernandez had gone, McKinsey continued to quietly work the smudge. After a few moments, he said, "If this gets out...I'll lose everything."

Lucas lowered himself back into his chair. "If what gets out?"

McKinsey glanced up and said, "Not just my job...my

wife. My kids." Another long pause, then, "Agent Foley, I have a very tough job."

"It's a big company," Lucas said.

"No, I mean, the pressures that go along with a job like this are enormous."

"I'm sure it's intense."

"I'm away from home almost eighty percent of the time. Traveling all over the world."

"Sounds exciting."

McKinsey let out a short laugh and gave up on the table. "It *was* exciting. At least when I was your age. Hong Kong, Singapore, Italy, Buenos Aires. It all sounds so glamorous. But mostly, I go from the plane to the office for long meetings. To a restaurant for a boring business dinner and then to some hotel for a few hours of lousy sleep. That's if I sleep at all. And then back to the airport and on to the next place." McKinsey sat back and added, "It's a grueling existence."

Lucas felt as if McKinsey had given this speech before, and he was amazed at the attempt to elicit sympathy.

"My wife used to come with me," McKinsey continued. "At the beginning. But then the kids came along, so…" His eyes grew glassy. "She'd be devastated if she knew."

"Knew what?" But the picture was already coming into focus.

"I'm getting there," McKinsey said, seemingly annoyed that Lucas would interrupt his train of thought. His shoulders relaxed, and he continued. "It was always harmless."

"Okay," Lucas said.

"I don't have affairs," he said. "At least not real ones."

Ah, there we go, Lucas thought. *At least not real ones.* McKinsey wouldn't be the first lonely road warrior to engage with call girls.

"Nothing like this ever happened when I did it before. San Francisco. Miami. Dallas."

"Did what?" Lucas asked, pushing for him to put a name to it.

McKinsey made eye contact. "It doesn't mean anything. It's simply companionship."

Lucas was getting impatient with the roundabout answers. "Sir, were you with a prostitute?"

McKinsey leaned back, his eyes fierce as he snapped, "I don't consort with hookers!"

"It sounded like that's where you were heading."

McKinsey relaxed his glare. "It's a discreet arrangement. It's not about sex." Lucas shifted in his seat as McKinsey continued. "These women are not into the normal dating scene. They're not looking for a long-term relationship. They just want...an intellectual conversation. Someone who can guide them." McKinsey paused and rubbed his chin. He was staring out the window again. "These are women who are looking for... help."

"What type of help, Jim?"

"Financial, mostly," he said, still looking away. "Some just want to be pampered. A night out in a fine restaurant. They always come from very simple means. They're hoping to meet men who...understand."

"And in return?" But again, McKinsey didn't really need to answer. Lucas had read about these so-called sugar daddies, wealthy men connecting with young women. Sometimes these men paid for their sugar babies' apartments and included a living stipend for clothes and nights on the town. It was clear that the men generally expected some type of sexual relationship in return. The FBI had investigated several sugar daddy platforms as high-end prostitution rings. But almost all the cases had been thrown out of court—too hard to prove the quid pro quo. Lucas had heard of at least one grim encounter. A Google executive overdosed on heroin administered by his sugar baby. The woman was convicted of involuntary manslaughter.

McKinsey said, "She seemed like a very nice young lady. Her name was Deirdre. At least that's how she was registered on the website. Incredible green eyes. I was amazed at how much she knew about technology."

"That's a strange thing to talk about on a date."

"She was very smart." McKinsey paused. "And very beautiful." He looked down toward his shoes and added, "I didn't have sex with her."

Lucas suppressed the urge to roll his eyes.

"At least, I don't think I did."

"What does that mean?"

McKinsey sat up. "I had arranged to meet her at the Signature Lounge in the Hancock building. That's how I like to meet these women the first time. Out in the open. There are plenty of scammers out there. If she doesn't match the profile picture, I make up an excuse—fake an important call—it doesn't matter. I slip them a few bucks and send them on their way. They get it. They know I'm on to them. But this Deirdre—if anything, she was even more attractive than her picture." McKinsey's eyes glassed over, as if in a trance, as if he could see the woman he knew as Deirdre in his mind.

"We had a drink and then a car took us to a French bistro on Sheffield. We had a very nice time."

"How do you think she got access to your computer?" Lucas asked.

McKinsey continued flatly, "After dinner, we went back to the Drake for a nightcap. We talked some more and then we…"

"Then you took her up to your room?"

"No. That's just it." His eyes now clear, he looked at Lucas and said, "I remember being in the bar. It had to be after ten, but I can't be sure. The next thing I knew, I was in bed. The sun was coming in behind the curtains. I was naked. But I was all alone."

"So you did have sex with her."

McKinsey rapidly shook his head. "I don't remember anything from the time we were in the bar until I woke up. It's all a complete blank. I assumed I had too much to drink, though I can hold my liquor, and I don't ever remember passing out like that in my life. A few days later, the company was attacked by ransomware. And later that week, my IT team informed me—and the board—that the malware originated from my computer."

"Did you have your computer with you at the Signature Lounge?" Lucas asked.

"As I said, it's always with me."

"I'll need the name of the dating service," Lucas said. "And any other similar services you've used." This time Lucas would need a judge to grant a subpoena to see how this Deirdre had registered on the site. "I'm also going to need you to provide a description for our sketch artist. Did this Deirdre have a foreign accent?"

McKinsey shook his head. "Nothing noticeable." He checked the time on his watch and said. "That's really all I can tell you, Agent Foley."

Lucas picked up his cane and rose as McKinsey extended his hand. "You know," Lucas said, shaking McKinsey's hand. "Why didn't your company report the attack when it happened? Why wait three months until a whistleblower came forward?"

McKinsey hesitated, then reached into his pocket and pulled out his phone. He scrolled through and handed the device to Lucas. "She knew how to keep me quiet." He placed his hand on Lucas's shoulder. "Please. When you find her, don't tell her I was the one that spoke with the FBI."

Lucas flipped through several pictures, all featuring the body of a naked woman, carefully excluding any portion of her face. But the CEO's profile was clear as the voluptuous woman splayed her body in various poses next to an apparently sleeping James McKinsey. The final photo was of a handwritten note. "We should keep our little rendezvous a secret. Otherwise, I'm sure your wife would love to see these…"

CHAPTER
TWENTY-NINE

THURSDAY MORNING, Alina checked her computer. The malware she'd embedded in the file she'd given to Donny the night before had yet to be activated.

She put on a long-sleeved blouse and slacks and walked over to Horizons. But Donny Brodsky didn't show up that day. Or the next. She stayed in her apartment the entire weekend. What if he had discovered she had forged the business plan?

Thankfully, by Monday, Donny was back.

"Got a little sidetracked," he said when she asked him where he'd been. "My mom died. I was in New York taking care of her affairs."

"Did you share my business plan with your brothers?" she asked, trying to look calm and firm. But her insides were shaking.

"Not exactly, Ana," he said. "I did look at it. But did you hear what I said? I was at my mother's funeral."

Alina tried to put on a more sympathetic expression. "Oh, no, I didn't hear you say that. Oh, I'm sorry to hear that."

"Well, I did speak to my brothers about it while I was there. At least with one of them."

"And?"

"Not a good time for him to make investments."

"He didn't like my business plan?"

"I didn't get a chance to show it to him."

"Why not? You didn't like it?" she asked, her heart racing.

"That's not it at all," Donny said, holding her arm. "Your plan was terrific. I'd really be very interested in doing this with you. I think it has huge potential."

"Just not enough potential to show it to your brothers." She pulled her arm away. Donny continued to make excuses but Alina wasn't listening. It was time to push him, hard. "I don't understand why you didn't show it to them," she said. "Especially if you're really interested in working with me."

Donny looked away as he seemed to be thinking. Finally, he said, "Okay. I'll send it to them tonight. I'm sure they'll take a look."

Not good enough. She leaned in closer. "Why don't you send it now?"

"Now?"

"Aren't you a man of action?" she asked, playfully punching his arm. "Isn't that what businesspeople do?"

Donny smiled and removed his laptop from his backpack. "I'll send it to them both right now," he said as he inserted her memory stick into his computer.

"Excellent." And Alina watched him hit the Send key on an email to both of his brothers with her infected business plan attached.

As she left Horizons for the last time, Alina walked briskly and confidently to her apartment, looking forward to finally texting Gagnon the encrypted message she had envisioned for the past three days:

TWO incoming.

CHAPTER
THIRTY

LUCAS RUBBED his tired eyes before pouring himself another cup of decaf coffee. It was almost one-thirty a.m. and he should probably call it a night. He needed to get a few hours of sleep before his early-morning rehab session. Instead, Lucas hobbled back to his kitchen counter and restarted the clip of the surveillance footage Agent Fernandez had compiled from McKinsey's night at the Drake.

The hotel's state-of-the-art, high-resolution color system captured McKinsey and his date at 8:46 p.m., arm in arm, entering and crossing the lobby of the Drake. Another portion started at 9:02 p.m. and showed them standing in the hotel bar, and another at 9:38 p.m., which caught them riding in the elevator to the penthouse suite. And then there she was, McKinsey's girl, all alone, crossing the hotel lobby toward the exit. The time stamp on this portion began at 11:04 p.m., thirty minutes after IBC recorded the malware breach from McKinsey's computer, confirming the woman was with McKinsey at the time of the IBC ransomware attack.

Each clear image also proved something else—the woman who called herself Deirdre was stunningly beautiful.

Lucas had watched the brief video compilation dozens of times over the past few hours, mesmerized by her image. He'd scrolled back again and again, studying the shapely suspect wearing a short, tight black dress, absorbing her arresting facial features. She had full lips and high cheekbones. Her bright green eyes moved nervously around the lobby as she made her way to the exit.

Agent Fernandez had done a superb job compiling and editing the footage. If the junior agent was still upset about being asked to leave the session with McKinsey, it didn't show in her work. Still, on the ride back from IB Corp. the previous day, Fernandez was like a yellow jacket whose nest had been stepped on.

"You should have fought to have me stay in the room with McKinsey," Fernandez had said.

"Come on, he opened up, didn't he?"

"Thanks to me. I was the one who pressured him. I had a feeling he was involved with another woman."

"I don't see what the big deal is. If McKinsey were female and had been involved in a sexual assault, I'd understand if I were asked to leave."

"I wouldn't equate what she did to him as a sexual assault," she snapped.

"She stripped him naked, didn't she?"

With that, Fernandez had shaken her head, blown out a breath, and stared out the window at the cars coming up the northbound lane of Lakeshore Drive. And she didn't say another word until they reached the office. Lucas had worked alongside junior agents at the FBI. He couldn't remember any, including himself, who would have been that outspoken with a senior officer. But he had to admit, he liked her edge.

Lucas decided to watch the sequence of videos one last time, this time, pausing it each time the woman came into the frame. He studied her closely, looking for any clues in her expression or mannerisms. Anything he might have missed over the past few hours. When the footage came to the final sequence showing her crossing the hotel lobby toward the exit, Lucas zoomed in on her expression. He peered into her green eyes. Over the past few hours, Lucas assumed her darting glances were a sign of nervousness. A sign she was worried about being discovered. But now, as Lucas's own tired eyes locked with hers, he considered an entirely new explanation.

The beautiful sugar baby hacker in the black dress was looking for someone.

CHAPTER
THIRTY-ONE

ALEXI ROMANOFF PACED IMPATIENTLY in his office with the fifty-two-page document in hand. What was taking Dmitri Fedorov so long to arrive? They had important business to discuss.

Over the past few months in Chicago, Alina Petrova had been exceptionally productive, well beyond Romanoff's expectations. Her well-placed ransomware attacks had yielded the equivalent of several million US dollars in cryptocurrency. He never expected more from her than the filling of his private coffers. In fact, suggesting that Fedorov's keylogger software ride along on the back of Alina's malware was simply an afterthought, a mere curiosity to see what they'd learn by capturing the follow-on keystrokes of ransomware victims. Romanoff was still glad they'd kept Alina in the dark. There was no need to increase her level of anxiety.

But judging from the report in Romanoff's hand, Alina Petrova had found her way to a very different type of target.

He rubbed his eyes and read again the summary abstract prepared by Dmitri Vladimirovich:

TITLE: Computerized Human Experienced as
Real Life (CHERL)
PRESENTATION SIZE: Fifty-two pages
PRESENTER: Dr. Josh Brodsky, Project Director
AUDIENCE: Board of Directors, Sway Corporation, Inc.
PURPOSE OF UPDATE: Inform the board on
top-secret project leveraging advanced artificial
intelligence (i.e., neural networks, inference
engines, machine learning, deep learning, and
natural language processing)
PROJECT GOAL: Deliver humanlike re-creation
of the greatest leaders in world history. The
CHERL AI engine will infer how these brilliant
minds would tackle modern-day challenges in
selected disciplines, including politics,
international affairs, business, and science.
INITIAL TARGET: A growing segment of
today's political leaders who lack historical education and perspective
SUCCESSFUL PILOT SUBJECT: Ulysses S.
Grant
SUBJECTS IN PROGRESS: Winston Churchill,
Napoleon, Franklin D. Roosevelt
FUTURE SUBJECTS: Abraham Lincoln,
Mahatma Gandhi, John F. Kennedy
INPUT REQUIREMENTS: Extensive written
and oral histories—autobiographies, biographies,
letters, memoirs, history books, interviews, articles,
papers, and other significant and relevant
background
DEPLOYMENT STATUS: Upcoming introduc-
tion to the US Secretary of State
FUTURE CLIENTS: America's entire political
and economic establishment

Romanoff heard the electronic hum emanating from

his private elevator. Moments later, Fedorov emerged. Romanoff waved the document at him and asked, "Which target did this come from?"

Fedorov shook his head. "It appears that Alina Grigoryevna took it upon herself to improvise." He went on to explain what he had learned from Gagnon about the Horizons boot camp. "She claimed she was simply trying to keep her AI skills fresh." Fedorov shrugged. "I am sure it was harmless. But that is where she met Donny Brodsky, a student who started bragging about his two successful brothers. She enticed him to forward a doctored-up business plan to these brothers." He laughed. "She told him she was looking to open her own AI training school but needed seed capital. Donny Brodsky obviously thought his brothers would be interested investors. I must say, very creative on her part."

"Indeed." Romanoff remembered another female agent from long ago with similar imagination and agility. "Perhaps I underestimated our Alina. Her DNA clearly equipped her with some innate skills."

"I would imagine a bit of luck was involved," Fedorov said. "But Sway's project director obviously opened his brother's email containing our malware just as he was preparing that board presentation, never suspecting his brother would forward a contaminated attachment."

"Was our ransomware attack launched?"

Fedorov nodded. "But unfortunately, Sway had the technical skills to defeat our malware, so no payment is coming our way. Yet Sway never discovered my stealth keylogger. It sat on the computer of Sway's project director, capturing and transmitting every word as he developed his board presentation."

"Incredible," Romanoff whispered. He sat behind his desk and drummed his fingers on the sheet of paper. "How feasible do you think this is? This CHERL project. Do you think they can re-create this kind of cognitive function from history books?"

Fedorov pulled up a chair. "Sway is a very powerful company. They are known to be visionaries, leaders in every area of AI they touch. The board presentation contained an appendix with high-level design schemes and details on technical approaches. It all looks very feasible."

Romanoff stood again and walked to his observation window. He stared down at the massive gathering of talent he had assembled and recalled his many accomplishments for the motherland. The denial-of-service attacks. The propaganda machinery. Ransomware attacks. With each event, he'd thought his superiors in the SVR would recognize his contributions, elevate him to his rightful place. But the megalomaniacs in charge never did. So here he stood, overseeing the incredible work performed in this old KGB warehouse, still waiting for a call. It had taken him years to accept that this call would never come.

So he had continued to omit Alina Petrova's mission from his periodic reports. The SVR leadership did not need to know about her presence in America or how many millions his scheme had netted so far. Even after accounting for Fedorov's twenty percent cut and expenses to cover the American operation, there would be plenty left to fund his comfortable retirement on the Amalfi Coast. Not quite up to an oligarch's standard of living, but good enough. Ironically, he had actually been thinking it was time to bring Alina home. Now with Fedorov's report in hand, Romanoff's mind churned with possibilities.

"Alexi Igorevich, do you think we should bring this to the attention of our superiors?"

"I am afraid it is too late for that, Dmitri Vladimirovich." Romanoff had witnessed men executed for far less than placing an unauthorized Russian agent inside America. "And I have a more interesting thought."

Fedorov joined Romanoff at the observation window.

"This is what I need you to do," Romanoff continued. "Take your best people and comb through that fifty-two-page Sway document. See if you can reverse engineer those technical details you found in the appendix. I want to know exactly how it works."

"I'll assemble our AI experts," Fedorov replied. "If need be, we will find a way to steal the code."

Romanoff grinned. "You are not thinking broadly enough." He placed a hand on Fedorov's shoulder. "I am not interested in stealing the code. I want you to learn how to *use* it!"

CHAPTER
THIRTY-TWO

ALINA TILTED her face toward the sky, allowing the early spring sunshine to warm her skin. She heard a high-pitched squeal and nearly jumped off the park bench. But when she turned, she saw only a young mother chasing after a toddler in front of the bird exhibit. The child's giggles should have made Alina smile, but she felt much too jittery to enjoy the scene. Alina worried that she might have blown her chance to stay in America—that she would never learn what she had come to discover.

It had been over two weeks since Donny passed her contaminated business plan to his well-placed brothers. And two weeks since Gagnon had admonished her for the improvised attack.

"Irresponsible!" he'd messaged when she revealed her scheme. "This was not approved! You may have risked the entire enterprise!"

In those first few days after Donny forwarded the malware, she had hoped a lucrative payoff would diminish Gagnon's hostility. More importantly, she had hoped the windfall would lead Romanoff to decrypt the remaining files about her mother. But Alina had received no confirmation that any ransomware attacks had been initiated, nor any indication that multiple five-million-dollar ransom payments had been made. And now Gagnon had summoned her for a meeting here at the Lincoln Park Zoo. Would he be conveying positive developments that would expedite the decryption of the files? Or would he be sending her home before she'd completed her AI scout program?

Alina bought a bag of popcorn and headed for the primate house. She stood in front of an exhibit of black-and-white colobus monkeys swinging from a series of vines. A larger monkey was sitting to the right of the cage, picking at the fur of her offspring.

Gagnon came up beside Alina, wearing a blue jogging suit and a wool cap.

"Very playful animals, don't you think?" he said.

"To me they look sad, locked up in a cage, so far away from their home."

"Indeed," Gagnon said as he stared ahead. After a moment he asked, "How are you?" Alina thought his tone sounded surprisingly cordial. Without answering, she held out the bag of popcorn, but he shook his head and strode away. Alina followed several steps behind as he moved quickly past the South Pond. He slowed when he reached the pedestrian bridge crossing Lakeshore Drive. Alina caught up and kept pace.

"Did they pay?" she asked.

Gagnon shook his head, and her heart sank. Her plan hadn't worked after all.

"But," Gagnon continued, his expression light, "it appears you may have stumbled onto something far more interesting."

"I don't understand."

Gagnon revealed what he knew about the keylogger program that had been riding along inside the malware Alina had been distributing, including Ana Dafoe's fictitious business plan that Donny Brodsky had emailed to his brothers.

"Wait." Alina stopped at the top of the pedestrian

bridge and faced Gagnon. "The keylogger program Fedorov demonstrated for me in the lab?"

Gagnon stopped and shrugged. "I assume it is the same."

Why hadn't they told her she was planting more than just ransomware? She thought back to the hacking maneuvers she'd been shown at Fedorov's secret lab, wondering what other tools she had unknowingly installed. Another of Romanoff's deceptions, like holding back the files about her mother. But this was not the time to confront her handler.

"Each of your malware attacks contained this keylogger," Gagnon continued. "But the transcripts created by the keystrokes of your victims were not very useful. There was little, if any, intelligence gleaned." He paused before adding, "Until now."

Gagnon motioned for them to continue walking and led her down the footbridge to a path that separated the highway from Lake Michigan. The sky was filling with dark clouds that threatened to block the sun's warmth. They continued southbound along the lakefront as bikers and joggers passed in both directions. Alina buttoned her jacket to ward off the brisk gusts of wind coming off the water. When they were finally alone, Gagnon explained. "Your infected business plan reached your intended targets, Alina. The malware did, in fact, lock up the files of two separate corporations. The first was a company called Virtual Bank, which we gather, was a client of one of the Brodsky brothers. But the other attack penetrated the Sway corporation."

"The man in my coding class said one of his brothers worked at Sway," Alina said. "That's why I thought he was a worthwhile target."

"And you were correct." Gagnon waved his hand dismissively. "Not for a ransomware attack, which their technologists defeated. But Sway never discovered the keylogger riding along with the malware, which revealed the true value hiding inside their massive computers. It appears they've built an extremely advanced system of artificial intelligence. A system that is capable of reconstructing people from the past."

Alina stepped back, almost losing her balance where the cement path met the adjoining beach. "How can it reconstruct...people?"

"The presentation to Sway's board tells of a system called CHERL. A system that has recreated the greatest leaders from the past. Brilliant minds they intend to bring back as AI avatars, capable of analyzing billions of records on recent world developments. I think the term the Americans use is 'supercharged.' Sway expects these AI leaders will help shape and advance the American agenda."

Alina pulled her coat more tightly around her, struggling to decipher Gagnon's words. She understood artificial intelligence was advancing at an exponential pace. She had experienced many state-of-the-art applications at university. But Sway's idea was beyond normal technological advancements. In discussions in her master's program, professors had always declared *this* type of cognitive system to be far off in the future. "Today's AI cannot think like a human." A statement she'd heard on multiple occasions. "AI is limited to replacing complex functions."

Functions like efficiently searching through thousands of documents and data files to locate an individual who disappeared more than twenty years ago.

"Do you think it's real?" she asked.

Gagnon shrugged and motioned for them to continue walking. "Romanoff believes that it is. And he fears America will use this tool against your own country."

"How?" she asked, walking beside Gagnon.

"Alina, it is quite simple. You are smart enough to know that Russian leaders have certainly made their share of mistakes over the past decades. But Romanoff believes that today's Russian leaders view their contemporary counterparts in the West as inexperienced. Disorganized, but…predictable." He paused and looked out over Lake Michigan as dark clouds continued to roll toward the downtown skyline. "Romanoff also believes despite America's many flaws, its history has been shaped by brilliant leaders in the past, far more gifted than their contemporary counterparts. Men and women who, if alive today, could tilt the strategic balance in the West's direction." He looked at Alina and added, "This CHERL system may become the most important weapon in the American arsenal. Unless Romanoff learns how to manipulate it first. To disarm it from shaping American policies that would harm Russia."

"How can he manipulate something this…sophisticated?" she asked.

"He needs someone working on the inside of Sway, Alina. Working on the team in San Francisco building this CHERL system. Someone who understands artificial intelligence." He stopped and looked at her. "He needs someone like *you*, Alina."

Her entire body tensed. "Me?"

"Romanoff believes he can modify the outcomes," Gagnon explained. "Control the advice these digital leaders deliver to the American establishment before CHERL forever changes the balance of power between your two countries."

Alina turned away and looked out over the vast lake, watching the wind-fueled waves crash onto the shoreline. Of course Romanoff would want to manipulate this CHERL system, just as he had controlled *her*. The whole idea was ludicrous, she thought. Even if she could get inside Sway, how would her coding skills be good enough to change the system? Posing as a sugar baby and planting malware was one thing, as was building her own AI scout. But the idea Gagnon was describing was beyond her. She had no training in infiltration. She wasn't a *real* spy.

But Alina had already done things in America she never could have imagined doing, things she had never thought herself capable of. An hour ago, she'd thought Gagnon might be sending her back to Russia. Instead, Romanoff was asking her to take on this new mission. The idea was frightening. But she had to admit—the thought of working on this CHERL system, inside one of the greatest technology companies in the world, and truly helping her homeland, was also...thrilling! And this new mission would take her away from life as a sugar baby.

And possibly get her the help she needed to complete her search for her mother.

She took in a long breath and slowly exhaled. A sudden gust of wind blew grains of sand into her face. She rubbed her eyelids and looked up, squinting to regain her focus. Her eyes cleared as she looked south, toward the downtown skyline.

The marquee of the Drake Hotel came into view in the distance.

If Romanoff had other agents, more experienced agents like her mother, he would have called upon them. But it was *she* Romanoff had chosen.

It was *Alina* they needed.

"Tell Romanoff no more games," Alina said, turning back to Gagnon. "I want *all* the files about my mother unlocked."

Gagnon's eyebrows rose.

Alina placed her hands on her hips. "And then I want Fedorov's help launching an AI program I've developed."

"I will pass on your...request."

"And how exactly do you propose getting me inside of Sway?" she asked.

"There is an assignment you are quite familiar with, Alina. One that will set our new project in motion."

CHAPTER
THIRTY-THREE

ROMANOFF LEANED BACK and puffed on his cigar. He'd just finished reading Gagnon's communiqué describing Alina Petrova's AI scout program.

"It is very impressive." Fedorov's voice came from the speakerphone on Romanoff's desk. "Alina Grigoryevna is obviously quite skilled."

Romanoff rested the cigar in the ashtray, leaned over the speakerphone, and replied, "Gagnon reports she received guidance from an AI expert. An instructor in that Horizons programming school."

The phone line was momentarily quiet before Fedorov asked, "Do you plan to deal with the instructor?"

"I prefer not to. Alina assured Gagnon she had disclosed little about the purpose of her system. Nothing beyond generalities." Romanoff paused before adding, "But we will keep our eyes on him." He picked up the cigar smoldering in his ashtray and asked, "Do you think her search program will work?"

"Theoretically," Fedorov responded. "But whether her inference engine will discover the fate of her mother, this we will not know until it is unleashed to scour through the American systems."

Romanoff puffed on his cigar. Alina had toured their

cyber command center, so she'd seen their successful AI systems. Now, she was asking for help with completing her AI scout and the unlocking of the extensive archives on her mother that he'd had encrypted.

Fedorov spoke again. "Alina has requested my hacking software so she can insert her AI scout into government systems in America, so it can perform a high-speed search to probe for…candidates."

Alina Grigoryevna was asking for a great deal of assistance, indeed. "What about this CHERL system?" Romanoff asked. "Has your team completed their review?"

"We have been prototyping a detailed design as best as we can from Dr. Brodsky's report," Fedorov answered. "The system relies on pattern recognition. For each past leader they develop, AI analyzes massive amounts of historical data and identifies patterns of behavior, patterns of decision-making, patterns of communication, and so forth. Neural networks then use those patterns to infer how the historical figures would tackle new situations, the decisions they would make and the advice they would provide."

"And if we wanted to change these outcomes, do you need to modify the neural network?"

"There is a simpler solution," Fedorov answered. "If we can deploy an additional set of data—a different version of history—I believe CHERL would recognize a *different* pattern of decision-making." Fedorov paused before adding, "Influencing the behavior—and the advice —coming from whichever leader they decide to re-create."

Romanoff slowly rubbed his chin. After a few moments he asked, "What options do we have for intro-ducing this…alternative history?"

"It is as I expected, Alexi Igorevich. My team has tested various penetration tactics, but Sway obviously bolstered its cyber defenses since the ransomware attack,

To execute this plan, we will need an agent inside. And we will need that agent to be in a position to continually feed our alternative data, over time."

Before calling Fedorov, Romanoff had been reviewing a list of candidates to send inside of Sway, anticipating Alina Petrova might refuse to participate. The list contained several engineers with far greater AI experience, but few had command of the English language. And certainly none possessed knowledge of Western culture. A separate list contained agents Romanoff had worked with throughout the years, each of whom could easily place themselves inside the Sway corporation, but none had sufficient technical skill to masquerade as an AI engineer for any length of time.

So, if Romanoff was going to execute this plan to influence the output of America's CHERL system, he *did* need Alina.

"I will agree to her terms," Romanoff said. "We will decrypt the remaining files on Valeriya Petrova. As far as helping her plant her scout program, we will provide her with our most advanced hacking tools, but not before our mission with this CHERL system is complete."

"But it might take us a year or longer before our data achieves the desired outcome," Fedorov said. "Alina may not be pleased with such a delay."

"She will have to be patient," Romanoff said. After all, Alina would not be the only one delaying personal plans. He would be deferring his own disappearance, rescinding his offer on that dacha on the Amalfi coast. Because he knew if his new scheme was a success, he would retire with a much larger nest egg.

He might live the life of an oligarch after all.

CHAPTER
THIRTY-FOUR

LUCAS ENTERED the Chicago bureau's fourth-floor videoconference room. Agent Fernandez had already arrived and was sitting in one of three chairs facing a blank screen. Steam was rising from the two black coffees on the table in front of her.

"Agent Fernandez," Lucas acknowledged as he placed his cane down and sat beside her.

"Agent Foley," she said curtly, her eyes fixed ahead. She slid one of the coffees toward him, a sign, he hoped, that she wasn't still sore about the McKinsey interview.

"Thanks," he said. "Any sign of Burick?"

Danilo Burick was one of the lead engineers in the FBI's cybercrime lab. He had committed to spending the majority of his weekend analyzing McKinsey's laptop and the malware that had infected IBC.

"They said he's running behind," Fernandez said. She sipped her coffee. "How's the leg?"

"It's getting there." But Lucas had just come from a particularly grueling physical therapy session, and his leg was still throbbing. "Any luck with the sugar daddy websites?"

She scrolled through her tablet. "As we expected, there were no other Deirdres floating around out there, at least none matching our hacker's description. I'm working with the facial recognition team to compare the Drake surveillance image against photos posted on all the sites. I doubt she could change her appearance enough to evade the AI."

Lucas said, "Check her image against all the crime databases, too. CIA, Secret Service. Somebody out there might have picked up her trail."

"Will do," she replied just as the image of Agent Burick filled the screen.

"Sorry to keep you waiting," Burick said.

Lucas gave a two-fingered salute. "No issue, Agent Burick. Good to meet you."

"Same here. You're Alec Foley's son, right?"

Lucas nodded.

"Your father's a legend around here," Burick said.

Lucas stared at the table. He could see out of the corner of his eye that Fernandez was looking at him.

Burick's eyes shifted to Fernandez. "And who is this?"

Fernandez cleared her throat and replied, "Agent Sarah Fernandez, sir."

"It's nice to see a fresh face," Burick said. "They've partnered you with a Foley, so the brass must think highly of you. Interesting case, too. Here we are, investing millions in hardening cyber defenses, making it tougher than ever for the bad guys to get through, and your perp uses the oldest trick in the book—finding people's weaknesses."

"There's no cyber defense for human frailty," Lucas said. "Anyway, tell us what you found."

Burick flashed a wide grin. "It seems we have a match." Lucas leaned forward. "Your source code was identical to several attacks. Two in Chicago and one that came in only a few days ago from San Francisco and New York."

"Frisco and New York?" Lucas was surprised that his suspect had ventured that far outside of Chicago. He wondered whether the matching malware meant that the sugar baby had moved her operation or that there was more than one hacker using the same software.

"Rob Dennison out of the Frisco bureau is working the case. Do you know him?"

Lucas didn't recognize Dennison's name, but he met several other agents from the San Francisco bureau during his online training sessions when he joined the cyber team. There was an imperiousness about them, as if they believed important cybercrime didn't exist unless it happened in Silicon Valley.

"We've never met," Lucas finally replied.

"How were you able to make the connection?" Fernandez asked.

Burick's expression became serious as he launched into the excruciatingly detailed processes the crime lab had developed to reverse engineer malware code, find connections to previous hacks, and assign probabilities to the code's origin.

"Let me guess," Lucas interjected, if only to break Burick's lecture. "It wasn't the fat guy sitting at home in his pajamas."

Burick laughed, a loud rat-a-tat sound, before saying, "Sometimes a lone wolf can create quite a bit of havoc, but I doubt that's the case here. This is a very sophisticated piece of malware. Too advanced for one person to build." Burick paused then added, "Unless your sugar baby has extensive coding experience."

Fernandez asked, "How did you connect the cases?"

"Malware often has a design or coding sequence. In fact, some hackers purposely leave clues—a comment, or an additional coding flourish, just to show off. In your case, the signature that connected your malware with the hit on Sway, Virtual Bank, and the other Chicago cases was a very unique subroutine."

Lucas felt his pulse quicken. "Did you say Sway?"

"Yes. That's Dennison's Frisco case."

Lucas hadn't seen anything in the FBI's case management system about a breach of one of the largest technology companies in the world. "How did the hacker get access?" he asked. "Did Sway pay the ransom, too? Was—"

"Whoa. Slow down, Agent Foley. One question at a time."

Lucas let out a slight laugh. "Sorry, man."

"No issue," Burick said. "As far as ransom, apparently Sway didn't need to pay. It should come as little surprise that their IT group is pretty sharp. Their people were able to stop the attack and decrypt the infected files on their own. They even helped Virtual Bank do the same. As far as how the hacker entered, I believe it was a phishing attack."

Fernandez asked, "So it wasn't any type of dating scenario, like McKinsey?"

Burick shook his head. "It doesn't appear so. But Dennison will know more."

"Did you pick up anything else from the code?" Lucas asked.

Burick checked his notes. "Our scan gives this a seventy-eight percent probability of being Russian sourced."

"Russia," Fernandez repeated.

"And the money trail?" Lucas asked. "Any trace on the million in crypto that IBC sent to the hackers?"

Burick shook his head again. "IBC's payment went into a black hole. Whoever received the funds probably used some type of tumbler or mixer to throw us off." Lucas knew that even drug cartels had started using these same modern-day money launderers to hide their cash as digital assets. If Burick was right, the money trail went cold the day IBC wired it.

"Anything else?" Lucas asked.

"That's all I have for now," Burick said as he stood. "But we'll keep digging."

"Thanks, Agent Burick. This was very helpful."

Before signing off, Burick nodded and said, "Good luck."

"Thanks, man."

When the screen went dark, Lucas turned to Fernandez and said, "You did a great job with the surveillance video."

"Thank you," she said with a small hint of a smile. "I still need to finish the facial recognition scans against the criminal databases. To see if her image matches anyone already on the bureau's radar."

"Good," Lucas said. "It would be great if you could also dig into the two new Chicago cases. See what the bureau already has on file about the MO of the attacks."

"Will do," she said.

"In the meantime, I'll connect with the San Francisco bureau and see what they'll share about what happened at Sway. We can compare notes tomorrow."

"That sounds like a plan, Agent Foley."

CHAPTER
THIRTY-FIVE

WITH ALL THE alcohol and GHB in Buford Chambers's body, Alina thought the sixty-four-year-old CEO of Aztec Enterprises would have passed out as soon as they entered his hotel room. Instead, he went to the bathroom and reemerged suddenly revived.

After she managed to drain another vial into the drink that Chambers prepared from the minibar, she then tried everything in her power to fend him off. But it took time for the extra dose of GHB to counteract the cocaine slicing through the system of the man she hoped would be her final sugar daddy.

It had been the first—and last—time she would let one of these men inside her.

When he had finally passed out, Alina had gone to the bathroom to shower—which is when she had discovered the white powder and the rolled-up dollar bill that explained Chambers's earlier revival.

Fifteen minutes later she was standing next to the bed in a hotel bathrobe. She checked on the lump of humanity. He was out cold. With all the narcotics in Buford Chambers, Alina had plenty of time to finish what she had come to do.

She sat on the bed, trying to regain her composure.

Other than her encounter with Tuxedo, this date with Chambers had been the most difficult and humiliating of them all.

But at least it would be her last.

She retrieved Chambers's phone and laptop from his briefcase and brought the devices to the bed. When the sign-on screen on the laptop requested the CEO's authentication credentials and code, Alina grabbed his limp hand and placed his index finger on the computer's touchpad. She held his cell phone up to his face, and a four-digit code appeared, which she promptly keyed into his computer. The multifactor authentication process granted her immediate access to Aztec's network.

If this were to be like all her previous rendezvous, Alina would now reach into her handbag, retrieve her thumb drive, and insert it into the laptop's USB port to begin the process of loading her malware.

But this was not like any of her previous assignments. Instead, Alina searched through Aztec's network directory. She scrolled down until she found her target—the company's personnel database, containing information on all current and former Aztec employees. A red prompt resembling an eyeball appeared on Chambers's cell phone with the words "Retinal authentication required." She pulled back Chamber's eyelid and waved his phone several times in front of his eye before the oval prompt changed to green and an Access Approved message appeared.

She removed a thumb drive from her purse containing the scanning program Gagnon had provided, the one that would identify an AI employee suitable for Alina's planned deception. After less than thirty seconds, the scan returned three possibilities. Alina browsed the profiles. Each of these women was in her late twenties, with no more than an undergraduate degree in computer science. But Alina's eyes fixed on a photograph of the third, a woman named Nicole Ryder who had resigned from

Aztec midway through her maternity leave. "Expects to take three-year hiatus before resuming career" was the reason noted for the former employee's departure.

Alina removed one of the burner phones provided by Gagnon and sat next to the drugged CEO. She pulled the covers off and examined his naked body, highlighted by a reddish birthmark on his right inner thigh that resembled a map of Italy. She snapped three photos of the distinctive pattern. The mark was high enough on his leg to allow her to include another notable body part that Alina assumed his wife would recognize. As Alina had done after each of her previous dates, she proceeded to snap several selfies featuring his profile next to various parts of her own body, careful to keep her face out of each shot. After examining the pictures, she picked three that best made her point and texted them to Chambers with a brief note:

```
I'll keep my copies in a safe
place, along with the
washcloth I used to clean us
up. Just in case your wife—or
anyone else—comes asking about
our night together.
```

She fetched his pants, which lay crumpled on the desk, and removed his wallet. Out of habit, she pulled out his driver's license, $420 in cash—which she would add to her significant getaway fund—and all but one of his credit cards. She always made sure her marks had at least one credit card in order to get home safely. She wanted these men to feel embarrassed but not angry. Mad at themselves for being reckless, for sure. Like the others, Chambers could replace his license at the local DMV and concoct a story for his wife about why he needed to call the credit card companies and report lost cards. And for Chambers, there would be no ransomware attack on his company to raise the company's suspicions. If Aztec's team ever discovered her scan of the personnel file, well, she was sure Chambers would simply plead ignorance. And if the pictures weren't enough to convince him to hold his tongue, the washcloth in the plastic bag from the ice bucket would be.

Alina took the elevator to the lobby of the Waldorf and walked quickly past the front desk. She noticed an older gray-haired gentleman in hotel uniform standing by the exit. Their eyes locked in a way that caused Alina to slow her pace until she came to a complete stop. The seeming look of recognition in his expression left her frozen in place.

Her heart began racing as he started to approach. When he was just feet away, Alina stirred herself and moved quickly past him. She took a green scarf from her bag and wrapped it around her jet-black wig before pushing through the revolving doors and disappearing into the dark Chicago night.

CHAPTER
THIRTY-SIX

LUCAS TOSSED his empty coffee cup into the waste bin and waited while an administrator in the San Francisco bureau tracked down Rob Dennison. Twenty minutes later, the tan and narrow face of the special agent appeared on Lucas's tablet, an FBI insignia displayed in his virtual background.

"Agent Foley," Dennison said. He slouched back in his chair. "What's the urgency? I'm in the middle of a dozen things."

Lucas felt his neck muscles tighten. "We're all busy, Agent Dennison," Lucas said, firmly.

Dennison inhaled and placed his hands on the desk in front of him. "What do you need?"

"I was hoping you could fill me in on your Sway case."

"How did you hear about Sway?"

Lucas recapped his conversation with Burick and the matching malware. He also walked Dennison through the key points of the IBC case.

"And Burick is certain your hacker used the same malware that hit Sway and Virtual Bank?" Dennison asked.

"He is."

Dennison seemed to be thinking this over. He then asked, "Was it just the one incident?"

"McKinsey's the only victim we've spoken to," Lucas answered. "But Burick found two other smaller hacks in our region. I have an agent chasing those down. It's hard to say if there are any other victims that will eventually come forward." Lucas told him about the compromising photographs McKinsey shared. "That's why it took us three months to hear about IBC. We'd still be unaware if not for a company whistleblower. Speaking of which, I don't recall hearing anything about the Sway breach."

"The company asked us to keep this out of the news."

"A big publicly traded company like Sway? With all those customer records they keep on file, I would think they would have to issue some type of press release."

"None of Sway's clients were impacted," Dennison said firmly. "The incident was limited to an artificial intelligence project they're working on, so no customer files were involved."

"That's good," Lucas said as he made some notes on his tablet. "And the New York company?"

"Virtual Bank? Same deal. Sway sent a tech team to help clear the malware from their files, too."

"What about the method of attack, Agent Dennison? Any similarity to how my malware was planted?"

Dennison thought a moment. "It's possible."

"You seem…unsure."

"Well," Dennison said, "like IB Corp., Sway's attacker entered through one of their executives. A Dr. Josh Brodsky. But Dr. Brodsky wasn't on a date with a sugar baby. This looks like an old-fashioned phishing attack. The type we used to see all the time ten, twenty years back. Dr. Brodsky innocently opened an infected attachment to an email, which launched the ransomware inside of Sway. He wasn't suspicious because the email was sent by his brother, Don."

"His brother?" Lucas repeated. "So a woman wasn't involved."

Dennison shifted in his seat. "I didn't say that." He leaned his arms on the table. "The company initially thought Dr. Brodsky might have been involved, but we checked him out. He's clean. Thirty years with DoD before joining Sway. Top AI guy. He leads that special project team I mentioned earlier. But the brother who sent the file, Donny Brodsky—he's another story. A real loser. Twice divorced. He does piecemeal programming gigs but has been in and out of jobs." Dennison went on, "Now, this Donny character happened to be visiting Dr. Brodsky when we went to talk to him at a house they were renting in Menlo Park. They were gathering with their third brother, Louis, who had flown in from New York. It seemed like they were sorting out some type of family squabble. Anyway, we interviewed all three. So here's where there may be some connection, Agent Foley. Donny said the infected file was given to him on a memory stick. And that he was coerced into emailing it to his brothers."

"Coerced by—"

"By a very attractive young lady."

Lucas felt his pulse quicken.

Dennison checked his tablet. "A blonde by the name of Ana Dafoe. Donny met her at a place called Horizons. It's an artificial intelligence programming school." He paused. "And the school is back there by you. It's in Chicago."

"It's her! Did he give you a description of the woman?"

"Blonde. Attractive. I'll send you the composite sketch."

"Hang on." Lucas scrolled through his tablet, found the sugar baby's image lifted from the Drake's surveillance videos, and posted it in the videoconference's chat panel for Dennison. "This one went by the name of Deirdre."

Dennison studied the screen and shrugged. "It could be her."

"Where is this Donny guy now?"

Dennison shrugged again. "I assume he's back home in Chicago."

"Listen," Lucas said, "if Donny is back here, I should show him this photo. And I can get over to that coding school, check out everyone this Ana Dafoe had contact with."

Dennison was silent for a few moments. Finally he said, "I guess there's no problem with that. As long as you let me know what you find out."

"For sure," Lucas said. "Hey, one last thing. Did Donny say if he mentioned Dr. Brodsky's artificial intelligence project to Ana Dafoe?"

"We asked the same question. She couldn't have been targeting Dr. Brodsky's project. Donny said he knew nothing about what either of his brothers were working on prior to his California trip. I'm telling you, Agent Foley, the hacker was just fishing for dollars. This had nothing to do with Dr. Brodsky's project. And just in case she tries again, Sway's cybersecurity team assured us they've beefed up their IT defenses. I'm sure it will be a long time before anyone is able to penetrate the Sway company again."

CHAPTER
THIRTY-SEVEN

THE YOUNG BLUE-JEAN-AND-SNEAKER-CLAD recruits had their heads down, their thumbs working their smart devices. Over twenty men and women were jammed into a holding pen at Sway's corporate annex, a building on the far side of the sprawling campus where the People Experience team screened job applicants. On the other side of a strategically placed glass partition was a large recreation room where two ponytailed women competed at a foosball table while four young men in short pants and flip-flops played doubles in Ping-Pong. On the far wall, a helmeted man was strapped into a harness, readying himself to take a turn at the colorful climbing wall. Alina wondered how often employees came over to use this corporate playroom—or whether these people were just props to demonstrate the "coolness" of Sway, Inc.

After acquiring Nicole Ryder's credentials the previous week, along with a falsified driver's license, it hadn't taken long for Alina to apply for two different positions on Sway's special projects team via a popular employment website. It had taken less than a day for Sway to invite Nicole to fly to San Francisco for an interview.

Alina now sat in the crowded room of recruits,

nervously running her hands along the top of her skirt and pulling at her new suit jacket. She noticed the stares from the very casually attired applicants, as if they wondered whether she had stumbled into the wrong building. As she studied the welcome brochure with Sway's smiling CEO on the cover, clad in jeans and a simple black T-shirt, she felt a growing panic. Her choice of wardrobe might have been a huge blunder.

"Nicole Ryder," announced a mechanical sounding voice. "Please proceed to interview room X."

Alina stood, straightened her pencil skirt, and felt behind her head to make sure the twisted bun she had perfected this morning was still in place. A young Asian man whose eyes seemed to be locked on her legs looked up with an approving smile and gave her a thumbs up. She nodded back, unsure whether his thumb was a show of encouragement or simply approval of what he saw. Too many months of merchandising herself left her questioning the motives of men.

She proceeded down a long, narrow corridor with closed doors on either side marked with large letters. Toward the end, she stopped by the door marked X and took a deep breath. She checked her hair again and knocked.

"Come in," said a female voice.

Alina entered a small bright but windowless room. A large picture of a mountain range hung on the wall. A young—she was no more than twenty-two—slightly built brunette with curtain bangs was sitting behind a desk. Other than four bottles of water and a tablet, the top of the white desk was clear.

"You must be Nicole," the brunette stated with a broad smile as she came out of her seat. She extended her hand and said, "It's so nice to meet you."

Alina took the woman's hand and said, "It's nice to meet you too, ah…"

"Ashley. Ashley McMichael. I'm with the People Experience team. By the way, sharp outfit," she added as she released Alina's hand.

"I know," Alina said. "I'm really sorry that I dressed like this. I er...just came from another interview. They're not as casual as Sway."

"Really?" McMichael said, her smile fading as she sat and flipped open a keyboard attached to the tablet. She slid one of the water bottles over to Alina before keying feverishly with both hands. "How many other companies are you interviewing with?" McMichael asked stiffly.

Alina felt her stomach suddenly tense, fearing she had already said the wrong thing. Did McMichael think Nicole wasn't committed to working at Sway? Alina opened the bottle of water, unsure how to respond. After an awkward moment, McMichael looked up and said, "I understand if you don't want to tell me."

"No, that's not it," Alina said. She took a few sips of water. "Er...Sway is really my first choice."

She tried to steady her breath, anticipating another question. But McMichael's fingers continued to work the keyboard. She finally stopped, and her smile returned. "You have a very impressive resume, Nicole." She pushed the tablet aside and said, "Tell me a little about yourself. Where did you grow up?"

Alina exhaled. She was ready for this part of her performance, having practiced several times with Gagnon over the past few days. She had studied Nicole's background—the towns, colleges, and activities listed in her online profiles—and had internalized the person she needed to become. Still, Alina started carefully, telling McMichael about Nicole's childhood in Butte, Montana.

"Montana was a wonderful place to grow up," Alina said. "It's where I developed my love of the outdoors." Coming from a remote location was one of the many reasons Nicole Ryder had scored high on the scan of Aztec's personnel files, Gagnon had told her. A mountain community, he'd explained, has fewer personal connections to the coastal crowd that staffed America's high-tech companies.

"I took as many math classes as I could," Alina said, knowing the Butte school district would produce a perfect transcript to substantiate her tale. By the time Alina recounted Nicole's gap year with Teach for America, the words were flowing easily and naturally.

"It was amazing," Alina said. "With so little in their lives, these children in Sudan were so inquisitive."

Even with McMichael's occasional questions, Alina was able to weave her way back to the framework of Nicole's storyline. She relaxed, leaned back, and crossed her legs as she came to Nicole's time at Carnegie Mellon. "An exceptional learning environment," she embellished, that allowed her to "push the boundaries of artificial intelligence." Nicole Ryder's transcript and excellent GPA would confirm every detail Alina shared.

Alina felt she was giving a winning performance. Still, she knew this might be the easiest part of the deception. She didn't know how long—or how well—she could perform the job at the level Sway would expect from someone with the three years of AI engineering experience the real Nicole Ryder had from Aztec. Gagnon had said Alina would just need to hang on long enough to feed enough of Romanoff's alternative data into the CHERL system to affect its outcomes. Only then would Romanoff deliver on his promise.

As Alina started to recount Nicole's work experience at Aztec Enterprises in far off Austin, the door opened and two men entered, each carrying a folding chair. McMichael stood and said, "Oh, perfect timing guys. We were just about to talk about Aztec."

Alina felt her shoulders shudder, thinking she recognized the gray-haired man.

"I hope you don't mind, Nicole," McMichael explained. "I've asked our unit leaders to join us. This is Dr. Josh Brodsky and his project leader, Naveen Gupta.

We thought that we would move things along, given you're in discussions elsewhere." Then, smiling, McMichael added, "We don't want to lose our shot at you, do we?"

Alina let out a slow breath. Despite the creases in Josh Brodsky's forehead and his intense expression, the man McMichael introduced as the head of Sway's special projects team bore a strong resemblance to his brother Donny. While Dr. Brodsky's demeanor seemed far more serious than the shady programmer's back in Chicago, there was no mistaking the family connection.

"So pleased to meet you," Naveen Gupta said in a lilting cadence. Alina was sure the thin project leader with ropelike strands of dark hair was of Indian descent.

Alina took a long gulp of water, preparing herself for what would be her first technical grilling since graduating from Moscow State University. She hoped she'd brushed up enough over the past few days to get past this first round. But as her heart raced, Josh Brodsky started tapping on his cellphone while Gupta spouted his views on the benefits of working at Sway. As he proceeded through his enthusiastic and uninterrupted monologue, the realization slowly sank in: Josh Brodsky and Naveen Gupta weren't here to assess her knowledge—in fact, Gupta was already in full sales mode.

"We can't share too much detail, but trust me, Nicole, we are breaking new ground. Deep learning. Natural language processing. Your mind will expand each and every day. And we're growing rapidly, which of course means loads of advancement opportunities."

"That all sounds amazing," Alina said. In fact, it actually did sound exciting—the kind of place Alina had dreamed of joining when she had graduated, before her father had revealed the truth about her family's past. How her life had changed in such a short period of time.

"We've always wanted to hire someone from Aztec," Gupta continued while Brodsky sat by quietly, his attention still directed at his phone's display. "But people love Austin. Nobody ever wants to leave."

"Oh, that's true," Alina responded. In fact, Gagnon had already confirmed that no Aztec employee had joined Sway over the past five years. "But I'm ready for a change."

"Who did you work for at Aztec?" Gupta asked.

Alina hesitated then gave the name of Nicole Ryder's supervisor, Avi London. "We were very close," she said.

"You worked for Avi London?" Gupta asked. Brodsky finally looked up from his phone as Alina's shoulders stiffened.

"Ah…well, yes," she said. "Do you know him?"

Gupta laughed. "I wished I did five years ago. He's the one who built that avatar creation business." He snapped his fingers and looked away. "What was his company called again?"

"I don't—"

"Jaspar," Brodsky said.

Gupta snapped his fingers again and pointed at his boss. "Jaspar. That's right. We wanted to buy those guys, remember?"

Alina swallowed. She and Gagnon hadn't bothered to look into Avi London's history before Aztec. They had only checked to make sure he didn't have any social media connections linking him to people at Sway. She had no idea he had built an avatar company. She shook her head. "You know, I didn't know Avi before he came to Aztec."

Brodsky stared at Alina but barely blinked. "Surely he talked to you about Jaspar."

"Avi always focused on what was in front of him." She shrugged. "We never spoke about what he did before."

"That's crazy," Gupta said, smiling broadly, like a teenager discussing the latest pop star. "I heard he was a real braggard, always running his mouth off at conferences."

Alina shrugged, but she didn't respond. She couldn't just make things up about a company and a man they were so familiar with. She felt a bead of sweat drip down her back.

Gupta turned to his boss and said, "The guy made millions but stayed around at Aztec for three years."

Alina felt as if Brodsky's stare might bore a hole in her head when he turned to Gupta and said, "Maybe he had a retention agreement or an earn-out. Happens."

"Did Avi leave to build a new start-up?" Gupta asked Alina.

"I'm not really sure," she said. Gupta and Brodsky looked at each other, disbelief registering on their faces. She had claimed to be close to her former boss, yet she expected them to believe that Nicole Ryder didn't know what Avi London had done before joining Aztec or what he was doing now. She had to come up with something to salvage her chance to get a job offer.

"Okay, I'm sorry," she said, holding her arms out wide, as if surrendering. "Of course, I know Avi's plans. He even asked me to critique his idea. It's brilliant. I think his new venture will be a game changer."

Gupta's eyes widened with excitement, as if he were about to hear about his favorite movie star.

"But please," Alina said, "you have to respect that Avi asked me to keep his plans under strict confidence."

Brodsky's stare immediately softened.

"Do you think you can convince him to give Sway early access?" Gupta asked.

"He won't be launching for a few years, but if I was here, I'm sure he would. As I said, we're very close."

Brodsky nodded almost imperceptibly and said, "Confidentiality is critical in our space, Nicole. We're pleased to see you respect that."

She slowly exhaled as Gupta scrolled through his device and said, "Why didn't he take you with him."

"Oh…he tried," Alina said. "But…well, I like the idea

of working on something new but inside the walls of a larger, more established company. I'm not sure a pure start-up is for me."

Josh Brodsky pocketed his phone and stood. "Look, Nicole, we can see you have excellent credentials. We have a great need for talent like yours."

"Thank you, Dr. Brodsky," she said.

"It's Josh," he said, extending his hand. "As soon as our people team finishes reference checks, you can expect us to take a hard run at you."

Alina shook his hand and replied, "Oh, that's very flattering."

Once Brodsky and Gupta left, McMichael escorted Alina to the lobby. "You're really impressive, Nicole. They're desperate for talent. Assuming everything checks out on my call with Avi, do you think you'll be able to start right away?"

"I'm sure that won't be a problem." Alina knew Aztec's human resources team would verify Nicole's dates of employment. And Gagnon's scan had already ensured that Nicole Ryder was clean on all the major criminal background checks systems. As Alina exited Sway's complex, she texted Gagnon a simple, innocuous message to "be ready"—ready to intercept McMichael's reference call.

After all, Avi London was obviously a busy man. And Gagnon was in a much better position to provide the very best references for Nicole Ryder.

CHAPTER
THIRTY-EIGHT

THE NONDESCRIPT ARTIFICIAL intelligence coding school was located above a Taekwondo studio on Fullerton Avenue. Brownish water stains streaked the suspended ceiling tiles above the large classroom. Five rows of desks faced an electronic whiteboard. Four small, windowless meeting rooms framed Benjamin Colias's cluttered office. Horizon's bespectacled, gray-bearded founder, who said he opened the AI boot camp five years earlier, parked Lucas in one of the meeting rooms to wait. Donny Brodsky had agreed to meet him there at three o'clock, but Lucas had showed up early to get a sense of the school and the students shuffling in and out of the facility.

Lucas also reviewed the updated case files Fernandez had uploaded, including the forensics investigation into Horizons. He spent an hour pouring through FBI background checks on each student and instructor. The core system and student files were clean. There was no sign that any malware development had taken place at the AI programming school. And no red flags on the students and instructors, other than Ana Dafoe—the driver's license the hacker had used to sign up for Horizons was a complete fabrication.

Lucas placed an enlarged image from the Drake's security footage on the desk and asked Colias to join him. It didn't take long for the school's owner to identify his former student as IBC's sugar baby hacker.

"That's her," Colias said. "I can't believe it."

"She never raised any suspicions?" Lucas asked.

Colias shook his head. "Ana was with us for a few months. She made a very positive impression."

Lucas eyed the photo. "I'm sure."

"No. Not only that," Colias said. "I'm telling you, she was wicked smart. Ana kept to herself at the beginning. But after a couple weeks, she started mingling with the others—after they were broken up into project teams. And that was around the time she started spending extra time with Logan."

Lucas asked whether Logan was a student.

Colias let out a brief laugh. "No. Logan Greig is our lead instructor."

"I'd like to meet with him. In fact, I wouldn't mind spending some time with some of the students on her project team."

"No problem." Colias rose. "I'll go see who's here."

"Before you leave, anything else about Ana that you found out of the ordinary?"

"Not really," Colias said, scratching the back of his head. "Well, other than that she was the only student to pay my five-thousand-dollar course fee in cash."

"Cash?"

"Yep. All of it in hundred-dollar bills. Strange, right?"

Lucas rubbed his aching leg. While a hacker might steer clear of the banking and credit card systems, five thousand dollars was a lot of cash to throw around.

Colias's eyes widened. "Hey, you don't think that money is counterfeit, do you?"

"The bank would have told you when you made the deposit," Lucas explained.

"I never went to the bank. I've been using it as part of the petty cash I keep lying around."

Lucas shrugged. "If you have any of those bills left, I could check 'em out."

"I'm sure I do."

———

THAT AFTERNOON, Lucas met with an eclectic procession of Horizons students while waiting for Donny Brodsky. All appeared to be big fans of their beautiful classmate.

"Ana had a quick mind."

"She was extremely knowledgeable."

"Ana carried our team, for sure."

A student named Oscar, his long slick-backed hair tied in a ponytail, said, "She knew her shit, man. Greig will tell you that."

"Your instructor," Lucas confirmed.

"Yeah. Ana was always staying after class to do extra work with Logan."

Lucas made a note and checked his watch as Oscar left the room. It was already close to four, but still no sign of Donny Brodsky. If he didn't show up soon, Lucas would go to his apartment. For now, he asked Colias to send in Logan Greig.

Lucas pulled out the background check performed on the instructor. Greig had been one of the first employees at a company called AI Solutions. The company had gone public three years ago, and Greig cashed out his equity for a huge windfall. Married, two kids, no loans or debt to speak of, house fully paid off—not exactly the profile of a ransomware conspirator. Lucas would dig through Greig's full file later. For now, the instructor was standing at this door.

"How well did you know Ana Dafoe?" Lucas asked after brief introductions.

"Obviously not well," Greig replied. "I had no idea what she was up to."

"But you spent a lot of one-on-one time with her."

Greig shifted in his seat. "Ana was a very eager student," he said. "Smart, too. You can't fake that."

"Did you feel her level of knowledge to be…out of place?"

"What do you mean?" Greig asked.

"Did she know more than Horizons' typical student?"

Greig picked a piece of lint off his jeans and stared at the floor. "She had a strong foundation…" Lucas waited for Greig to finish. The instructor finally looked up and said, "Yes. Ana knew more than our usual clientele."

"Any theory as to why she enrolled in the boot camp?"

"It seemed like she was brushing up on a few things. But best I can tell, that didn't take very long." Greig shrugged. "Maybe she was sizing us all up for that cyber-attack. Guess Donny was the unlucky fellow."

"Tell me about your time together," Lucas said. "What was that all about?"

Greig cleared his throat and said, "Ana had a special interest in advanced inference engines."

Lucas had learned enough in his brief cyber training to know that inference engines apply systemic rules to deduce new knowledge from a reservoir of data. Certainly not the kind of tech used in ransomware attacks.

"Were inference engines part of her school assignments?" Lucas asked.

Greig smirked. "Not at the level she was getting into. Maybe if she was in a sophisticated program like MIT, but not here. From the questions she asked, I thought Ana had to be doing some consulting work. Whatever the project was, she was querying—or planning to query—a ton of data. Trying to infer the identity of something." He paused and added, "Or some*one*."

Lucas thought back to the Drake surveillance footage

and how the sugar baby's eyes were darting around the lobby.

"Do you have any idea what or who?" Lucas asked Greig.

The instructor shrugged. "Not without seeing the data she was planning to query against."

"It was nice of you to spend that kind of time with her on an outside project," Lucas commented. "Do you always provide that level of...extra assistance?"

"Nothing unseemly happened here, Agent Foley. I'm a happily married man. I take what I do here very seriously."

Lucas held his hands up. "No offense intended. I'm just covering all the bases." He was about to ask his next question when he heard a quick rap and the door opened. A heavyset middle-aged man wearing a LIFE IS GOOD sweatshirt stepped in and nodded at Lucas. "Sorry I'm late."

COLIAS HAD NOTED that Donny Brodsky was not your typical Horizons student. Still, seeing the middle-aged, balding man standing in the doorway surprised Lucas.

"I told the agents in California everything I know," Donny said. He slowly lowered himself into the chair vacated by Greig.

Lucas nodded. "Agent Dennison said you were very cooperative, Mr. Brodsky."

"It's Donny."

"Okay. I read Dennison's full debrief. But he didn't realize Ana Dafoe had been involved in multiple incidents."

"Oh?" Donny said. His eyes seemed immediately drawn to the photograph placed on the desk. "She found another moron like me?"

Lucas suppressed a chuckle and continued, "I appreciate your coming in, Donny. I do have a few follow-up questions."

Donny continued to stare at the image.

Lucas asked, "Is this the same woman that gave you the thumb drive?"

Donny snickered. "That's her," he said.

"How many times did you meet up with her outside of the Horizons classes?"

"Like I told the FBI guy in California, the class went out for drinks at McGee's Tavern. One time at Gibson's Steakhouse." Donny motioned toward the classroom. "Other than here in class, those are the only times I ever saw her."

"So you never ran into her around town?"

"I don't get out much, Agent Foley. These millennials have a lot more energy than I do. I was just trying to get a better tech job." Donny looked away. "But I shouldn't have bothered."

Lucas asked, "Why not?"

Donny frowned. "I'm retiring from the tech world. I don't like where it's all going. Cyberattacks. AI humanoids? I'll leave all that to my brother."

Lucas thought about Dennison's comment about Josh Brodsky's special project. "Is that what your brother Josh is developing? An AI humanoid?"

"Didn't your San Francisco friends tell you?" Donny asked.

"Not really. Is there any way Ana Dafoe knew what your brother was working on?" It was worth checking, despite Dennison's assurances.

"I don't see how she could have," Donny replied. "I didn't know anything about his contraption before my visit out there, after I got conned by Ana."

"Fair enough. And when was the last time you saw her?"

"A few weeks ago. Right before I went to California. I

kept trying to reach her after that, but she didn't answer her phone or text messages. Good thing for me."

"Did Ana say anything about where she might be heading after the Horizons boot camp?"

"She made up that bullshit story about opening up a string of AI coding schools across the country. Maybe she's out there doing that someplace. Although I wouldn't waste a lot of FBI time trying to chase down that lead."

"Point taken." Lucas checked his notes and said, "You told the San Francisco agents you thought Ana was trying to seduce you."

Donny waved his hand toward the picture. "She didn't have to try very hard."

"Did you sleep with her?"

Donny smiled slightly. "I would have. She put me off. Said I had to show what I could bring to the 'partnership' first. But she pushed me to send that file to my brothers." He groaned. "I'm such an idiot."

Lucas made a note on his tablet before asking, "Did you ever feel…woozy or drugged at any time you were with her?"

"No. Why? Is that what she did to the other guy?"

"Maybe. But you're certain you never felt you were under the influence of any kind of drug or narcotic?"

"Nothing more than the martinis we had at Gibson's."

They talked for another twenty minutes but mostly went over the same ground already covered with Dennison. The San Francisco agent was probably correct—Donny Brodsky was nothing but a sap. Lucas felt his cell phone vibrate on the desk and glanced over. It was Ramsey.

"I need to take this," Lucas said.

"No sweat," Donny said as he stood. He was about to close the door behind him when Colias appeared waving three hundred-dollar bills. He placed them in front of Lucas and asked, "Will I get this back?"

"Give me a day or so," Lucas said, motioning for

Colias to close the door behind him. Lucas answered his cell. "Hey, Hank."

"Lucas. Are you still at Horizons?"

"I'm just finishing up. Why?"

"I'm here with Agent Fernandez."

"What's going on?" Why was the junior agent meeting with his boss?

"Gilroy wants to meet with you and Dennison. Her office set up a videoconference for tomorrow morning."

Sonia Gilroy was the FBI's assistant director of counterintelligence.

"Since when does Gilroy get involved in our cases?" Lucas asked.

"Oh, I don't know, Lucas. Maybe it has something to do with counterintelligence flagging your sugar baby as an international spy."

CHAPTER
THIRTY-NINE

THE SUN PEEKED through the lifting fog as the white bus with dark privacy windows crawled along the thirty-six-mile route from Alina's new hometown of Santa Cruz to Sway headquarters in Silicon Valley. Every seat of the shuttle bus was occupied, including the one to Alina's left. Feeling the guy's stare since he'd taken the seat next to her over an hour ago, she kept her face turned away, dark sunglasses covering her eyes as she watched cars inch along in this Monday morning rush hour.

Alina tried to relax, but her insides were churning. She couldn't believe she was about to start a job inside the largest tech company in the world. Her interview had been just five days earlier. After Nicole Ryder's clean background check and a glowing reference from the supposed Avi London, McMichael had called to extend the job offer.

Alina had pulled it off. She had convinced Sway that she was Nicole Ryder.

So Alina had packed some essentials and taken the next flight back to California. Gagnon would follow by car with her limited belongings, including her laptop computer. But she no longer needed the cylinder-shaped computer storage device.

Her laptop now held the fully decrypted files about Valeriya Petrova.

Romanoff had delivered on the first part of their bargain. She would take her time loading her AI scout with her new treasure. She would diligently test and retest, preparing her creation. But Gagnon had convinced her of the need to wait before hacking into America's vast data networks and deploying her program to search for her mother.

"Small incursions might draw scrutiny," Gagnon had argued. "Romanoff insists you delay until your new mission is complete. Then he will provide all the tools you'll need to insert your AI scout into the target systems."

Alina had waited this long to run her search program. She could wait a little longer to find the truth about her mother.

The shuttle exited the highway and picked up some pace. Sway's new-hire package had pronounced the Tech-Shuttle as "the most cost-effective and stress-free way to commute to our complex." But after having already sat through an hour of interminable traffic, Alina checked her navigation app—Sway's headquarters was still thirty minutes away. She watched as a gray-haired bicyclist with a wicker basket full of groceries outpaced the bus. The new-hire orientation session was scheduled to start in five minutes. Alina hoped she would be able to sneak in without being noticed and blend in with the crowd of other newbies.

Alina briefly scanned her fellow passengers. All seemed lost in whatever they were listening to through their earbuds. Thankfully, the guy next to her had closed his eyes. No one seemed concerned with the traffic or the time. Alina felt the bus slow again and glanced outside. She saw a small crowd of people, their expressions animated as they waved handwritten placards at the bus. The slogans written on the signs were clear, however.

AI, SAY GOODBYE.

TECHSPLOITATION IS TOXIC.

STOP KILLER ROBOTS!

She felt a nudge from the seat next to her. "There they are again."

"I'm sorry?" Alina said, still facing away. "I don't—"

"They know a lot of Silicon Valley shuttle buses pass through this intersection," the guy said. "You've never seen them before?"

"No," she said. "I mean, well...it's my first day?"

"Ah. I *knew* it," he said, loud enough to invite stares from some of the earbud-clad riders. "I'm pretty good with faces. I didn't think I'd seen you before."

The bus picked up speed, and the placard toting crowd disappeared from view.

"They're against technology?" she asked.

He laughed, but it sounded more like a school-boy giggle. "They're against all of us." He nodded toward the other passengers. "You know, artificial intelligence engineers." He rubbed his hands together and lowered his voice, as if mimicking an old lady, and said, "We're taking over the world, my pretty."

Alina held her hand to her mouth to suppress her own laugh. Growing up, she and her friends had watched *The Wizard of Oz* dozens of times.

"Seriously," he continued, "you name the problem, and those people blame AI. In their minds, we eliminate their jobs. We listen in on their conversations. Shoot smart missiles at children. Oh, and don't forget the money we're paid, forcing middle-class people out of their homes when we bid up real estate prices." He puffed out his chest and deepened his voice. "Destroying truth, justice, and the American way." He giggled again, clearly enjoying himself.

"So that's why they're out there?" she asked.

"Every day," he said. "I think they're just pissed we get

to ride these free shuttle buses instead of the crappy public transit system." He extended his hand. "I'm Dan. Dan Barry."

Alina shook his hand and said, "I'm Nicole. Nicole Ryder."

"Cool. Welcome to Sway," he said, still holding her grip. "You're gonna love working for the Death Star."

Alina's shoulders relaxed. Dan Barry had a nice smile that accentuated his dimples. Dark, wavy hair touched the top of his round wire-frame glasses.

"Where are you working?" he asked. "I mean, which division?"

"I'm assigned to strategic initiatives," Alina said.

"Wait," he said, his smile gone. "You're in Naveen's group, too? He never hires off the street." He retrieved his smartphone and started texting. "I had to work in the drone group for three years before Naveen would let me transfer in."

"Please!" Alina said, grabbing his hand again and squeezing it.

He looked down and said, "You're crushing my fingers."

"I'm sorry," she said as she released her grip. "I didn't mean to—"

Dan Barry shook and flexed his hand. "You know, when they ask for strong coders, they didn't mean body builders."

"I'm really sorry. I just don't want to get in trouble."

He seemed to think this over, then said, "Okay." He pocketed his device. "It's just that I know a lot of good internal people trying to get a job with us down there."

"Down there?"

"Yeah. The basement lab. That's where the CEO keeps his top-secret project team." He leaned over to Alina and whispered, "Except what we're working on is not so secret."

Alina removed her sunglasses. "Really?"

"Whoa!" Barry said. "Killer eyes!" Alina smiled as he leaned in closer and whispered, "If you think those protestors back *there* were angry, wait until they find out we're bringing back dead people."

"What?" Alina feigned shock. "What are you talking about?"

"Yep. We're bringing back people from our history books," he said. "I'm telling you, it's true." Barry looked at her over the top of his glasses. "We're going to change the world."

Alina felt the bus make a sharp right-hand turn, and an elliptically shaped glass building came into view. A chiseled granite sign announced their arrival: SWAY, INC. WORLDWIDE HEADQUARTERS.

As her shuttle approached the building, Alina saw swarms of people disembarking from a line of buses and moving like a wave toward the main entrance. This complex was separate from the People Experience facility where Alina had interviewed the previous week, so she didn't recognize the headquarters. When her shuttle came to a stop, Alina stood and followed Barry down the steps, up the walkway, and through the revolving doors into the main entrance, a sixty-foot-high atrium of steel and glass. Casually clad employees were scattering in all directions. Alina felt an energy, a vibrancy to the young men and women making their way down one of four corridors marked A through D.

Barry pointed out where new employees needed to register and turned to say goodbye. She found herself clasping his handshake, holding his gaze. Dan Barry's eyes exuded a warmth, a genuine comfort she hadn't experienced in her brief time in America. Certainly not from any of the sugar daddies, nor from Gagnon or Donny Brodsky or the other students at Horizons. And Barry said he had many friends on the CHERL project.

Perhaps she would figure out a way to become his friend, too.

CHAPTER
FORTY

HEATHER BLACKRIDGE, a petite brunette from Sway's People Experience team, escorted Alina to a room at the far end of the cavernous headquarters. Blackridge explained that she had expedited Alina's onboarding process so Alina could join the orientation session already in progress. Yet, even as they rushed down the corridor, Blackridge made time to point out the company's employee cafeteria ("Free lunch on Tuesdays and Thursdays," she shared), fitness center ("Andy's Zumba class is awesome"), and, behind a large soundproof glass window, the dog babysitting center ("We're launching one for cats next month").

Finally reaching their destination, Heather opened the door and motioned for Alina to step in. The room was dark, but a spotlight shined brightly on a man standing on a stage. His voice echoed as he spoke into his headset. A giant screen behind him projected the words *STRATEGIC INITIATIVES*.

"You can join the others," Heather whispered, pointing down the aisle.

The man on stage walked to the edge and squinted through the lights. "Another of our recruits?" The sound system accentuated his booming voice, making it seem as if he were shouting each word.

"Sorry I'm late," Alina meekly called out. As her own eyes adjusted, she could make out around twenty people seated in the front two rows of the otherwise empty auditorium. They all turned to watch her walk down the aisle. So much for sneaking in and not drawing attention.

The man said, "Well, you must be our Nicole. Welcome! I'm Carl Townsend. Anyway, you've missed the company overview and introductions." He waved toward the audience and added, "I'm sure you'll meet the rest of your peers at dinner tonight."

Tonight? Alina hadn't remembered anything in the welcome email about a dinner. Townsend returned to the center of the stage as Alina inched into a seat in the second row next to a young Black woman, her hair in neat rows of braids. Alina immediately feigned scribbling notes, keeping her face turned away.

"So, as I said earlier," Townsend continued, "you are all now part of our Strategic Initiatives group. But in reality, there is only one initiative that we are focused on."

The words on the screen behind him dissolved, replaced by *CHERL: Computerized Human Experienced as Real Life.*

Alina stared at the words as her throat went dry.

She was on the inside of the project they called CHERL.

"Maybe not the most elegant acronym," Townsend continued with a shrug. "But it does the trick. Let me ask you: What if our leaders could discuss today's challenges with the greatest minds in history?"

Alina saw several people shake their heads, so she mimicked their reaction. Townsend motioned to his audience with his palms up. "Impossible, you'd say? Well you, my friends, are joining the team that has already brought our vision to life!"

Alina heard a few whispers and murmurs as

Townsend launched into a long discussion of the science behind the CHERL project. The woman next to her leaned over and whispered, "I'm Jada Tyler." Alina whispered back, "Nicole Ryder."

"This is some cool shit," Tyler whispered.

"Wild," Alina agreed as Townsend paced the stage, describing the computer processing power now available to CHERL.

"Crunching billions of pieces of data—history books, diaries, letters, biographies—all in a nanosecond," he said. He talked about the advancements in machine learning and neural networks that "make it possible to replicate decision processes, personalities." He paused and looked at his audience. "Even to replicate the exact voice that makes it all real." His pacing resumed as he continued his lecture. Everyone had their heads down, taking copious notes. Alina scribbled along, but Townsend was adding very little to her own knowledge of CHERL. After all, she'd memorized Josh Brodsky's board report, analyzed the strategy and early successes re-creating people like Ulysses S. Grant, Churchill—even Gandhi.

"Learn as much as possible about how system works," had been one of Gagnon's instructions.

Along with: "Position yourself for data input and editing role."

Townsend paced back and forth across the full length of the stage. "Think about the impact we will have on political discourse. On domestic and international affairs." He paused before adding, "But many of you will be assigned to our emerging corporate sector." He cupped his hand over the microphone and whispered, as if letting everyone in on his little secret, "But I'd hold out for science and medicine." He widened his eyes and said, "You never know if Mr. Einstein or Mr. Newton may be in your future."

He headed toward the side of the stage. "We will now hear from our CHERL leaders. Each will describe the role of their respective teams. Oh, and at the end, we will have you rank the teams in the order of preference of where you'd like to start your journey. There is no guarantee, but we try to match everyone with their first or second choice."

Over the next hour a series of presenters paraded onto the stage, describing the technical components of CHERL. And while Alina noticed a few of her peers slouching in their seats, she sat straight up, captivated by every word, riveted by the science, the AI techniques, the sheer genius of CHERL's design. Each succeeding presentation ignited Alina's mind more than the last.

A long-haired project manager named Kyle Fraser presented the CHERL neural networks that controlled empathy and aggression. Fraser was followed by an Asian woman named Sol Kim. As Kim started speaking, Tyler leaned over and whispered, "It's nice to finally see a sister up there."

Alina smiled and whispered back, "Sure is." Kim gave a description of natural language processing and how neural networks recreated voice and inflection. She demonstrated samples of voices her team had recreated, asking the audience to identify who they belonged to. No one guessed right. Still, to Alina, the voices sounded authentic, amazingly real.

A man named Faisal Khan followed with a rundown on his work re-creating personality. "If we fail to re-create the temperament of our subject, CHERL will have no credibility. The whole system collapses without us."

From the yawns and body language of her peers, Alina knew the final presentation on the Tower Operations team was viewed as the least compelling of all. This didn't stop project manager Enrico Alvarez from trying to excite the crowd. "We are at the core of what makes CHERL work," he asserted. "Our team deals with memory. Our team deals with history. The richness of the information we acquire, how we organize and present the data to the neural networks. We are the difference between CHERL presenting a caricature or something our clients will *experience as real life!*" Alvarez moved to the front of the stage. "With my team, you will work alongside our best engineers inside the Tower, our massive server farm—with enough processing power to crank out over one trillion calculations per second."

Alina sat forward, making a mental note of this server farm.

"More importantly," Alvarez continued, "you will learn how even small modifications in the data can have a dramatic impact on the advice the system provides our clients." Alvarez paused and held his arms out as if welcoming a throng of believers. "Come. Join the Tower Ops team and see where the magic happens!"

As Alvarez exited the stage, Alina felt her tablet vibrate. Townsend had texted his mini-survey—it was time to indicate her top two selections.

"Which one you going for?" Tyler asked as conversations broke out among the recruits.

Alina knew she would do anything to work on Fraser's neural network team. Even working on Khan's personality team would be thrilling. Yet, as she replayed Gagnon's directive (*Position yourself for input role*) and Alvarez's comments about Tower Ops and how his team will "learn how even small modifications in the data can have a dramatic impact on the advice the system provides," Alina knew which team she would be ranking first.

CHAPTER
FORTY-ONE

LUCAS BOUGHT a black coffee at the corner street vendor and walked two blocks to the Green Line, which would take him to the Roosevelt Avenue FBI building. He'd spent the previous evening on the phone with Fernandez and Dennison, preparing for this morning's video call with the assistant director of counterintelligence, Sonia Gilroy. Fernandez's revelation about the identity of their hacking suspect kept churning through his mind.

"I used the bureau's facial recognition system against the criminal databases," Fernandez had explained. "Just as you asked, Agent Foley. I even checked with Interpol. No matches. I reached out to Homeland Security, and they tapped into their systems. TSA, Secret Service. They ran the Drake's surveillance image against ICE files. The next thing I knew, Ramsey summoned me."

Lucas spent the ride downtown using his phone to search for articles to familiarize himself with Sonia Gilroy's meteoric rise through the bureau. Like most senior DC staffers, she had been plucked out of a productive career in the field. But Lucas had observed changes in field agents once their lungs had filled with the rarified air of DC—many turned into bureaucrats, more focused on their careers and on coddling politicians and their staff in the Beltway than in solving cases. Lucas didn't have any reason to expect that Sonia Gilroy would be different from the rest. Yet he had to admit, she had an impressive background.

After earning degrees in psychology and criminology, Gilroy had started as a special agent in the Philadelphia field office, busting up high-profile drug rings. She had built a reputation as an agent with uncanny instincts, strong discipline, and maniacal focus, an agent who developed a broad network she shielded like a mother hawk protecting her young. Coworkers commented on her unique sources, which kept her one step ahead of the bad guys. After a brief stint on a task force investigating foreign corruption, she had moved on to counterespionage, where she had thwarted some of the most high-profile plots of the past ten years. Gilroy had been elevated to the top job in counterintelligence this past fall.

After passing through security in the FBI building, Lucas went directly to the secure video conference room. The call was scheduled to start in five minutes, but Gilroy's secretary, Sarah Lake, was already connected and displayed on the screen.

"She's finishing up a call," Lake said. "I'll patch you in when she's ready."

At precisely ten o'clock, Gilroy's image appeared. The assistant director was behind her desk, eyes focused on her computer as her hands raced across the keyboard.

"I'll be right with you," she said flatly while her fingers tapped away.

"No issue," Lucas said. But where was Dennison?

While he waited for the meeting to begin, Lucas studied the assistant director. She wore a white button-down blouse open at the neck, and her sleeves rolled up. He had seen Gilroy on video presentations, but now her face appeared to be thinner than he recalled. At fifty-two, Gilroy was quite striking. In fact, her high cheekbones, accented on one side by a small beauty mark, and short blond hair, styled in a side part, brought to mind a middle-aged fashion model more than an FBI agent. The background behind Gilroy was clear enough for Lucas to view her sparsely decorated office. A few awards lined the wall, along with photos of the assistant director shaking hands with several of DC's most notable dignitaries. He observed few personal items on her immaculate desk—none of the standard photos of family or vacation destinations that he could see.

"I've heard good things about you, Agent Foley," Gilroy finally said when she looked up and pushed the keyboard away.

Lucas felt his shoulders relax. "Thanks," he said. "It's an honor to meet you, Assistant Director Gil—"

"Sonia's fine," she said. "How's your leg healing up? I read about the Rojas Cartel operation."

"It's a slow process. But I'm getting stronger."

"That's good. The bureau is in short supply of top-quality undercover agents. It's nice to see you've gone into the family business. How's your father enjoying life on the beach?"

Lucas shifted in his seat. "How do you know my father?"

"Only by reputation," Gilroy said as her image shifted to the left side of a split screen as the right side filled with the image of a smiling Agent Dennison. Lucas exhaled a sigh of relief.

"Sorry," Dennison said. "Technical difficulties."

"That's quite all right," Gilroy said. "I know it's early in California. Thank you for joining us, Rob."

"No issue, Sonia." Hearing Dennison and Gilroy use each other's first names was jarring. Lucas assumed Dennison had worked with the assistant director in the past. "I didn't know we were tracking one of your spies," Dennison said. "Who is she?"

"Hold on," Gilroy said. "I'd like to hear what you've both learned about her first."

Dennison held both hands up and said, "Sorry."

Gilroy leaned forward and rested her arms on her desk. "Agent Foley, why don't you start us off? Tell me what you know."

Lucas opened his tablet and proceeded to describe the sugar daddy dating services and the senior executives the hacker had targeted. "These are powerful men," Lucas explained. "She obviously believed they would be vulnerable, looking for companionship."

Dennison interjected, "The promise of sex has a way of making men lower their guard."

Lucas ignored the agent's comment and moved on to details of the McKinsey case—the fancy dinner with the woman who called herself Deirdre. The drinks the woman presumably spiked with a narcotic. How the hacker used McKinsey's laptop to sign on to his company's computer system and load her malware. And the naked pictures she took to make sure her victim remained silent.

"McKinsey instructed his company to pay the ransom, and they swept the whole episode under the rug."

"How much?" Gilroy asked.

"One mil."

Gilroy looked down, seemingly lost in thought. After a few moments she asked, "I assume she scrubbed the fake profiles from the dating sites."

Lucas nodded. "SugarConnections.com, Seeking-Companions.com. All history, deleted. We found no traces of a profile fitting her description. We're lucky she didn't think to delete the Drake's surveillance footage."

Gilroy leaned back and asked, "Why did she choose the Drake?"

"She didn't choose it," Lucas replied. "McKinsey liked to stay there when he was in town."

Gilroy looked away. She seemed to think this over

before asking to see the photo taken from the surveillance video. Lucas punched a few keys on his tablet to share the still image of the hacker. Gilroy stared at her computer for a long while before shaking her head. "She looks... younger than the passport photo," she said softly.

"What passport photo?" Dennison asked.

"I'll get to that, Rob," Gilroy said. "Go on, Agent Foley."

"Okay," Lucas continued, now referencing Fernandez's notes. "The hacker mostly used wigs to change her appearance. But not well enough to defeat the facial recognition system. And my partner got a positive ID from two other Chicago victims. And from Donny Brodsky."

"Who?" Gilroy asked.

Dennison jumped in. "He's the guy that she used to get to Sway."

"Another sugar daddy?" Gilroy asked.

Dennison took his cue and gave Gilroy the same summary he had given Lucas two days earlier, practically verbatim. When he finished, Gilroy glanced to the side as she quietly processed the information Lucas and Dennison had conveyed. After a few moments she turned back to the screen. "Certainly she didn't enroll in the Horizons coding school just to find a new vector of attack. Is that where she built the malware?"

"She didn't build it," Lucas jumped in. "The FBI cyber lab is sure the code is too complicated for one person to have built it alone."

"Then what was she doing there?"

"The Horizons instructor believes Ana was working on some type of AI search engine," Lucas said. "He assumed she was hired by a client to create a system to query large data files. He said she was obviously searching for something. Or some*one*."

Gilroy seemed again to be quietly taking in this last

piece of information. Maybe it was worth adding his own suspicion.

"I'd like to show you something else," Lucas said as he tapped at his tablet and the surveillance video from the Drake appeared on the conference screen. The three of them watched as the sugar baby emerged from the hotel's elevator and slowly walked toward the exit. When the suspect was almost to the stairs leading down to the street, Lucas froze the image. "You know," he said, "I can't help noticing the way her eyes dart from side to side. I don't know about you, but it seems to me she is looking for someone in the lobby."

"Run it again," Gilroy said. After replaying the video two more times, Gilroy said, "I don't see it the same way as you, Agent Foley. She's making sure no one is watching her. It's as simple as that."

Lucas shifted in his chair, now wishing he hadn't brought up his theory. Gilroy looked at her watch, so Lucas checked the time, too. The meeting had been scheduled for an hour, and it was already ten forty-five. They had fifteen minutes to learn why counterintelligence had flagged their hacker.

"Assistant Director Gilroy," Lucas said. "If you wouldn't mind, can you share how our suspect became of interest to your team?"

Gilroy leaned back, tented her fingers, and tapped at her pursed lips.

"Four months ago, a woman entered the country with fake passports from Latvia and America, using the name Brianna Danis. Hackers had inserted Danis's fictitious profile in our immigration systems ahead of her arrival. US Customs has been piloting a set of AI algorithms that run overnight. AI picked up patterns that didn't match expectations of a dual American-Latvian citizen so they alerted the FBI."

"Amazing," Dennison said.

Gilroy nodded. "My team has been trying to locate

her ever since. It wasn't until your associate ran images from the Drake's surveillance video against our databases that we made the match."

"Ana Dafoe," Lucas said. He remembered Burick's analysis of the malware's origin and asked, "Is Russia involved?"

"Possibly," Gilroy said. "And your sugar daddy hacks might only be her warm-up assignment."

"Any theories on what she's searching for with the program she was working on at Horizons?" Lucas asked.

Gilroy looked away but did not offer an opinion.

Dennison chimed in. "Maybe she's looking for new victims for her malware scheme."

Given the ease with which she had found her initial targets, Lucas couldn't see why the hacker would build a sophisticated AI search engine to find new victims. And from the way Gilroy slowly tapped her fingers on the table, Lucas suspected she might be thinking the same thing.

"Why don't we go public with the Drake images," Dennison suggested. "Set up tip hotlines. Someone will spot her."

"That's not how we do things over here, Rob," Gilroy said. "If we release her photo, she will surely be extracted by her handlers—as will other operatives who might be in America—and we'll miss our chance to potentially break up a larger network. It's critical that she be brought in so we can interrogate her." Gilroy leaned forward, and her eyes narrowed as she said, "No harm can come to her at any cost. Is that understood?"

"Yes, ma'am," Lucas and Dennison said in unison. Gilroy checked her watch again as her expression softened. "Sorry, gentlemen, but I have another appointment." She tapped on her keyboard. A phone number appeared in the chat window on the screen. "This is my private cell phone number. If you discover anything more, I want you to call me directly."

"Will do," Dennison promised. Suddenly, the voice of Gilroy's assistant was heard off-screen.

"Excuse me, Sonia. I have Agent Hank Ramsey calling in. He says he has urgent information you and Agent Foley need to hear."

"Put him on speaker," Gilroy instructed.

Lake appeared at the edge of Gilroy's screen, pressed the speakerphone button, and said, "Agent Ramsey, you're on with Assistant Director Gilroy and—"

"Lucas," Ramsey said, his voice shaking. "Those hundred-dollar bills you brought in from Horizons. The bills Ana Dafoe used to pay her tuition. They weren't counterfeit."

"Okay," Lucas said. "Why is that relevant to—"

"The serial numbers match the money we lost at the failed Rojas Cartel bust! The money in the Samsonite suitcases! Lucas, if your sugar baby had that cash, that means she—"

"The date gone bad?" Lucas called out.

"That's right, Lucas. Your sugar baby hacker may have murdered Henry Garcia!"

CHAPTER
FORTY-TWO

FOR THE FIRST time since Alina had come to America, she found herself following a daily routine.

Each day her alarm and coffee maker kicked into gear at six thirty sharp. After a quick shower, she donned a pair of khaki slacks and a polo shirt embroidered with the company logo, poured coffee into her Sway-issued insulated thermos, and walked three blocks to catch the Tech-Shuttle. Despite the predictable traffic, the seven-fifteen bus deposited her in front of Sway before eight thirty—the time Enrico Alvarez expected his team to be firing up their workstations in Tower Operations, which was located in a secure space in the basement next to the room of giant high-speed computer servers, stacked wall to ceiling.

She focused on the assignments that Alvarez spooled out each day, mostly involving loading fresh data and recoding basic logic algorithms. She finished these early drills quickly. But the tasks became more complex during the second week, and Alvarez partnered her with a freckle-faced engineer named Ted Kavanaugh who demonstrated knowledge of more advanced machine languages.

"Enrico likes to keep his code fast and efficient,"

Kavanaugh repeated after each of their brief sessions. Alina tried to stay late to make sure she was keeping up, but at six p.m. each day, she was expected to join her fellow new hires for after-hour "bonding events."

"The company likes to create some esprit de corps among incoming classes," Alvarez had told her on her first day. So there was the three-hour wine-tasting tour along the Silverado Trail in Napa and a twilight hike in Palo Alto's Baylands Nature Preserve—complete with flasks filled with tequila and lime Gatorade. From the way everyone stumbled onto the van at the end of the hike, Alina assumed her flask was the only one that had *not* been returned empty. Each event was followed by dinner and more cocktails and incessant banter about hot new San Francisco clubs and the latest Silicon Valley billionaires. As the end of this two-week marathon neared, Alina was exhausted.

When she finally had a free moment, she decided to work on her friend from the shuttle.

"Hey, I thought you forgot about me," Dan Barry said as soon as he answered the phone.

"I'm sorry," Alina said. "I've had to go out every night with the other new hires."

Barry laughed. "Ah, the bonding thing. Yeah, it's big out here. I hope you played nice in the sandbox."

Alina paused, remembering some of the tech bros hitting on her at the nature preserve, then said, "Don't worry. I was a good girl."

She heard Barry clear his throat before asking how she was enjoying the work.

"Actually, Dan, I feel like I'm being spoon-fed. I'm being assigned these small projects. But the system is so massive, I'll never understand how it comes together."

Barry said, "I don't think Dr. Brodsky *wants* his minions to understand how the whole thing comes together. That's why he has all these separate teams."

Alina tried to sound glum. "But I'm feeling very frustrated."

Barry was quiet. After a few moments he said, "Listen, what are you doing tomorrow?"

"I think Naveen is taking us out for a final celebration."

"How about tonight? I'll invite some of my friends over. The ones who work on CHERL. We can order in some tacos. I'm sure we can get you up to speed."

DAN BARRY LIVED on the fourth floor of a five-story building in San Jose near a small marina that jutted out over the San Francisco Bay. When Alina rang the buzzer, she heard laughter coming from inside. She took a deep breath just before the door swung open.

"Heeey, you found it," Barry said, grinning broadly. He kissed her on the cheek and guided her into the apartment. "Everyone's excited to meet you."

Alina followed Barry into the small, sparsely decorated living room. Two young men wearing identical fleece vests were sitting on a faded brown sofa talking with a pale-skinned, compact woman perched on one of two wicker barstools. Half-empty bottles of bourbon sat atop a metal coffee table next to a bucket of watery ice. From the glassy look in their eyes, it was obvious Barry's friends had started without her. Barry introduced the sofa guys as Bobby Kang and Andy Bonner. They waved but didn't—or couldn't—rise from their comfy positions, while the woman stood and shook Alina's hand.

"So, you are new kid," Agnes Nowak said in a clipped accent. Alina tried not to make direct eye contact with the woman she made for a Pole.

"Two weeks in," Alina said slowly, taking extra care with each word so as not to reveal any hint of her own accent. Barry brought over another stool and offered

Alina a drink. "We're having bourbon but I have beer if you want."

"Bourbon is fine," Alina said as she slid the stool closer to the couch. Kang, pudgy-faced, with dark hair and fashionable green eyeglasses, raised his cup and said, "Welcome to Team CHERL."

"Thanks," Alina said. Barry handed her a glass of the whiskey, which she promptly raised. "It's good to be here."

Kang asked, "How do you like the work so far?"

"It's great." Alina rolled her eyes and said, "But I feel like I have so much to learn."

"Yeah, the curve is quite steep," Bonner said. He had shaggy brown hair and an overgrown beard that glistened around his upper lip after each swig of bourbon. "CHERL is extremely complicated."

Alina took a sip, then asked, "How did you ever learn it all?"

"We know it because we built it," Bonner said.

Kang swirled his drink. "It eventually comes together. I'm sure they'll rotate you around to the different pods. Where do they have you starting out?"

"Tower Operations," Alina answered.

"I started with Alvarez too," Kang said. "Pretty boring. But at least I was able to use the test partition to run my homework."

Alina shifted in her seat. "What do you mean?"

"For my thesis, I built this crazy AI chess master that blew up Stanford's computers, so I borrowed the Tower. Alvarez doesn't care what you do in the test partition, as long as you don't mine crypto coins and—"

"Where did you come from?" Nowak interrupted, her eyes narrow. "Nicole. Is that right?"

"Yes. It's Nicole." Alina shifted on her stool. "You mean where did I work before?"

Nowak shook her head. "Where did you grow up?"

Alina took a sip and launched into a brief summary

of Nicole's childhood, sticking with the generalities that worked for her during her Sway interview.

"Interesting," Nowak said, rubbing the side of her face. She opened her mouth as if about to probe further when Barry said, "And Nicole used to work for Aztec."

"In Texas?" Kang beamed. "Really. Did you know my bud, Spencer Metcalf?"

Alina looked up as if in thought before shaking her head and saying, "I don't think so. It's a big company."

"Spencer's not really that happy there," Kang continued. He swallowed some bourbon. "He says the CEO is a real dick."

"It's that Chambers guy, right?" Bonner asked.

Kang nodded. "Yep. Buford Chambers."

Alina kept the glass in front of her face and said, "I didn't get much exposure to him." She almost winced at her accidental double entendre. "But Aztec was a good place to learn a lot about AI."

Kang said, "Their tech is top-notch. Spencer says—"

"You ever work outside US?" Nowak interrupted. Her brow was furrowed.

Alina shook her head slowly and sipped on her bourbon, wondering what signals she might be giving off to draw Nowak's pointed probes. She had to steer the conversation in a different direction. "How long have you all been at Sway?" she asked.

"Five years for me," Kang said. "About a year on CHERL."

Bonner raised his hand and said, "I'm the senior citizen. Two years on CHERL. And I was on Sway's drone team before that."

Alina waited for Nowak to answer, but the Polish woman just stared at her, as if trying to decipher a puzzle. Alina felt her heart beating faster. She turned her chair slightly to face Kang and Bonner, keeping Nowak out of her sight line.

Barry waved his hands and said, "It took four years for Naveen to let me join."

Kang laughed. "Well, Danny boy, you might be the last internal hire. I don't think corporate is letting Brodsky steal any more internal talent." Then, pointing at Alina, he added, "Nicole's part of the new vanguard."

Bonner swallowed the rest of his bourbon and let out a long breath before adding, "If you ask me, the factory is about to break down." His comment brought Nowak into the conversation.

"Why would you say that?" she asked.

"The pressure is on, Agnes," Bonner said. "Management is no longer satisfied with re-creating political leaders. They're pushing us into the business sector. We're about to stamp these things out on a conveyor belt."

"It will not be...conveyor belt," Nowak responded. "Every subject will be different."

Bonner poured more bourbon and said, "How can you be so sure? You know we used to care much more about the quality of the information that trains the system. And the quality of the code." He glanced at Alina and added flatly, "Developed only by engineers who had proven track records at Sway."

"Whoa," Barry said. "Back off, man. Nicole's not going to be a problem."

Alina felt her stomach twitch but kept her eyes steady. Bonner put down his glass and held his hands up. "No offense, man. I'm just saying."

Alina shook her head and said, "None taken," before Bonner continued.

"We all know there are holes in this business version. Now we're bringing in untested engineers from the outside, bodies to get the assembly line moving." He crossed his arms and said, "Our CEO had a vision to help fix our system of government. Now he expects us to clone a bunch of fat cat business dudes to help companies make more money."

Kang raised his glass. "*Cha-ching*, baby. I hear there are already forty clients in the pipeline. At least there'll be *some* form of intelligence running those places."

Alina hadn't realized how rapidly the project had shifted away from the government realm.

Bonner shook his head. "There won't be any intelligence if we lose control of what CHERL recommends."

"How would you lose control?" Alina asked.

Bonner reached for his glass. "These business titans we're bringing back. With our billion lines of code and all that data, all those neural networks projecting what strategies they would offer, projecting their advice." He climbed off the sofa and walked toward the kitchen. Other than reaching for his drink, it was his first movement since Alina entered the apartment. "When it was just a few of us, we could stay on top of every line of code. But I've seen the new plan. Every week there will be a new batch of engineers. Just like Nicole. Being thrown right into the mix. Without the knowledge and experience we all have." Bonner looked at Alina. "You said it yourself. You told Dan you were frustrated. Well, it's going to get worse. Without an understanding of the intricacies of what we've built, I don't see how CHERL's output won't suffer."

"Don't be such an ass, Andy," Barry said.

"No. It's okay," Alina said. "I understand what he's saying. I mean, it's true. I've been trained to do my job, but I only know what's going on in Tower Operations. How can I be expected to know the system if all I do is data input and a few scrubbing algorithms? I should know as much as all of you do about CHERL."

"That's why I thought maybe we could help her get up to speed," Barry interjected, looking at his friends. "You know, take her through each of our areas of expertise."

Alina shrugged and said, "I've never even seen design specifications. I have no idea how the data is used to make CHERL recommend what she does. I have no—"

Nowak interrupted. "If Brodsky wanted you to know this, he would have arranged for it."

The two women locked eyes for several seconds. Alina felt a bead of sweat dripping down her spine. She hoped she hadn't made a huge mistake by exposing herself to this Nowak woman.

The room stayed silent until Bonner cleared his throat. "I don't agree, Agnes. I think Dr. Brodsky is up to his eyeballs."

"I agree." Barry nodded.

Nowak pursed her lips and took in a deep breath. She rose and slowly walked to the kitchen. After rinsing out her glass, she turned and looked back at Alina. Her icy stare made Alina shiver. After a few uncomfortable moments, the Polish woman walked out of the apartment without saying another word.

"What's bugging her?" Kang asked.

Bonner shrugged and finished his drink. "Who knows. But I better get going."

Kang stood and said, "Right behind you."

Bonner and Kang said their goodbyes as Alina sat frozen. What had she done to raise Nowak's suspicion? Dan started clearing the coffee table of bottles and glasses. After a few moments he said, "You know, I have access to all the CHERL specs." He squinted at Alina, as if mulling over his thought. "I guess there's no harm in lending you my copy for a few days."

Alina finally rose and started helping him load the dishwasher. When they were done, she tossed a dish towel in the sink, reached for Barry's hand, and turned him toward her. She had been through so much over the past year. Learning about her father's lies. Her narrow escape from Henry Garcia. The demeaning encounters with sugar daddies. And now, impersonating Nicole Ryder, possibly drawing the suspicion of Agnes Nowak. And despite Gagnon's support, she had been on her own every step of the way. She had no idea how long she would remain inside Sway. How long until she could unleash her AI scout. But as she looked into Dan Barry's soft eyes, one thing was clear.

She did not want to be on her own any longer.

She pulled Barry closer and slowly removed his glasses. She brushed the hair back from his forehead, caressed the side of his face, and kissed him. Gently at first, testing to make sure she hadn't misread his signals. But moments later, their lips were pressed together, their bodies locked in a passionate embrace.

And then he took her by the hand and led her to his bedroom.

CHAPTER
FORTY-THREE

THE VAN WEAVED through downtown San Jose as
the sun set behind several tall buildings. The vehicle came
to a stop in front of a bright green awning announcing
they had arrived at the Island Taste restaurant. Jada Tyler
was sitting next to Alina, peering out the van window.

"Do you think that guy owns the restaurant?" she
asked Alina.

Alina's stomach growled as she leaned over and
looked at the thin Indian man with the long dark hair
waving at the van. "Actually," Alina said, "that's our
boss."

"Wait. That's Naveen Gupta?"

"Yep. He came in at the end of my job interview."

"What's with the hair?" Tyler asked. "I thought
Naveen was Indian. He looks like a Rastafarian."

"A what?"

"It's like a religion, but they smoke a lot of weed."

Strange, Alina thought.

"Hope the food is good," Tyler said.

"I'll go for anything right now." The day had been so
busy that she hadn't eaten a thing since Barry had made
her breakfast that morning, more than twelve hours ago.

Alina had never tried Jamaican food, but she was so famished she would eat anything.

As they disembarked from the van, the jovial Gupta welcomed each of the twenty new hires and directed them into the restaurant.

"Island Taste!" Gupta smacked his fingers with a chef's kiss as Alina passed. "The best, mon!"

Alina thought she noticed a pungent odor, and Tyler rolled her eyes and said, "Told ya. That dude's been partying."

Rhythmic music washed over Alina as she entered the restaurant, a combination of steel drums and guitars filling the empty establishment. Gupta, who apparently had rented out the restaurant for the evening, shimmied his way to the head of a long rectangular table and called out, "Please sit, everyone." Alina and Tyler walked around and took seats at the far end. Several chairs remained empty, including the one to Alina's right.

"Let me do the ordering," Gupta called out as he started punching at the restaurant's ordering tablet.

"I'm a vegetarian," a woman said.

"Me, too," said another.

Gupta started counting the raised hands and said, "I've got us covered. You all like spicy, right?"

"Just don't kill us," someone shouted, and everyone laughed.

The standard Russian diet didn't include much in the way of spice, so Alina didn't know what to expect.

"I'll have them dial it down on the ackee," Gupta promised.

"The what?" Tyler asked.

Gupta giggled. "Don't worry. You'll love it."

The waiters started placing bottles of Red Stripe in front of each place setting, even in front of the chair Alina hoped would remain empty by her side. She started taking long gulps of beer.

"Take it easy, girl," Tyler said.

"I have to put something in my stomach," Alina said. She tried to join in the collegial banter around the table but was content to let Tyler carry the conversation. Why weren't they at least bringing some bread? Finally, the waiters arrived with large platters filled to the brim.

"What is this?" someone asked.

Gupta jumped up and pointed to a dish containing a yellowish stew. "This," he said, "is ackee and saltfish. A Jamaican staple." He nodded toward a greenish mixture. "And that's for my vegetarian friends. It's Jamaican callaloo. I hope you like spinach." He continued his tour of the platters—jerk pork, brown stewed chicken, and curried garbanzo beans. Alina stopped listening and filled her plate. When she sampled the pork, she immediately started coughing from the spice. Feeling the sweat beading on her brow, she guzzled the rest of her beer, trying to wash the burning from her throat.

"Everyone, take it slow." Gupta laughed as he chewed, his mouth seeming to move to the beat of the drums, which was almost drowned out by the cacophony of coughing. Apparently Alina wasn't the only one unused to the dish's heat.

The waiters kept the beer coming as quickly as the new recruits emptied them. And the more Alina drank, the easier the food went down. She found herself swaying to the reggae beat. For the first time since arriving in California, she felt relaxed.

Alina had made it through the first two weeks as Nicole Ryder. She was working in a real artificial intelligence company, positioned on the control and data management team, just as Romanoff wanted. And thanks to Dan Barry, a copy of the CHERL system's specifications was on the way to Romanoff. Alina thought of their impassioned night together. Barry was a kind and gentle man. It had felt good to be with someone who might care for her, even if he had no idea of her true identity.

Tyler leaned toward her and said, "Well, I hope you're

enjoying yourself, 'cause we're not coming back here anytime soon."

"I don't know," Alina said, wiping the sauce dripping from the side of her mouth. "I could get used to this." But Tyler's attention had shifted to the restaurant's entrance. Alina followed her new friend's gaze. Josh Brodsky had just walked in, followed by several people Alina didn't recognize. But she gagged on a bite of saltfish when she saw the last person now entering the restaurant.

It was Agnes Nowak.

The chatter quieted as Gupta stood and walked over to speak with CHERL's leader and the late arrivals filled the empty chairs. Alina nervously kept her eyes locked on Gupta and Brodsky. She sensed the chair next to her sliding back.

"I see you are still here," Nowak said as she sat down beside Alina.

Alina took a swig of beer, then forced a smile. "What a surprise to see you here."

Nowak said, "Dr. Brodsky likes senior engineers to mingle with his new hires," Nowak said before turning to introduce herself to the woman to her right. Alina took the opportunity to reengage with Tyler, hoping to minimize any interaction with the Polish woman. A few minutes passed before Alina heard the clink of silverware on glass.

"Excuse me, everyone," Gupta said. The few conversations that had persisted came to a sudden halt.

"I know it's been a long day," he said. "I hope you're enjoying the…tasty food." Gupta bowed toward the kitchen, and everyone clapped. He turned back to his boss. "And thank you, Dr. Brodsky, for joining us tonight." Brodsky's stoic expression hadn't changed since he entered the restaurant. "I'm sure you're all anxious to get some rest this weekend. Monday starts another long week." Gupta shrugged. "As some of our senior staff here will tell you, it will be another long week after that one too." There was the brief sound of nervous laughter. "But you've heard a lot about our special project during these two weeks. Hopefully you're excited about the teams you've been assigned to." Heads nodded all around. "Good. Well, this is your chance to ask our fearless leader any questions on your mind."

Gupta stood to the side, and Brodsky moved forward. He surveyed the room, waiting for someone to speak. After a few awkward moments, a blond man in the far corner raised his hand.

"Dr. Brodsky," he started.

"It's Josh."

"Um. Well, I think I just wanted to say—and I think I speak for everyone here—we're all so excited to be part of this." Everybody clapped and nodded. Brodsky rolled his eyes and looked for another hand.

Alina sensed Nowak leaning toward her. "A brown nose in every batch," she whispered. Alina started to smile before Agnes added, "Just like military leaders in *your* country."

Alina felt as if something heavy were suddenly pressing on her chest.

"These historical leaders," a dark-haired woman called out. "How do you select who you plan to bring back?"

"Good question," Brodsky said. "For CHERL to be effective, we require a very rich supply of historical information. Biographies. Textbooks. Correspondence. So the list of possibilities narrows fairly quickly. You see..."

"You know," Nowak whispered to Alina as Brodsky continued, "I can smell a Russian a mile away."

"Shhh!" Alina tried to wave off the Polish woman, but she felt as if the room were spinning. She took a long gulp of beer.

"I cannot say why," Nowak continued. "Maybe centuries of knowing our enemies."

Brodsky pointed to Tyler, who had her hand up. Alina shifted her seat so her back was to Nowak.

"How will we know if the advice is sound?" Tyler asked. "Will all the recommendations be tested?"

"As much as we can in a lab environment. One of the reasons you've all been hired is to help us deploy CHERL to an actual set of clients. Exposing the AI to authentic situations. Unfortunately, that is the only way we'll learn how the advice plays out in the real world."

Tyler followed up. "And clients will be okay with helping us shake out how well CHERL works?"

"Look," Brodsky said as he leaned his hands on the back of an empty chair. "Certain recommendations will be no-brainers. For example, one of the jobs of any leader is to allocate resources, right? CHERL can optimize this allocation much more effectively than any human. I plan to be at each client rollout, at least in the first year. Even clients must be trained." He pointed around the room. "I might even bring a few of you, too."

An excited murmur filled the restaurant.

When Brodsky turned to answer another question, Nowak whispered, "I'm wondering who trained *you*?"

"Stop," Alina whispered firmly. "I'm trying to listen." Alina kept her eyes glued to Dr. Brodsky as he spoke, but to Alina his voice sounded muffled, while every whisper from Nowak sounded like a scream.

"To fully explain our computations would be extremely difficult," Brodsky was explaining. "Certainly, in any terms that humans would understand. CHERL analyzes far too many variables—the inference engine games out thousands of scenarios, just as an AI chess master would." He shook his head. "It may be beyond our clients to ever really understand CHERL's logic tree."

A man in a hoodie stood and asked, "Dr. Brodsky—I mean, Josh—if you can't explain what CHERL is doing, how can anyone really trust what she's recommending?"

Brodsky pulled out the chair and sat. "Trust will only

come with experience." He looked out at his audience, his expression firm. "And I have personally had this experience with CHERL. I can say with confidence that the interaction will change you. The interaction will build the trust you're referring to."

"It is *you* I do not trust," Nowak whispered. "I do not know what you are doing. But I will find out."

"Excuse me?" Alina finally said, loud enough that Dr. Brodsky stopped speaking.

All eyes turned to look at Alina.

"Is there an issue?" Gupta asked.

Nowak put her hand in the air and said, "Small misunderstanding. It is my fault. Please...continue, Dr. Brodsky."

Dr. Brodsky glared at Alina and Nowak for a few seconds before shaking his head. "Where was I? Oh yeah, you see..."

"What happened?" Tyler whispered to Alina.

"Nothing," Alina whispered back. "I'll tell you later."

The questions continued for another forty-five minutes. Alina kept her head down, slowing picking at her food. Nowak had stopped whispering her accusations, but how did the Polish woman know Alina was a fraud? Or was she just probing to see how Alina would react? Maybe Nowak somehow knew the real Nicole Ryder. In any case, Alina didn't want to risk going back to the Sway complex until she knew. She needed to alert Gagnon. And she needed to get away from this table before Nowak told Brodsky and Gupta about Alina's deception. But maybe it wasn't even safe to return to her own apartment.

She heard Gupta say, "Let's take one more question." Alina looked around. Thankfully, no more hands went up. After a few silent moments, Gupta clapped his hands together and said, "Very well. Why don't our recruits hop on the van, and we'll get you on your way."

Alina slid her chair back and texted Barry.

> Can I stay at your place
> tonight?

As everyone boarded the van, Alina took a seat and kept her head low. When she shifted her eyes to look out the window, she had difficulty drawing in a breath.

On the street outside the restaurant, Agnes Nowak was waving her hands in excited gesticulations as she talked to Josh Brodsky.

FORTY-FOUR

ALEXI ROMANOFF LEANED BACK and observed the changes flashing on the giant, flat-panel screen. Fedorov had assembled four engineers from his AI team in this private and secure conference room to demonstrate their CHERL simulator. Of course, this AI model was a modest replica of the system described in the specifications Alina had passed to Gagnon. This version did not contain the complexity nor the depth of Sway's AI system, but Fedorov had assured Romanoff that with enough money and manpower, they could build a full-scale version of CHERL.

"Alexi Igorevich," Fedorov said now. "It is not too late to steal their code. Think of what it could mean if we provided the Kremlin with this tool. They could seek guidance from the greatest leaders in Russian history! Peter the Great. Alexander the second!"

But what purpose would it serve to provide such a robust capability to his superiors? There was little anyone could do to help those currently in charge of Mother Russia. Even CHERL couldn't extricate the cancer that had metastasized within the Kremlin. Besides, Romanoff ruled out source code theft as being far too risky. An audacious plan to steal the CHERL code would require the approval of his bosses. They would need to know how Romanoff had learned about this CHERL system. They would need to know he had been running an off-the-books ransomware scheme to line his own pockets.

No. Romanoff had no intention of letting them in on any facet of Alina Petrova's secret mission. Fedorov's dreams of stealing the CHERL code were best reserved for another day. Perhaps, after Romanoff was gone, when someone else was in charge of his band of cyberwarriors —which, if all went according to the plan formulating in Romanoff's mind, would not be long from now. He just needed to keep his personal asset embedded in the Sway corporation until he had what he needed.

Romanoff lit a cigar as the AI team continued their demonstration. With each change to the data model—that is, the information fed into the simulator—Fedorov pointed out subtle differences in CHERL's output recommendations. He illustrated how to make the simulator spin advice that could be more aggressive or hostile. He manifested other recommendations that appeared tamer and diplomatic. Romanoff took particular note when modified data led the recommendations to be more favorable to certain Russian causes. Not only political causes.

But business and financial causes.

With each succeeding demonstration, Romanoff grew more confident in his latest moneymaking strategy. A tactic that would secure a rather extravagant exodus to that Western European dacha. Romanoff struggled to keep his usual unreadable expression in place as he rose. Adjourning the session, he asked Fedorov to stay behind. When the room was cleared, Romanoff shut the door. He spent the next hour with Fedorov, revealing his new scheme—far more complex than the relatively simple ransomware attacks. And then he outlined the size of the opportunity.

And how much Fedorov's twenty percent share could be worth.

When Romanoff was done, Fedorov looked away, seemingly in deep thought. Dmitri Fedorov had been Romanoff's loyal and trusted lieutenant for over a decade, a Russian patriot to the core. But as Romanoff waited patiently for Fedorov's response, he worried that he might have taken too great a risk in revealing this new idea. But what choice did he have? Romanoff had learned over his career that a plan was nothing without the expertise to bring it to fruition. After a few more moments, the two men faced each other. A small smile appeared on Fedorov's face as he extended his hand, and the two men shook.

"I will need more specifics on your scenarios, Alexi Igorevich. But it should not be difficult preparing data loads for each. As long as Alina Grigoryevna is able to merge them into CHERL's workstream."

"I will have my framework to you tomorrow," Romanoff said. "But we will need to adapt as we learn more about CHERL's client list."

They left the conference room together, and Romanoff went immediately to his office. He had been waiting to respond to a message he'd received earlier in the day.

> GAGNON:
> A Polish woman at Sway is
> suspicious of Alina's origins.
> Please advise.

Now that Romanoff had confirmed they absolutely required Alina to remain securely inside of Sway, he keyed in his response to Gagnon:

> You must rectify the
> situation.

CHAPTER
FORTY-FIVE

THE NEXT MORNING, Alina called in sick while Barry went to work. They had made love into the early-morning hours, but part of Alina's mind had been elsewhere. It had been only their second night together, but Alina feared it might be their last. She just couldn't shake the words whispered in her ear by Agnes Nowak at the Jamaican restaurant: *I can smell a Russian a mile away* and *I do not know what you are doing. But I will find out.*

Alina was afraid to leave Barry's apartment. What if Nowak had already told Dr. Brodsky of her suspicion? Was Sway's People Experience team digging further into Nicole Ryder's background? Had they already discovered Alina was an impostor? If so, the news hadn't reached Barry, who had been texting her all morning.

> DAN:
> Feeling better?

> > ALINA:
> > I think so. Must have been the spicy food.

> DAN:
> I should have stayed in bed with you.

> ALINA:
> Better off keeping away.

> DAN:
> Impossible.

His last text was followed by a kissing emoji.

Alina got out of bed and paced Barry's living room. She decided to get dressed. She would go back to her apartment and retrieve the hoard of cash she had stashed away for just such an emergency. She still had over thirty thousand dollars. If Gagnon didn't extract her by the end of the day, she would leave on her own.

She wouldn't just wait to be arrested.

Alina was about to leave when she heard her laptop ping. She opened her computer and read Gagnon's message.

> GAGNON:
> It is safe to resume
> assignment.

> ALINA:
> How can you be sure?

> GAGNON:
> That woman returned to home
> country. Family emergency.

> ALINA:
> What about when she comes
> back?

> GAGNON:
> She's decided to stay in
> Poland.

Decided? She asked what Gagnon had done to make Nowak "decide."

> GAGNON:
> Presented her with better
> opportunity.

Alina shook her head. Did she really want to know more about this "opportunity"?

> ALINA:
> What if she told Sway her
> suspicions?

> GAGNON:
> She did not.

> ALINA:
> How can you be sure?

But Gagnon did not respond.

CHAPTER
FORTY-SIX

EIGHT MONTHS LATER...

LUCAS STARED at the scene playing out on the TV screen hanging above the diner's counter as he washed down the last of his toast with lukewarm coffee. Fire engines were dousing a blaze consuming a house in Oak Park, west of downtown. A burly waitress used the remote to flip to a local sports channel. The Blackhawks had lost again, sinking Lucas's favorite team into last place.

"Bunch a losers," the waitress barked before offering Lucas a refill.

Lucas shook her off and said, "That's harsh." Glad she didn't know how long his own losing streak was running. It had been eight months since his meeting with Sonia Gilroy, where he learned the sugar baby hacker was on the radar of the bureau's counterintelligence unit. Eight months since Ramsey had matched the FBI's money stolen by the Rojas Cartel to cash the hacker used to enroll in the Horizons AI boot camp. Eight months and the hacker's trail had gone completely cold. Yet barely a day went by where Lucas didn't study the image from the Drake's surveillance video. He'd gaze at the hacker's mesmerizing features as if it would enable him to conjure up clues about her whereabouts. Her image was posted in police departments all across the country, as were descriptions of Mateo Lozano and his two bodyguards. Over two hundred sightings had been reported, each a false alarm.

And every day he read through the latest in the bureau's case management system, but few meaningful notes or leads were posted by Agent Dennison in San Francisco or by Assistant Director Gilroy's counterintelligence team. Lucas checked in with Agent Fernandez, who was busy with her own expanding caseload. She was in high demand inside the cyber team but still made time to monitor the facial recognition software that scanned the sugar daddy websites, looking for any women resembling Brianna Danis. But the software hadn't found any additional hits. In fact, Fernandez's scans of the sites had come up empty since confirming that Henry Garcia had indeed been playing the sugar daddy circuit. Fernandez had turned up three separate relationships in which Garcia masqueraded as a "senior executive in a midsize company." But the dating website he had frequented the night of his death had been wiped clean of the sugar baby hacker's profile.

When Ramsey had first connected the hundred-dollar bills the hacker had used at Horizons with the cash taken from the failed drug bust, Lucas had wondered whether the sugar baby hacker had known she was dating a member of a drug cartel. But he surmised that she had stumbled onto Henry Garcia and fallen for his deception, just as real executives had fallen for hers. After all, her hacking scheme had gone after multimillion-dollar ransom paydays. She had targeted fat cat CEOs and their corporate backers and launched her attacks from the relative safety of a computer. Why would she take the risk of mixing with someone from the Rojas Cartel?

But now, the woman who had entered the country as Brianna Danis—and later became Ana Dafoe—seemed to have disappeared without a trace. It was possible she had already fallen into the hands of the cartel, her body chopped up and weighted down to sit at the bottom of Lake Michigan. Ramsey's undercover team continued setting bait, hoping to draw out Lozano and his bodyguards. But it was as if the Lozano team had pulled up stakes.

Yet Lucas's instincts kept signaling that the sugar baby hacker was still alive, probably working on the bigger mission Gilroy had worried about. Perhaps the hacker's Horizons software program was helping her find whoever it was she was looking for.

Which meant she was still alive. And still in America.

Certainly, Gilroy seemed to share that opinion.

"We have to find her before the cartel does" had been one of a series of messages from Gilroy over the months immediately following their initial meeting, as if Lucas needed a reminder. But as more months had passed, even Gilroy's requests for updates had stopped appearing on Lucas's phone. And no breaks materialized.

No clues. No leads.

Lucas tossed a ten note on the counter, exited the Pearl Diner, and crossed Broadway, walking briskly toward the field office. The pain in Lucas's leg had largely subsided, and his gait had improved enough to ditch the cane. The bureau's medical team was about to clear him to resume his work as an undercover agent.

Which meant his time with the cyber unit would soon be coming to an end.

He had some paperwork to complete on a business email scam before joining a ten o'clock briefing on a cryptocurrency manipulation ring. But as he crossed the threshold of the FBI building, he felt his phone vibrate. He pulled it from his pocket and read the text from a name he didn't recognize.

> Are you the agent working the
> sugar baby hacker case?

CHAPTER FORTY-SEVEN

THE CEO LEANED his elbows on the mahogany desk and rubbed his forehead as if trying to smooth the deeply etched worry lines there.

"So you see," he said, "this is quite a complex situation."

Alina and five other CHERL engineers had spent the past two hours seated in the gallery above CHERL's control room, observing Edward Bordelli on the twenty-foot-wide video display as the CEO spoke from two thousand miles away in Nashville, Tennessee. Bordelli had barely taken a breath as he rambled on about the situation he'd been managing over the previous three years. The meeting prep notes had described his company, Westfield, as "the largest insurance empire in the world, with agencies across the US and on three continents." Bordelli had been most animated when chronicling his digitization strategy, which he credited for slowing the revenue decline and client defections that had plagued his company.

"Still, every day another insurance-tech start-up comes out of the woodwork," Bordelli said before moving on to complain about regulators who believed Westfield's size presented systemic risks to the economy. "A bunch of bureaucrats trying to break up my company."

As Westfield's CEO droned on, Alina glanced at the indicator lights flashing at the lower left-hand corner of the giant screen. All CHERL performance measures were hovering in the green. Sway's AI creation was barely breaking a sweat. Alina felt her phone vibrate as a message came through from Jada Tyler, who was sitting three seats to her right. They had both been invited as part of an engineer rotation to monitor implementations.

```
TYLER:
Will this guy ever shut up?

                              ALINA:
                     He likes to talk.

TYLER:
First system crash caused by
boredom.
```

Alina chuckled. This was the fifth implementation she had been allowed to observe as part of her rotation. As she had in the prior four sessions over the past few months, Alina listened carefully for signs that Romanoff's data was working—information she had been secretly loading into each CHERL creation. While she never knew exactly what Romanoff's alternative data contained, Gagnon assured her that these new facts would lead CHERL to produce recommendations "helpful to Mother Russia." So far, in those previous sessions, the recreated leaders had never so much as mentioned her home country. She hoped today would demonstrate the result Romanoff was looking for and Romanoff would finally deliver the hacking tools needed to launch her AI scout.

Still, working as an engineer at Sway had been thrilling. And CHERL's recreations were absolutely mesmerizing. Alina had listened as CHERL's version of Henry Ford, the automobile pioneer, seemed to express real empathy toward a CEO from the aerospace industry. Alina especially enjoyed the AI portrayal of Steve Jobs, probably because everyone in Russia knew about Apple

Inc.'s founder. CHERL's version was extremely inquisitive, as if trying to feed the AI engine with greater and greater amounts of information. Andrew Carnegie was charming, though she had no idea who the steel industrialist was. Nor did she know much about today's AI recreation, Jack Welch—a man Bordelli claimed was his favorite CEO. The prep notes said that Welch had run the General Electric Company for more than twenty years at the end of the twentieth century. And that's who they would be hearing from today. That is, if Bordelli ever stopped talking.

Finally, after close to two hours, as the client paused to pour himself some water, a gravelly voice came from the audio system.

"Ya looking for a medal?"

Bordelli's eyes widened, like those of a kid who had unwrapped a new train set on Christmas Day. "Is that—"

"I asked if you're looking for a medal?" the voice repeated. "For your tough situation."

Bordelli still stared into the monitor, but his smile was gone. Alina and her fellow engineers had observed that each of these AI "experts" came with a certain edge. "It's impossible to dial down," Naveen Gupta had said during the last post-session debrief. "Not without pulling out CHERL's personality engine." Still, today's client seemed rattled by the AI's harsh tone.

"No...ah," Bordelli tried. "I was simply trying to give my point of view so—"

"I had your point of view over an hour ago. I can already see the missteps you've made with this company."

"Missteps?" Bordelli said.

"I see you playing defense. Trying to protect legacy businesses while the competition is reinventing your industry."

Bordelli stood and walked to his office window. The miniature cameras embedded in the top of the device Sway had provided him with swiveled to keep him on screen. According to Gupta, CHERL's visualization engine was interpreting the client's facial expressions and body language.

"That legacy business spins off a lot of cash for our shareholders," Bordelli said as he stared out the window. "Dividends that they count on."

"The hell with the dividends," the CHERL system responded, its volume rising. "Why are you still paying dividends? That's valuable cash that you should be reinvesting—"

"We are reinvesting!" Bordelli said, turning back to the computer. "Plenty. But our dividend is sacred."

"That's a load of crap. Not when your company is shrinking. You should be using capital to buy some of those upstart companies you're worried about. Ignite your innovation engine!"

"We've made plenty of acquisitions," Bordelli said.

"Yeah? Well, you bought the wrong ones. I've seen the numbers. You should be going after Hydra P&C. They're a perfect fit. It's plain as day!"

Alina did a quick search on Hydra while CHERL's Jack Welch continued lacing into Westfield's CEO. Welch's recommended acquisition was a public insurer based in Switzerland.

"Fire those business development people," the voice continued. "They keep bringing you the wrong deals. I looked at their backgrounds. You need heavier hitters in those roles. Go out and pay up to get some real talent."

Bordelli stuck his chin out. "Carol and Thomas have run through walls for me."

"Do you want loyalty or results?"

```
GUPTA:
I hope you're all having fun.
```

She was continually surprised by the project leader's playfulness, but neither Alina nor the other engineers responded to his message. She kept her attention on the oversize screen and tried not to smirk while concentrating on her role to document common themes emerging from these sessions: Move faster! Stay aggressive! Be decisive!

Alina tried to imagine the reaction Russian oligarchs back home might have to this type of feedback. She pictured Bordelli's speakerphone smashed into several inoperable pieces.

When Bordelli had finally been bludgeoned into submission, he returned to his desk and started to furiously write down notes. And after another hour in which "Jack Welch" dissected each Westfield division—and something he referred to as the "flat side" of the unit leaders that sat atop each—Bordelli made a motion with his hand.

"That's enough for today," he said, looking like a boxer who had just gone fifteen rounds.

———

ALINA STARTED to pack up as Gupta closed down the session with Bordelli. She had now listened in on more than twenty gripping hours of "conversations" between different business leaders recreated by CHERL and Sway's clients. Each recreated personality came across as cutthroat—sometimes gentlemanly but always very assertive. Every suggestion more like a directive as CHERL pushed the CEOs to make operational changes, restructure business units, strengthen balance sheets, and pursue mergers, acquisitions, and/or divestitures. Steve Jobs had even given a thirty-minute browbeating to Sway's client for its "inferior brand design."

As with the other sessions Alina had monitored, she'd personally loaded all the historical data that fed the CHERL AI. In the case of Westfield, that included information on the company's eight competitors in the property and casualty insurance industry. Alina's upload included more than twenty years of financial results, annual reports, regulatory filings, customer premiums, and claim behavior, each cleaned and formatted by her very own algorithms. She was proud that Enrico Alvarez trusted her to build code that interpreted executive presentations, along with weather patterns and projections on global warming, information which would help predict future insurance events for Westfield and their competitors.

With millions of pieces of information passing through Nicole Ryder's work stream, it had been simple for Alina to provide smooth passage for the alternative data provided by Romanoff. Yet, as with the previous four sessions, Alina had heard nothing from CHERL's Jack Welch to indicate that Romanoff's alternative facts had influenced CHERL's output. Actions were demanded in international markets throughout Asia and Europe, yet the Welch AI made no mention of Russia. While she worried that CHERL's extensive edit and security routines had washed away Romanoff's data, just as the body's immune system protects it from outside germs, Gagnon's encrypted communiqués always insisted everything was going according to plan.

After completing her notes on the Westfield session, Alina packed her laptop and made her way toward the TechShuttle pickup. As she stood in line, she heard her laptop ping. She boarded the shuttle and moved to a seat in the rear. When she opened her computer, she felt her spine tingle. She could not take her eyes off the text message, as if she needed to make sure the words were real.

> Your package will arrive in
> two days.

After all her efforts, Gagnon was finally delivering what she had been waiting for.

FORTY-EIGHT

WHEN LUCAS ENTERED the secure conference room on the second floor, the video feed was already live. The lawyer on the screen sat behind a metal table, wearing a white shirt and black tie, his black hair slicked back. At the lower right of the screen were the words *Southern District of Texas.*

"Agent Foley?" the lawyer asked.

"Mr. Sterling?" Lucas said as he removed his jacket and draped it across the table.

"Call me Skip."

Lucas lowered himself into a chair and opened his tablet. "Thanks for reaching out."

"For sure," Sterling said, shifting in his seat. "The higher-ups thought there's enough here to bring your unit under the tent."

Something about the way the lawyer emphasized the word *higher-ups* signaled that Sterling might not have agreed with the directive.

"Always appreciate help from Justice. What have you got?"

"Have you heard of a company called Aztec Industries?"

"Artificial intelligence company, right?" Lucas asked.

"That's right. Anyway, we're getting set to indict a guy named Buford Chambers. He's Aztec's CEO."

Lucas had never heard of Chambers, but at the mention of the CEO, he assumed they finally had another sugar daddy victim. The Justice Department attorney explained that Chambers had been a partner at a global accounting firm when Aztec hired him ten years earlier, and that this background had come in handy when the CEO started inflating revenues and misleading shareholders with fictitious client contracts.

"To investors and regulators," Sterling said, "it looked like Aztec was growing fast, and the share price skyrocketed. But when the short sellers started sniffing around, they found evidence that Chambers was manipulating results." Sterling explained that Buford and his CFO were about to be charged with four counts of embezzlement. "Staring at twenty years in prison tends to make people want to cooperate. Chambers has been divulging all his business and personal shenanigans, including his habit of feeding his 'sweet tooth' with company funds."

"Sugar daddy?" Lucas asked.

"Yep. He's been riding the circuit for the past five years," Sterling said. "And in one of his many encounters, Chambers claims he was drugged unconscious by one of his dates."

Lucas leaned forward. "You don't believe him?"

"I'm still questioning everything he's telling us."

"Why would he lie about that?"

"Oh, I don't know." Sterling smirked. "He's a liar, for one. Looking for negotiating ammo to plead for a lesser sentence. Maybe he caught wind that your hacker was in circulation and he's trying to cover up some other BS he was planning."

Lucas couldn't see how a corporate CEO would have learned about a hacker trolling for victims on sugar daddy websites. As Gilroy had instructed, the hacker's MO of drugging her victims with GHB had been kept out of the media.

"But there's just so far we're willing to negotiate with this guy," Sterling continued. "Especially with my boss having his suit pressed for a splashy news conference." His jaw jutted forward. "I've been told to pass on what I know. But before you boys get too excited, nobody sees any room at the podium for you guys."

Lucas had been stiff-armed by other parts of the bureau, especially by the agents working financial crimes, but he was surprised to hear this attitude from the US Attorney's Office. Despite the cyber unit's poor arrest record, ransomware had garnered a lot of media attention over the past few years, while the press had grown bored of the never-ending stories detailing corporate malfeasance. If the sugar baby hacker was involved with Buford Chambers, it seemed Sterling wasn't going to let the FBI share his headlines.

"Funny," Lucas said, letting out a quick laugh. "I don't think you have anything to worry about. We're not close to making any arrests." He wished that weren't the case.

"Anyway," Sterling said. "We dug into his bank records, phone records, private internet searches. I'll give him credit. It doesn't appear Chambers ever messed around with women at work. But he did a lot of business travel over the past five years." He lifted his tablet and turned it to show Lucas at least a dozen female head shots. "He took pictures of everyone who passed through his harem. Seems like he had a sugar baby in every port."

Lucas squinted. "Can you email those to me?"

"None of these is your suspect," Sterling said, placing the tablet down. "At least not according to Chambers."

"Did he identify all those women?"

"Yep. He'll talk all day about each of his *relationships*. Says they usually lasted two or three months. Except *your* gal. As much as he wanted her, he claims he never got past the first evening. Dinner and back to his hotel. Then she was gone."

Lucas scribbled notes, then asked, "Was there a ransomware attack or hack at his company?"

Sterling slowly shook his head.

"No malware of any kind?" Lucas said.

"Aztec's IT team scrubbed through everything. There's nothing there."

Strange, Lucas thought. If she was the hacker, why would she drug him but leave Aztec completely unscathed? "Maybe it was a near miss," Lucas said, more to himself than to Sterling. "Where and when does Chambers say he met with her?"

Sterling checked his notes. "He said it was in Chicago at the Waldorf. His expense reports place him there on April eighth."

Lucas texted Fernandez to pull and review the Waldorf security footage from the date in question.

"He had an expensive dinner at an Italian place on Michigan Avenue," Sterling continued. "He ran up quite the bill, so apparently someone *was* with him. He says he took her back to his hotel room, had a drink. Next thing he knew, the sun was shining and he had missed his morning flight to LA."

"Does he remember the website he used to set up the date?"

Sterling checked his notes. "He liked to frequent SugarHigh.com. But we didn't find any record of Chambers having a date through the site that night."

"She never leaves a trail. Usually hacks in and scrubs her profile and dating activity." Lucas checked his notes. "Did she send Chambers any naked pictures of the two of them? Any threatening notes?"

"He didn't mention any," Sterling said. "Is that what she does?"

"Apparently. Did anyone contact Aztec? Threaten them in any way?"

"Nothing."

"And Aztec's systems were clean," Lucas said, closing his tablet, disappointed with yet another dead end.

"I didn't say that," Sterling said as he leaned back in his chair. After a few moments he started again. "We had a local forensics team trace Chambers's digital fingerprints."

Lucas knew the drill. They would have done a full examination of the corporate financial systems, including any money transactions initiated by Chambers.

"And?"

"There *was* a system Chambers accessed that night."

"On April eighth?"

Sterling nodded. "We didn't think anything of it. Chambers and his CFO monkeyed around with their financial systems all the time. But that night, it looks like Chambers accessed the company's personnel files."

"Personnel files?"

"Yeah," Sterling said. "Over a thousand employees were exposed. Current and former. But it was nothing. It's not like he downloaded or transferred any records. He was just snooping around for something."

"Or some*one*," Lucas said.

"What's that?"

"Did you record the time and date stamp?" Lucas asked.

"It was close to midnight on April eight." Sterling glanced down. "At eleven forty-two p.m., to be exact. He was in there for a good twenty minutes."

Lucas took in a slow breath. Sterling had been told to check the box by his superiors, and he had done that by reaching out to the bureau. But if the sugar baby had a reason for searching through Aztec's personnel records, Lucas would only know by organizing his own examination.

"Listen," Lucas started, "I understand your skepticism

here, but why would a CEO want to look through his own employee records at eleven forty-two at night?"

Sterling shrugged. "Digging for dirt? Something he could use to bring others into his orbit?" He admitted, however, that there was no evidence of anyone else's involvement in Chambers's embezzlement scheme, other than his CFO.

"Did Aztec alert their employees?" Lucas asked. "Have them watch out for fake activity using their names?"

Sterling shook his head. "As I said, no information was downloaded."

Lucas tapped his fingers on the table. "Listen, Skip. You may be right. Your case may have nothing to do with my hacker, but your bosses are going to look pretty foolish at their press conference if we don't follow up on a simple lead."

The mention of the upcoming media event and the word *foolish* seemed to get the attorney's attention. "Exactly what do you think I *missed*?"

"It may be nothing. And I know you said no data was downloaded or copied. But what if she found a different way to use those names? A new type of monetization scheme?" Lucas paused before adding a further embellishment to stoke Sterling's anxiety. "What if Chambers helped her and something significant is revealed after you guys negotiate a plea deal?" He shook his head and exaggerated a grimace. "That wouldn't look good."

Sterling looked away.

"But listen, I may be able to help," Lucas said. "Can you have Aztec pull a copy of their personnel file from their archives—the way the data looked on April eighth?"

"I can probably get that done. What do you have in mind?"

"Something low-tech for sure," Lucas promised. "But we'll need to reach out to Aztec's employees for help."

CHAPTER
FORTY-NINE

A LARGE TOSSED salad was waiting on the dining room table next to two unlit candlesticks and an open bottle of pinot noir. Alina drew in a deep breath, savoring the aroma of fresh garlic wafting in from the kitchen where Dan was preparing her favorite, pesto shrimp. One of the many fringe benefits of moving in together early last summer—Barry was a fantastic cook. She poured herself a glass of wine and said, "It smells delicious."

Barry smiled as he sautéed the shrimp. "You're so easy to please."

Alina sipped the wine and came up behind him. She leaned over and planted a soft kiss on his cheek. "Not *so* easy," she whispered. He let out a quick laugh and continued to stir. Beyond preparing delicious meals, Barry provided her something else she hadn't expected. Something she had been missing those first months in America. A sense of comfort. A sense of normalcy.

During the work week they took the TechShuttle together. At night, after devouring Barry's latest culinary delight, they would drive down to Santa Cruz and walk along the wharf, watch the sea lions, and grab some dessert at Penny Ice Creamery. On weekends they took day trips down to Monterey or the beaches of Carmel by the Sea. Barry guided her on his favorite hiking trails on the Big Sur and took her on scrumptious food tours along Fisherman's Wharf, where his friends from Sway would join them. All except Agnes Nowak. Barry said he had been surprised by her sudden and unexpected departure last spring. But Alina tried not to think about the role Gagnon had played in Nowak's "resignation."

As Barry plated the shrimp over wild rice, Alina filled their glasses with more wine. When he joined her at the kitchen table, she stroked his cheek and kissed his lips.

"What's that for?" he asked.

Alina waved both hands over the table. "For keeping me watered and fed."

Barry laughed as he lifted a shrimp with his fingers and placed it in Alina's mouth. "Want to take a ride to Sausalito tomorrow? It's the last day of the art fair."

Alina wiped her mouth, and the lightness she had felt these past few moments quickly faded. "Sorry. I thought I told you. I need to work tomorrow."

Barry sat back and raised his palms. "Come on, Nicole. It's Sunday. Can't it wait?"

She shook her head. "Brodsky has a big session with a manufacturer this week." She moved the rice around on her plate and added, "Why don't you take Andy and Bobby?"

He shrugged. "Yeah. Maybe."

They finished their meal in silence. Barry hated when she worked on the weekends, and she felt bad disappointing him, especially tonight. For this would be the last lie she would ever tell him as Nicole Ryder.

The life she had built with him was coming to an end.

It was true she was going to Sway's server farm to load data detailing Lee Iacocca's rise as an automobile executive. But also true was that Gagnon had finally delivered Fedorov's hacking tool kit, along with a very specific direction from Romanoff:

Your mission at Sway is now complete. System contains ample data for our needs. Time to execute AI scout before extraction.

Alina was ready. Over the past nine months working on Alvarez's team, she had learned the intricacies of the vast server farm known as the Tower. She had meticulously prepared and blocked off a secured area in the test partition where she could launch her AI scout. Launch it on a mission of discovery across the US for anyone—dead or alive—matching the profile of a Russian spy who had disappeared twenty-five years ago.

Gagnon had planned her extraction to commence Sunday afternoon. Once she had the AI scout results in hand, Alina would take a taxi to the San Jose train station, where she would board the evening express to Sacramento. After another taxi deposited her at the airport, she would fly to Denver, where Gagnon would meet her at the Hyatt Place hotel. From there, he would move Alina to a temporary location, where she would study the output from her AI scout and plan her next move. Alina felt a sudden shiver as several realizations settled in. It might be only a matter of hours before she knew the fate of her mother. And as she watched Barry soak up pesto with a piece of bread, she knew these were their last moments together.

She pushed her plate away. They opened but didn't finish a second bottle of wine. They didn't clear the plates from the table. Instead, she moved him to the bedroom and ended the evening as they had many others since moving in together: in each other's arms, grabbing for each other like two hormonally charged teenagers. These were the moments when she tried to drop the facade of being Nicole Ryder, letting go of her act, releasing the tension she'd lived with every day since arriving in America. Savoring these moments, Alina had convinced herself that what she had with Barry *was* real. But how was that possible when Nicole Ryder wasn't? Still, being held tightly, being caressed, being cared for—in these moments with Barry, Alina almost forgot about Romanoff and sugar daddies and nearly cleared her mind of CHERL and AI scouts and the fear of being discovered. In these moments, Alina felt she was where she belonged.

After Barry fell asleep, Alina lay on her back and stared at the blades of the rotating ceiling fan. She took in a deep breath and enjoyed the calm that always washed over her after making love with Barry. Perhaps this explained the Russian government's rationale for sending her parents together as a couple all those years ago. Immersing yourself in a foreign country, impersonating someone you're not. The risk of being discovered, arrested, even tortured. The stress was extreme, but even more so when you were alone. Had she not been with Barry, she doubted she would have survived. Thanks to their time together, Alina had slowly come to believe—to accept—that her parents' relationship had not been solely a cover story. Alina's mother had to have cared for her father. Just as Alina—not Nicole Ryder, but Alina—had grown to care for Dan. Even if her parents hadn't known each other well when they started their mission, being together on the front lines had to have created a deep bond. They would have needed one another. Cared for one another. Which meant something else was possible.

Alina's birth was *not* merely a prop of the Russian intelligence service.

Maybe Alina *had* been conceived out of…love.

CHAPTER
FIFTY

LUCAS RAPPED TWICE on the door and entered the small, dimly lit FBI interview room where two junior agents, their ties askew, sat at a long metal table with their heads buried in computer screens.

"Anything?" Lucas asked.

The first agent, a young Black man named Darius Maddox, said, "We're almost done scouring through the popular dark web sites. We haven't found any Aztec employee names or personal information."

The second agent, George Lim, removed his headset and tortoiseshell glasses and added, "And just a lot of noise from the credit bureau reviews, for sure."

"Noise?" Lucas asked, lowering himself into a chair.

"Employees leaving messages on our hotline about credit card charges they don't remember or loans they didn't apply for."

It had been a few days since Agent Fernandez had asked the three major credit bureaus to send free credit reports to every current and former Aztec employee. Aztec had followed up with emails urging the employees to inspect their reports and call the special FBI hotline if they noticed unusual or suspicious activity.

Lin continued, "So far, I've spoken directly with

twenty-six employees, each swearing they found fake accounts on their reports. But most were opened by members of their own families. Spouses, brothers, teenagers. One woman I spoke with didn't even hang up before starting to yell at her son."

Lucas smirked and said, "Guess it wasn't his first time in trouble."

"I have a few more messages to listen to," Lin said. "But so far, nothing of significance."

Lucas tapped his fingers on the metal table. "Okay, let me know when you've finished. Where's Fernandez?" he asked.

"She's down the hall," Maddox answered. "She wanted a quiet space to review the Waldorf surveillance footage."

Lucas walked down the corridor lined with empty interview rooms until he found Fernandez in the last room with her back to the door, staring intently at her laptop. "How are you making out?" he asked, but Fernandez didn't look up. Lucas approached and spotted the wireless earbuds in her ears. He tapped her on the shoulder, startling the junior agent.

"Oh, Agent Foley," she said. "I didn't hear you."

"My fault. I was just checking in."

Fernandez pulled an empty chair over for Lucas to sit. "This is the Waldorf's surveillance video from the night of Buford Chambers's date." She paused and ran a small portion of the footage in slow motion. "I don't think we need the facial recognition software this time," she said. "It's definitely her. The same woman that hit McKinsey."

Lucas peered at Fernandez's laptop as the color video played in slow motion. It was clear from the very first frame that Fernandez was correct. While the sugar baby had chosen a green scarf and jet-black wavy wig as a disguise, she made no other attempt to hide her distinctive beauty. Even if she had, there was no mistaking those alluring green eyes.

"Should I play the close-up again?" Fernandez asked.

"Let it run through to the end first," Lucas said. "And I want to see all the angles."

Over the next hour, Fernandez brought up footage from each of the seven surveillance cameras positioned around the Waldorf's lobby and entranceway. Lucas had her play each portion in slow motion so he could take in every movement. The last of the seven cameras showed their suspect exiting the elevator by herself and quickly moving past the unstaffed concierge desk. But as she approached the hotel's exit, an older gray-haired man came into view. He was wearing a suit and a very visible Waldorf badge.

"Pull back the shot," Lucas said. "I want to take a closer look at his face."

Fernandez moved the video around the older man's features. "What are we looking at?" she asked.

"Don't you see it?" Lucas stared back at the screen. "Look at his wide eyes, locked with hers. His expression—open mouth, slack jaw."

Fernandez shrugged. "Old guy ogling pretty girl?"

Lucas shook his head. "He's not ogling, Agent Fernandez. He looks like he's seen a ghost!"

"I'll get over to the Waldorf and see if I can speak with him," Fernandez said. "Hopefully he still works there."

The door to the conference room flew open, and a breathless Agent Lin stuck his head in.

"Agent Foley. I'm glad you're still here. I have an employee voicemail message you should listen to."

CHAPTER
FIFTY-ONE

IT WAS seven fifteen on Sunday morning, and the parking lot at Sway headquarters was deserted. The taxi dropped Alina at the side entrance, where she swiped her ID. She walked down the hallway and took the elevator to the empty Tower Operations center. She sat in front of one of the five workstations arrayed along the glass wall and signed in to the CHERL system, as she had every day since being assigned to the Tower Operations team almost a year earlier. Alina viewed the vast information prepared for the Iacocca sessions. A 352-page autobiography, a 192-page book on leadership, and a catalog of more than three thousand newspaper and magazine articles. She thought the autobiography would be a good place to spend her time this morning. She would use Sway's standard ETL process—Extract, Transform, and Load—the same process she had followed countless times, supplemented, of course, with Romanoff's hidden files. Today's work on Iacocca would be no different.

Alina had delivered her end of the bargain, and finally Romanoff delivered his. It was time to move on. But not before she had her chance to unveil the true fate of her mother. That notion sent Alina's heart galloping.

As the autobiography digitization process

commenced, Alina opened her laptop. She navigated to the protected folder that contained Fedorov's package, and then she used her Sway security credentials to sign on to the Tower's test partition.

She uploaded the final version of her AI scout, fully trained by the vast archive of documents about her mother. The scout knew all there was to know about her mother's education, upbringing, career, family lineage. Everything ever documented about her mother's various missions in America. Each piece of intelligence her mother had ever gathered for Russia. Alina's AI scout knew it all.

Minutes later, she uploaded the contents of the second folder, this one containing Fedorov's hacking software. His encrypted messages had assured her that the massive Tower Ops processors held more than enough firepower to launch the AI scout across the hundreds of government agencies Alina had identified. Census records, employment records, marriage licenses, birth and death certificates, prison records, motor vehicle registrations, taxing authorities—Fedorov's hacking software would provide the AI scout safe passage to those files and more, across each and every state in the nation. Across every federal system. Fedorov's hacking tool would open the doors, allowing Alina's scout to search through millions of names and analyze every profile until it discovered the secret identity of the mother who had disappeared more than a quarter century ago. If these files contained answers, her AI scout would find them. Every possible candidate, alive or dead, would be returned and consolidated in a single file. She would give her program exactly one hour to perform its task. Any longer and Sway's cybersecurity detection systems were sure to kick in.

The AI scout was ready. Fedorov's hacking program had its targets. Alina knew she would only get this one chance.

She initiated the search.

"This is a surprise."

Alina closed the laptop and spun around. Standing in the doorway was CHERL's project director.

"Oh, I didn't hear you come in," Alina said, her heart pounding.

"Sorry," Josh Brodsky said, pushing his hair to the side. "I didn't mean to startle you." He checked his watch then asked, "What's so important this early on a Sunday?"

"Um…I promised Alvarez I'd finish Iacocca."

"Hmm," Dr. Brodsky said. He stared at the workstation screen in front of Alina. "I didn't think we were doing Iacocca for a few more weeks."

Alina shrugged as sweat started running down her spine. "I like to stay ahead of schedule."

Dr. Brodsky nodded. "I like it."

Alina cleared her throat and said, "I don't think I've ever seen you in here, Dr. Brodsky."

The executive director put his hands in his pockets and looked around at the glass walls separating the data room from the flashing colored lights of the server farm. "I love it in here," he said. "The quiet hum of hundreds of servers working in concert. If you didn't know, you would never realize what's happening behind that glass." He looked at her, but his eyes seemed foggy as he continued. "So much power and intelligence. Millions of problems and calculations being solved simultaneously. But all anyone can hear is that hum. Sometimes I just come in here to marvel at the enormity of it all."

"It's quite remarkable." Alina glanced at the workstation screen filling with Iacocca's autobiography in digital form.

Brodsky removed his hands from his pocket as his eyes became clear. "Listen, as long as you're here, why don't you join us in the control room next door? Naveen is walking me through the first set of diagnostic results."

"Diagnostics?"

"From the first year of CHERL installations. Naveen's analyzed client performance for the six-month period after engaging with CHERL. This is our first chance to see we've made an impact."

Alina motioned to her workstation. "I really should stay and fin—"

"Don't be ridiculous," Dr. Brodsky waved his hand. "Iacocca can wait. This will only take an hour and will be a great learning experience." He turned and held the door for her.

Alina nodded. "Let me just finish up, Dr. Brodsky. I'll be right there." As soon as Brodsky left the Tower Ops room, Alina spun back to the desk and opened the laptop. She wanted to abort her search, try again the following weekend. But the AI scout and hacking tools were already executing. If Sway's cybersecurity routines activated, the clock might already be ticking. The test partition might get locked down before she had another opportunity. She couldn't take the chance of aborting now. Dr. Brodsky had said the diagnostic review would last only an hour. That was all the time the AI scout needed.

She grabbed her phone and walked through the door to the control room.

CHAPTER
FIFTY-TWO

"PUT IT ON SPEAKER," Lucas instructed.

Lin pressed an icon on his phone and held it up. Lucas heard the voice of a young woman who spoke so fast, in a rapid, staccato fashion, that Lucas asked Lin to stop and restart it twice so he could adjust to the cadence. On the third try, they let the recording play through to the end:

"Hello, FBI. The human resources department at Aztec told us to call you if we noticed anything unusual on our credit reports. I used to review my credit score all the time. You wouldn't believe how many mistakes they make. But everything's been crazy in our lives since I had the baby. Now that things have calmed down, my husband and I plan to apply for a mortgage. We haven't applied for new credit in a long time. So when I saw that personnel background check on my credit report, I was upset. I know employers will pull credit bureaus, but I haven't applied for a job since I resigned from Aztec over a year ago. And I know for sure I never applied to Sway. I'm worried the inquiry will hurt my credit score, so I called the background check company and told them it must be a mix-up. But they said no, it was a legitimate request. The credit bureau help line said I shouldn't worry about it because background checks don't impact credit scores, but I'm telling you, that wasn't me. Maybe you can call the bureau. They wouldn't listen to me."

There was a pause on the recording before the woman continued:

"Oh, and one more thing. I'm not sure if it has anything to do with your investigation, but I recently checked LinkedIn and didn't find my profile. I think it was deleted. My name is pretty common, but you can see for yourself. None of the Nicole Ryders listed on LinkedIn ever worked for Aztec."

CHAPTER
FIFTY-THREE

ALINA'S HEART was still pounding as she stepped through the doorway connecting Tower Ops to CHERL's control room. She leaned on the wall and saw Brodsky standing in front of the twenty-foot-wide video display. She examined the screen but could not make sense of the multitude of graphs and numbers. A door opened at the far side of the room and Naveen Gupta entered, three of his team leaders in tow—Townsend, Fraser, and Khan. As they joined Brodsky and surveyed the flashing statistics, Alina felt a tap on her shoulder.

"Dr. Brodsky told me you were here," Enrico Alvarez said when she turned, his eyes squinting. "I don't remember pushing for Iacocca to be loaded this early."

Alina felt her mouth go dry. "I—"

Alvarez placed his hand on her shoulder. "At least someone is on top of things." He told her to take a seat anywhere. "This should be enlightening," he promised, before joining Brodsky and the others.

Alina took a deep breath and slid into the back row. She checked the time—the AI scout had already been running for fifteen minutes.

She saw Gupta wave his hand and a motion activated sensor transformed the giant screen into sixteen block-shaped segments. Each block displayed month by month trend lines labeled REVENUE, GROSS PROFITS, and MARKET SHARE, along with a paragraph or two of commentary in a font too small for Alina to read from her position at the back. Still, she recognized the client names at the top of each block, and at the bottom, the identity of each historical leader she'd helped bring to life. As she scanned the metrics, she couldn't help feeling an inkling of pride at what she had been a part of—almost all the colors were flashing green, virtually every trend line moving up within months after the CHERL implementation. Only two of the charts flashed red. The first, for a semiconductor company called AMVIA, continued to lose money even after an audience with Thomas Edison. And the market share of the second, an entertainment streaming company advised by CHERL's Walt Disney, portrayed a steep downward slide. Still, Alina could tell from the murmuring coming from the front that Gupta and his project managers were pleased. The men moved closer to the screen. All except Brodsky, his head moving side to side as he digested the information.

Alina read some of the commentaries, looking for signs of any impact Romanoff's data feed might have had. The first three blocks contained paragraphs on company successes—acquisitions, business unit improvements, and product launches. She was reading through the fourth block when Gupta and the project managers reassembled in front of Brodsky. She overheard Townsend remark, "Pretty damn good!" as Alvarez patted Khan on the back. She stopped reading and listened.

"Naveen," Brodsky said, "have we verified all these calculations?"

"Yes, boss. But we'll double-check everything again."

"Come on, Josh," Townsend said, placing his hand on Gupta's shoulder. "Naveen's numbers always check out."

Brodsky pointed to the screen. "Any more commentary than what you're showing?"

"Absolutely, boss. We can drill down to the next layer."

Brodsky crossed his arms. "Bring the details of each client up one at a time."

Maybe now Alina would see what Romanoff's data had done for her country.

Gupta waved at the motion sensor, and the information block for BrightStar Energy enlarged to consume the entire wall. BrightStar's CEO had been advised by John D. Rockefeller. The commentary was mostly about BrightStar's accelerated pursuit of renewable energy sources, including a new investment in offshore wind farms. With another wave of his hand, Gupta changed the screen to display the results of a financial firm that had been advised by CHERL's J. P. Morgan. A lengthy paragraph described the rationale behind its decision to exit the slowing business in Europe. Next, a retailer advised by Sam Walton was pursuing the acquisition of a Midwest competitor. As there was still no mention of anything to do with her homeland, Alina's thoughts returned to the AI scout running next door. She checked her watch again.

Twenty-five minutes left.

"What the hell is that?" she heard Brodsky say.

He walked closer to the giant screen. When Alina read the commentary for InPharma at the bottom of the chart, her mouth went dry.

New joint venture created with Polynef Industries, a Moscow-based conglomerate.

Alina heard Brodsky say, "Moscow?"

"What's wrong?" Gupta asked.

Brodsky said, "Moscow companies are still on the sanctions list."

"There are still some Americans operating over there," Khan said.

"Maybe it's for humanitarian assistance," Townsend offered.

Or maybe this was Romanoff's doing, Alina thought. Maybe this was *her* doing.

Brodsky turned to Gupta, his eyes squinting as he seemed to process the possibilities. "Have government affairs check that out," he instructed.

"Will do, boss," Gupta said. "Should we keep moving?"

Brodsky nodded, and Gupta waved his hand to advance the screen. While she didn't understand many of the details, Alina carefully read each line, searching for any other signs of her mission's success. When Brodsky held his hand up during the review of the chart for Orbit-world, a space tourism company that had been advised by the astronaut Frank Borman, Alina felt her neck muscles tighten.

New joint venture created with Polynef Industries, a Moscow-based conglomerate.

"Holy shit," Alvarez said.

Gupta walked up to the screen and said, "A coincidence?"

Brodsky looked at his project leader. "Coincidence? Two different clients entering joint ventures with the same Russian company?" He pointed at the monitor and said, "What happens if you drill down on that comment?"

Naveen clicked on the Polynef sentence and the screen filled:

Polynef Industries was formed two years ago by two Russian oligarchs, Ilya Romanoff and Mikail Volkov, former members of the Soviet-era KGB, who merged their family interests in oil and gas.

Alina struggled to breathe as her mind flashed back to her first meeting with Romanoff under the fish store.

"Do you have family?" Alina had asked him.

"Yes. A brother, Ilya," Romanoff had replied. *"We worked together in the old KGB. He's now a businessman, of all things."*

Was *this* what her entire mission had been about? Romanoff lining his own family's pockets? Gagnon had said Romanoff wanted to manipulate the CHERL system to "disarm it from shaping American policies that would harm Russia." But was this moneymaking scheme Romanoff's plan all along?

Brodsky stared at the screen and read the second paragraph out loud. "'Profits will be shared—sixty percent for Polynef, forty percent for Orbitworld. Orbitworld will transfer all intellectual property needed to operate the joint venture.'" He turned to face the project managers. "Transferring aerospace IP?" he said. "To the Russians?"

"How could CHERL let this happen?" Alvarez asked.

Brodsky faced Alvarez. "*Let* this happen? What if CHERL *made* it happen?"

The room was silent as Alina eyed the door behind her. Fifteen more minutes until the AI scout finished. She had to get back to Tower Ops in time to retrieve her laptop with the results before her chance to escape evaporated.

"Go back to the InPharma slide," Brodsky directed. "I want to see the details of its Polynef comment."

Gupta waved the charts back to InPharma and drilled into the Polynef comment, finding the same commitment to transfer IP to Russia.

Gupta said, "I'll have the system perform a diagnostic comparing results across all our clients. Let's see if there are others involved with Polynef."

"And run a search on news feeds about Polynef," Brodsky said. "See what it turns up."

Gupta went to one of the computers, and his fingers

raced across the keyboard. Within seconds, the results appeared:

Commonalities in Client Results

At the very top was the same comment about Polynef, listing only InPharma and Orbitworld. But when Gupta scrolled down, the words Alina read sent a jolt down her spine.

"US officials investigating Russian hacking ring that reaped over $300 million trading on insider information. Hackers bought stock in certain publicly traded companies just days before public announcements of significant transactions—transactions that drove these specific company stock prices higher by 30-40 percent."

Below the commentary were the names of the American companies that had made the announcements referred to in the commentary. Alina recognized all six of the companies listed.

All were clients of Sway.

Each of their CEOs had been advised by the CHERL system.

CHAPTER
FIFTY-FOUR

"WE'VE GOT HER!" Lucas shouted over the sound of heavy rain pelting his driverless sedan. But there was silence on the other end of the line. "Are you there, Dennison?" Lucas asked. "I said—"

"Slow down, Agent Foley," Dennison said. "You have her where?"

"No. I mean, I know where she is," Lucas replied quickly, the adrenaline surge still rushing through his veins. "She's out there in San Francisco."

"What? How do you know?"

"She's masquerading as an AI programmer named Nicole Ryder, using credentials she stole during a date with Aztec's CEO. Something bigger must be going on. She's infiltrated the Sway corporation. She's—"

"What makes you think she's inside Sway?"

Lucas was overexcited. After almost a year, he finally had his break. "Sorry," he said. "A lot came together in the last few days." He backed up and slowly revealed what he'd learned from Sterling at Justice about Buford Chambers, the Aztec employees' credit report reviews, and the phone message from the real Nicole Ryder.

"That explains why she went dark," Lucas continued. "Whatever was on the ransomware she planted through

Donny Brodsky somehow introduced her to the inner workings at Sway. She learned something from that failed attack, something that led her to position herself inside the company. Remember what that Horizons instructor, Logan Greig, told me?" he asked. "He said his student, Ana Dafoe, had extensive training in artificial intelligence. Gilroy had said the sugar baby hacking was just the warm-up act. Infiltrating a company like Sway—using her AI skills inside—who knows what her endgame is!"

"And if Burick was right," Dennison said, "and the malware was built by the Russians…" He paused before asking, "Have you called Gilroy?"

"Not yet." Lucas knew that as soon as he alerted Gilroy, her counterintelligence team would take control and Lucas's role in breaking the case would be relegated to a footnote. He might view an arrest photo of Nicole Ryder's impersonator in the bureau's case management system. And if the sugar baby was a foreign spy apprehended by Gilroy's team, Lucas would never come face to face with the woman he had obsessed over the past ten months.

"I thought you and I should call Gilroy together," Lucas said, hoping the attention-grabbing Dennison would go along. "In the morning. Once we have our perp in custody."

Dennison was quiet again for a few moments. Finally he said, "I'll call over to my Sway contacts and let them know our suspicion. We'll pick her up as soon as she shows up at Sway's headquarters in the morning."

"Listen," Lucas said, "I don't think we should arrest her at Sway's offices. If other spies are involved, a perp walk in front of thousands of employees would send up the kind of warning flairs Gilroy was worried about. Once Sway confirms Nicole Ryder is employed there, get her home address. I'll fly out tonight. We can pick her up at the crack of dawn."

Dennison cleared his throat and said, "Don't trouble

yourself with a late-night flight, Agent Foley. My team can handle it."

Lucas knew Dennison would envision himself the hero, extolling the brilliance of his Silicon Valley agents who broke up a major foreign hacking ring.

That was not how this would end.

"It's no trouble, Agent Dennison. I'll meet you at your office at five a.m."

CHAPTER
FIFTY-FIVE

ALINA URGED herself to move through the door
leading back to Tower Ops, but her body felt leaden and
the walls seemed to spin around her. Brodsky was talking
into his cell phone, but whatever he said sounded garbled.
When he finished, he pointed at Gupta, and said, "You
need to take your lieutenants and scrub through every
piece of data. Every line of code."

Gupta said, "Let's not overreact, boss. There may be a
logical explanation."

But Alina already knew there was no logical explanation. After all of Romanoff's bluster about protecting
Mother Russia, her mission hadn't been about the "balance of power." Her mission had been all about lining
Romanoff's pockets. Greed. That's all it ever was.

She had been Romanoff's pawn from the beginning.

"Yeah," Khan said. "Maybe InPharma and Orbitworld decided to work with Polynef before engaging with
CHERL."

Brodsky stared at the screen. "I don't believe in coincidences, gentlemen. Our country has had nothing to do
with Russia for years. Now we have two clients forking over
intellectual property to former KGB agents at Polynef."

He pointed at the screen. "And six other CHERL clients involved in business transactions that the Russian stock traders knew about before any public announcement."

"Maybe the Russians planted a mole inside of Sway," Khan said. "Someone communicating information from client interactions with CHERL."

Alina's heart pounded in her chest.

Gupta started tapping his phone. "I'll call internal security."

"What we have here is far worse than a mole passing information," Brodsky said.

The project leaders stared at Brodsky. "I think CHERL *directed* InPharma and Orbitworld to form joint ventures with that Russian company, Polynef. CHERL's recreated business leaders urged clients to enter those other business deals. Deals the Russians knew about ahead of everyone."

Alina thought of all the data files Gagnon had her include with her massive information loads. Data that somehow manipulated CHERL to recommend business deals that would allow Romanoff to make millions! How soon before Sway discovered she was the source? She glanced at the door leading to Tower Ops. Her laptop was behind that door where she'd left it, about to receive the AI scout's results. She had to get in there before CHERL's leadership team discovered what she was doing—and what she had done. Yet her body remained frozen with fear.

"Insider trading leaks could have come from anywhere," Townsend said weakly.

"He's right," Khan tried. "Happens all the time on Wall Street. And if CHERL pushed joint ventures with the Russians, it's possible our AI was just getting ahead of the rest of America. Maybe we've done such a good job scrubbing out political biases that CHERL identified real opportunities."

Alvarez interjected, "Or maybe we accidentally built biases *into* the system."

Brodsky glared at Alvarez. "That doesn't explain insider trading. And I can't go to our board with conjecture. We need to do our homework."

"We will, boss," Gupta said.

Alina finally managed to inch her way toward the Tower Ops door.

"Review every line of code," Brodsky continued. "Every piece of data loaded over the past year. Some of these sessions occurred months ago, so go back to the beginning." He turned to Gupta and added, "If I wanted to change CHERL's outcomes, I would alter the training data. I'm betting hackers somehow corrupted the information."

Brodsky had already deciphered how his system had been attacked. It wouldn't be long before Alina's work would be discovered. She had her ID in hand, ready to unlock the Tower Ops door.

Gupta said, "I'll get everything prepared, boss. But we need resources to scour through the code and data sets. Let us bring in at least a small group of trusted employees."

Brodsky shook his head. "Can't risk it. The five of you will be enough. Nobody else from the team is allowed in the facility." He pointed at Gupta. "Lock down the Tower and make sure you deactivate everyone's sign-in credentials. Send a message out to the team. Tell everyone to stay home until we call them."

Gupta's hands ran over the keyboard just as Alina swiped her ID and pushed the door. She heard a click.

But the door did not release.

Panic spread through her like waves as Brodsky turned to Alvarez. "Do we employ any Russian immigrants?"

Alvarez shook his head. "I do have several eastern Europeans. A few from Ukraine and Romania."

"It doesn't have to be the Russians," Gupta said. "Anyone could have been paid off."

Alina had to escape before she and her laptop running the AI scout were discovered. She could tell Brodsky she needed time inside Tower Ops to shut down the Iacocca load before they locked everyone out. But Brodsky had already zeroed in on corrupt data as the most likely tool used to manipulate CHERL. Alina wasn't about to draw attention to her work in Tower Ops, where all the data loads occurred. She had no choice. She had to get away while she still had the chance. But the only other exit was where Brodsky and the others stood. She needed to create a distraction. And draw them away from Tower Ops.

"You know," Alina called out, "you might want look at Agnes Nowak."

All eyes turned and stared at Alina, their expressions startled, as if they'd forgotten her presence.

Khan said, "Agnes has been gone for months."

Alina cleared her throat. "I know. But Dr. Brodsky just said the data or the code could have been corrupted a while ago."

The project managers looked at Brodsky, who said, "I remember her."

"Me too," Gupta said.

"Agnes was from Poland," Khan said. "She worked for me. A very sharp engineer. She had been with the company for years. I assume the People Experience team cleared her."

Townsend pulled his phone out and started typing. "I'll see if I can find anything on her."

Brodsky's eyes stayed locked on Alina. "What makes you suspect her?"

Alina shrugged. "It was so odd when she just stopped coming to work."

"That *was* strange," Khan said. "Agnes was one of my most productive coders. After she didn't come in, I received a cryptic message saying she returned to Poland.

Something about a family emergency. But I never heard from her again."

"Dr. Brodsky, you said you don't believe in coincidences," Alina added, trying to stoke the embers. "I always thought she was hiding something."

Brodsky looked at Gupta and said, "Have your team scrub through Nowak's code." He looked back at Alina and said, "And Nicole, we'll need you to leave. We're shutting down the facility until we finish our investigation."

"I understand," she said, slowly descending the side steps as everyone moved toward the exit.

Suddenly, Townsend shouted out, "You're not going to believe this!" He held up his phone as everyone stopped in place. "I did a quick search on Agnes Nowak and found an English language article from Euronews Poland, published last year. Right around the time Nowak left the company, someone by the name of Agnes Nowak was found in an alleyway in Warsaw." He paused and looked around the room. "She had a bullet in the back of her head."

CHAPTER
FIFTY-SIX

ALINA EXITED the control room with the others and tried to calm her nerves as she rode the elevator up seven floors. She hurried through Sway's deserted lobby, but her legs were unsteady. How much time before Brodsky and his team discovered who had been loading corrupted data into CHERL? Data that had caused their AI to provide directives lining the pockets of Romanoff and his brother?

How long before they discovered Alina was using the Tower's test partition to hack into systems across America?

She made her way down the perimeter road surrounding the complex, bringing her onto the main thoroughfare. She walked away from the bucolic campus until her legs would take her no farther. She ducked into the restroom of a tire repair shop, locked the door and leaned against the wall, trying to slow her pulse. Her hands shook uncontrollably.

Where would she go now?

Think! Alina steadied her hands and checked her phone. Gagnon had broken security protocols by texting her:

> Why r u not responding? Why
> not on train?

Alina tried to keep her reply cryptic:

> They know about impact.
> reviewing code + data.

Gagnon finally responded after a long pause:

> Proceed to train.

She nervously tapped her foot against the bathroom floor. How could she trust Gagnon? Everything Romanoff had said about her mission inside Sway was a lie. And Agnes Nowak was dead! Killed in a Warsaw alleyway. Thinking back to that night at the Island Taste restaurant, Alina remembered being frantic about Nowak's threatening comments. She'd told Gagnon of the Polish woman's suspicions. Alina wasn't naïve. She had understood that Nowak had been coerced to leave America. Even threatened. But killed?

Which meant Alina was responsible for her death.

And now that Romanoff had earned his millions, was Alina about to be eliminated too? Was that why Gagnon wanted her on that train? She was so nervous her teeth were chattering.

Maybe she would still find her way to Denver. But not tonight.

Tonight, she needed to clear her head. She assumed her diversion about Nowak meant Brodsky's team would spend the night reviewing the Polish woman's code. They might not move on to examine Alina's work until the morning, which meant she had a few hours to figure out her next move. Her heart rate slowed as she texted Gagnon:

> Tomorrow.

Tonight she would return to the only person who had provided her a safe space over this past year.

———

ROMANOFF DOWNED another scotch as he studied the message displayed on his encrypted communication device:

> GAGNON:
> Breach discovered. Extraction
> negative.

He read it again and again, as if the words would suddenly morph into the message he had been expecting, the message confirming Alina Petrova was on her way to rendezvous with Gagnon's extraction team. Romanoff finally typed back, requesting details. How had their operation inside of Sway been revealed?

> GAGNON:
> No specifics. Subject dark.

> ROMANOFF:
> Find her!

> GAGNON:
> Tracking in progress.

There was still a chance Gagnon could find Alina before the Americans did. Alina did not know of the tracking device Gagnon had placed inside her phone.

Gagnon had been monitoring her every move since she'd arrived in America.

> ROMANOFF:
> Once secured, proceed as
> planned.

Romanoff then returned to his own exit preparations.

CHAPTER
FIFTY-SEVEN

LUCAS SAT in the passenger seat of a gray unmarked sedan as Agent Dennison drove into the back alley of the Sunnyside Terrace complex. An SUV pulled out of the passageway in the opposite direction as Lucas focused his attention on the apartment building bordering the alley. There were no fire escapes, no place for Nicole Ryder's impersonator to go if she tried to climb out the back window of the condo she shared with Dan Barry. Four stories was simply too high for anyone to jump.

Lucas hadn't slept on the late-night flight to San Francisco. In fact, he hadn't slept in over twenty-four hours. He'd arrived at the bureau's office on 7th Street in San Francisco around five a.m., where Dennison had debriefed him about what he'd learned from Dr. Brodsky at Sway the previous evening, about the deception perpetrated deep inside the company's artificial intelligence system. Dennison had shared the FBI's suspicions about Nicole Ryder with Brodsky, and the company had then provided Dennison with the impostor's most recent address. She had moved in with another Sway employee several months ago.

Despite Lucas's fatigue, the adrenaline rush of being this close to his prey charged him into a heightened state of alertness. Dennison parked, and Lucas left his cane in the back seat as he and Dennison got out. They approached Dennison's backup agents in the car behind them.

"You two stay here and cover the back," Dennison instructed. "Agent Foley and I will go in through the front."

Lucas checked his watch. It was six thirty-one a.m. Lucas asked everyone to take one last look at the photograph he had on his phone of the employee calling herself Nicole Ryder.

"Let's go," he said.

He and Dennison moved around to the front of the building and toward the door leading to the lobby. A man was coming out of the building to walk his Yorkie and held the door when they flashed their badges.

Lucas double-checked the chamber on his Glock as they rode the elevator to the fourth floor. They hung their FBI shields from their waistbands and approached apartment 4A, positioning themselves on opposite sides of the doorframe. Dennison pressed the doorbell.

After a few moments, Lucas heard shuffling from inside. "Get ready," he whispered as the footsteps approached the door.

When the door opened, Lucas held his arm up, holding Dennison back. A man with shaggy hair stood in the vestibule, holding an ice pack to his face, his expression confused. He removed the pack, revealing a swollen, discolored cheekbone, and said, "Did you assholes forget something?"

———

THIRTY MINUTES EARLIER, Alina had opened her eyes, bright sunshine glaring from behind the shades. The digital clock read six a.m. She rolled over and saw the indented pillow and rumpled sheet beside her. She leaned up on one arm and smelled the aroma of fresh coffee. But coffee would have to wait.

She didn't want to waste any more time.

She picked up yesterday's slacks and blouse from the floor, went into the bathroom, and started the shower, leaving the door open so Barry would hear. As the sound of water provided cover, Alina started rummaging through her dresser drawer, grabbing what remained of Garcia's money along with the fake IDs she had hidden away from her days as a sugar baby. She stuffed a few pieces of clothing into a satchel, enough to get her through the next twenty-four hours. She would buy what she needed whenever she arrived at her destination. Where that would be, she had no idea. She only knew that she had to get as far away from Sway and California as possible. The window for her escape would be closing very soon. It was only a matter of time before Sway discovered what Nicole Ryder had done. And until Gagnon proved he could be trusted—until he proved she would not end up like Agnes Nowak—Alina would be on her own.

She turned the shower off, got dressed, and padded into the kitchen. Dan Barry faced the stovetop, whipping a bowlful of egg whites.

"Hey," she said softly.

Dan turned. "Hey, yourself." He beamed as he held out the bowl. "Hungry?"

Alina shook her head. For the first time since she'd arrived in America, she wasn't the least bit hungry. The nausea that swilled in the pit of her stomach since she'd left the Sway complex had yet to subside.

"Come on," Barry insisted. "I'm making my egg white frittata." He nodded toward the refrigerator. "There's multigrain on the second shelf. Put in some toast."

Alina forced a smile, opened the refrigerator, and started the toast while Barry emptied the eggs into the frying pan.

"You need to relax, Nicole. They'll figure out what's going on. Naveen will probably want us back at our work-stations by noon, so let's enjoy our little break while it lasts. Grab some coffee. This will be ready in a few minutes."

"I forgot to brush my teeth," she said, feeling tears welling up in her eyes. "I'll be right back." But as she shuffled to the bathroom, her shoulders began to quake. She had thought about asking Barry to come with her, an impromptu vacation for as long as it lasted. But she couldn't bring herself to drag him into her charade any further. She had lied to him enough. She would not put his life at risk.

She'd started the water in the sink and wiped away the tears when she thought she heard a loud thump. She turned the water off.

"Dan?" she called out. But there was no answer. She inched to the bedroom door and slowly cracked it open. What she saw made her heart jolt.

Dan was being held facedown on the floor by a burly man in a dark suit.

An official-looking badge protruded from his belt.

Alina reached for the bedroom door, but before she could slam it shut, another large man barreled through and tackled her to the floor. Alina tried to kick herself free, to claw at the arms that were pinning her to the ground, but he was too strong. He easily pulled her wrists behind her back, and she felt the cold metal of handcuffs.

And as they clicked around her wrists, Alina knew it was over.

The man stood her up and silently led her past the other man, who was still holding Barry on the floor. She thought she heard him call the men fascist pigs, but it was hard to tell with his face planted in the carpet. She was led out of the apartment and into the hallway. They walked her down the four flights of steps and out the back toward a black SUV. One officer protected her head as he lowered her into the back seat of the car while the other got into the driver's seat.

At least they hadn't taken Barry.

"Where are you taking—" But her question was interrupted by the sharp needle plunged into the side of her neck. As she drifted off, she wondered whether she would ever see her father again.

FIFTY-EIGHT

THE MELODIC BEAT of steel drums filled Barry's kitchen. Naveen Gupta stood by the stove stirring ingredients in a frying pan, steam rising to the ceiling. The buzzer sounded, and Alina ran to the door.

"Hello, Alina," her father said. Barry came up behind her and said, "Her name is Nicole. Why are you calling her Alina?"

"Papa," she cried. "You've come to take me home!"

"I haven't seen you in so long," her father said as he moved past her and sat at the kitchen table. Gupta shimmied over and brought him a plate filled with a dark brown stew. The music grew louder.

"No, Papa. Don't eat it."

Alina heard a noise and looked up to see Henry Garcia in the hallway. "It's okay, Nina," Garcia said. "It will not be the food that kills him."

"Jamaican food is too spicy for him!" Alina shouted.

Her father took a bite, and the kitchen started to vibrate with a low humming sound. Alina felt as if there was a vise on her head. She wanted to take it off, but her hands were locked to her sides and wouldn't budge. "I can't get it off!" she cried. The front door swung open. Josh Brodsky entered holding a six-pack of beer and said,

"Of course you can, Brianna. If you change the data, CHERL will help you do anything you want."

Alina felt a sudden jolt.

She opened her eyes, her face wet with perspiration. She heard the hum of an engine. Her mind cleared, and she took in her surroundings. She was seated in a small airplane cabin, facing backward, opposite a single empty leather seat. Lightning flashed against a darkening sky visible out the left porthole as the plane bounced along the turbulent air. A miniature camera lens was perched on a low tripod in front of her. She felt something pressing on her head and remembered the sensation from her dream. She wanted to reach up, but her wrists were tied to the armrests with flex-cuffs, and her forearms and fingers were taped to several long electrical wires which led to a black device placed on the floor between her legs. Her ankles were also bound to the legs of the chair. She leaned back, trying to focus and calm her racing heart. Her last hazy memory was of being tackled to the floor, of Barry being restrained as she was rushed out of his apartment. Alina glanced at the lightning bolts outside.

Where were they taking her?

She heard a door creak open from behind and a large burly man with a dour expression came into view. The sleeves of his white button-down shirt were rolled up, revealing a pair of muscular, tattooed forearms. The cabin suddenly reeked of cigarette smoke. Alina pressed back into the seat as the plane rattled on.

"I see you are with us," the man said in a gravelly voice as he lowered himself into the seat across from her. "It can take a while for the sedative to wear off." He placed a briefcase on the metal table between them and retrieved a laptop from it. "But oh, yes, I forgot. You know all about narcotics, don't you?"

Alina's shoulders tightened as the man moved his hands across the computer keyboard. Did his comment mean the Americans had connected her to Chicago?

Connected her to the ransomware attacks? And was this man FBI? Or maybe CIA? She doubted he was local police or security, but why had she been sedated? She would see how much he would divulge. She tried to shift in her seat, but the cuffs made movement difficult. "Who are you?" Alina asked.

Without looking up, he responded, "My name is Franco. I have been hired by people who have an interest in your…activities." He squinted at his laptop. "How about you….*Nicole*? You want to start by telling me your real name?"

Alina struggled to stay calm, but her heart was still racing. Why had the Americans hired this man? A man who already knew she wasn't Nicole Ryder, but he clearly didn't know her real identity. She stared blankly ahead and said, "I want to speak with a lawyer." She heard her own voice crack.

Franco grinned. "You watch too many movies." He stared at his computer and said, "Let's go at this again. What is your *real* name?"

Another flash of lightning lit up the cabin. How could the Americans refuse her a lawyer? Maybe in her own country, but not here. Not from everything she understood about their government and legal system. And what was he examining on his computer? She again became aware of the pressure on her forehead. She moved her fingers.

"What's all of this?" she said as she gestured with her chin to the wires attached to her.

"Probes," he said. "They pick up neural activity when you try to bullshit. The one in the skullcap and the eye scanner are supposed to bring the accuracy level up to ninety-nine percent." He shrugged. "I don't know much about the science. But *you* should. After all, you're one of Sway's top AI experts, right?"

A lie detector. She took a long, deep breath and slowly exhaled as the plane bounced again.

"You can't hold me like this," she said, trying to sound calm. "I'm an American citizen."

Franco stared at his screen as his face broke into a grimace. "Not a good start," he said. "But if you insist. Does our *American* citizen have a name?"

Her stress response was already revealing her lie to his device. She needed to concentrate, to give this man something more, lock in on facts that her own body might not give away. She summoned the memories of those weeks preparing for her departure from Russia, internalizing the backstory she'd absorbed as if it were her own.

"My name," she said, "is Brianna Danis."

Franco focused on his screen. "Okay…Brianna. Let's see where this takes us. Where are you from?"

Alina took another deep breath and cleared her throat. "I was born in Chicago. But I grew up in Latvia."

Franco's expression didn't change. "Go on."

Alina slowly recounted Brianna's cover story, the same one she had learned before entering America. Franco's eyes never left his screen as she told him about her studies in AI at the University of Edinburgh.

"I came back to the US over a year ago," Alina continued, trying to control her body's vital signs. "To pursue my career in artificial intelligence." With that, she leaned her head back and looked away. "I won't say more until I see a lawyer."

Franco's eyes remained focused on his laptop. He finally let out a long sigh, reached into his briefcase, and pulled out a small plastic bag. He stood over Alina and started to tape small white squares to each of her wrists.

"What are those?" she asked, her heart thumping again.

Franco bent down and lifted the bottom of her slacks, taping the same white squares to her bound ankles. He returned to his seat. "There is some resistance to this approach, but I don't have a lot of time."

"What does that mean?" she asked, again trying to free her arms. "What are you doing?"

"Your story is well told." He pointed to the screen. "But my system—it is fairly certain this is a farce."

Alina's entire body tensed. "What are you talking about?"

"If you want to continue with your charade, you can forget that lawyer you were asking for. We'll take you to a detention cell where beautiful people like you should never be. Eventually," he added, "you will tell us the truth."

"You can't do that!" But she felt a lump in her throat.

"Now. Let's try again." His hands hovered over the keyboard. "What is your *real* name?"

"I told you. I'm Brianna Da—ahhh!!!" she screamed as her body convulsed in jolts of pain. Her legs and arms felt as if they were being ripped away from the bone. Once the electric current that cracked through her body stopped, the pain slowly subsided, but her limbs continued to vibrate.

Franco leaned over. "Let's not prolong this. We need to know who you are. Who sent you? Are you an assassin? Why did you kill the drug trafficker?"

Assassin? What drug trafficker? What was he talking about? She tried to raise her head, but the residual pain made it impossible to straighten her neck. She tried to speak, but her mouth was bone-dry.

"Tell me your real name!" he demanded before moving his hands across the keyboard.

"*No! Ahhhh!*" she screamed as he administered another jolt. Her body shook violently and her head lolled to the side. She was not trained to withstand this. America and Russia had always negotiated to trade captured spies. Alina never believed the Americans would resort to… torture. Telling the truth might be the only way she could get past that lie detector. The only way she would ever get home again.

She swallowed hard and managed to say, "And then…
you will…send me home?"

"Of course," Franco said. "But you must tell me
everything."

She slowly lifted her head. "My real name…is Alina.
Alina Petrova."

———

FRANCO'S GAZE remained on his screen
throughout Alina's account. The storm outside slowly
subsided as she revealed the existence of Alexi Romanoff's
hacking warehouse hidden in an old KGB bunker. She
detailed the names of the sugar daddies she had hacked
and the companies she had extorted money from. She
described Josh Brodsky's document revealing Sway's
CHERL program, the data Romanoff had her plant, and
the insider trading that had been discovered at Sway headquarters. As she recounted it all, there was one piece of
truth she fought to keep from the forefront of her mind,
and that was her original reason for coming to America.
With her capture, she accepted that she might never find
out what happened to her mother. But Alina would die
before sending the Americans onto her mother's trail.

Sharing her numerous revelations brought a growing
sense of relief. The pain from Franco's electric shocks had
subsided. And her days of living a life of deception and
lies were finally over. Her long journey home had begun.
She felt the plane making its descent. She still didn't know
where Franco was taking her, but she assumed once he
contacted the Russian embassy to confirm her identity, a
trade would be arranged and she would be on her way
home.

"That is everything." Alina said. She closed her eyes,
overwhelmed with complete and utter exhaustion. When
she opened her eyes moments later, Franco was glaring at

his computer screen, his brow furrowed. "What are you not telling me?"

"There's nothing," Alina insisted, gripping the armrests tightly as a tiny bead of sweat started dripping down the back of her neck.

"Who trained you to kill?"

"I didn't kill anyone!"

"Who have you been looking for?"

"What?" Alina cried.

"We know about your search program. Who are you looking for? Were you sent to kill—"

"I don't know what you're talking about!"

Franco reached for the keyboard.

"No!" Alina shouted, but another jolt of electricity shot through her, the force causing her entire body to quake. She couldn't hear the sound of her own voice screaming. When Franco finally made it stop, her head was still vibrating. "No...more," she muttered. "I...told you...everything."

Franco brought his face inches from hers and screamed, "No, you have not!" The wheels of the plane hit the tarmac, and Alina's head lolled from side to side, but Franco continued shouting. "Who sent you to look for—"

"I didn't," she sobbed.

"You are lying!"

"No one. Please...you must call...Russians..." Alina's mind was numb, but she thought she felt the plane coming to a stop.

"Not until you tell me!" Franco shouted.

"Nothing...to tell." Through the sounds of her sobs, she thought she heard footsteps. "I'm...not."

He leaned forward and reached for the keyboard.

"No!" Alina cried. "Don't. I—"

She heard the door behind her open and a woman's voice yell, "Stop this!"

Alina slowly raised her head to see a blond-haired woman walk into view.

"What the hell are you doing to her?" the woman shouted as Franco stood and shouted back, "They said they must know! I was told to make sure you are secure!"

The woman said firmly, "I never agreed to do this!"

Alina was still trying to control her convulsions and quiet sobs as the woman kneeled down in front of her.

"I am not done with her!" Franco shouted.

"Please...don't," Alina sobbed.

"She is done!" the woman commanded. She pulled an object from her pocket and flicked open a long blade. "I am putting an end to this right now!"

"Please...call Russia," Alina cried. She squeezed her eyes closed. "They...will trade..." She felt the cold steel of a knife on her right wrist. "Noooo..." she whimpered, but the knife had already shifted to her left wrist. Alina opened her eyes, expecting to see her arms covered in blood. Instead, the flex-cuffs were gone, the woman still kneeling in front of her.

"We don't need to call the Russians, *lyubov moya*," the woman said. "We *are* the Russians."

CHAPTER
FIFTY-NINE

"WHO DID YOU TELL?" Lucas fumed as he and Dennison got back in the sedan. Dan Barry was being walked to the other car to be brought downtown.

"Don't try to blame me, Foley," Dennison said as he put the car in gear and exited the apartment complex, the sound of screeching tires echoing off the buildings. "I called Dr. Brodsky at Sway, just as we agreed, to alert him and get Nicole Ryder's home address. He already knew the CHERL system had a serious breach but didn't suspect her. I told him to keep Ryder's name confidential until we had her in custody."

Lucas wondered whether other spies had infiltrated the Sway company. Maybe Dr. Brodsky was one.

"And I've had two agents with Brodsky all night," Dennison said. "He's been at his lab assessing the damage."

"Anyone else?" Lucas asked.

Dennison was quiet. After a few moments, he said, "I had to cover my backside."

"Come on, Dennison!" Lucas snapped.

"My boss, Foley. That's all. You didn't want me to call Gilroy—fine. But I had to make sure my boss knew. He goes by the book. He's the only one I told."

"Were those agents from your Frisco bureau? Are you already holding my suspect somewhere?"

"She's not *your* suspect, Foley. She's *our* suspect. And in case you hadn't noticed, she's here in San Francisco, which last I looked, is *my* jurisdiction. But no. We don't have her. Despite what you Chicago boys may think, we don't operate that way."

"So how do you explain it? Barry said they were FBI agents."

"Barry said they *looked* like FBI agents."

Lucas rubbed his temples. Dennison was right about that. Barry had said the officers hadn't identified themselves as they whisked Nicole Ryder out of his apartment. And other than the official-looking badges hanging from their belts, Barry's description of the men sounded eerily similar to what Lucas remembered about Lozano's bodyguards.

Big guys, wearing dark suits and ties. One bald with a beard, the other clean-shaven.

Lucas tried not to think about the real possibility that the Rojas Cartel had caught up with the woman who might have killed Henry Garcia.

He and Dennison rode in silence during the hour-long drive to Sway headquarters. The case had spiraled beyond their control. It was time to bring Gilroy up to speed. Lucas scrolled through his phone until he came to her number. He stared at Gilroy's contact information. She would probably tell them to stand down and turn everything they knew over to FBI counterintelligence. Most likely, Lucas would be on the afternoon flight to Chicago.

He returned the phone to his pocket.

He would at least learn what the hacker had been doing at Sway.

———

"WHEN WE SAW these crazy results, we pulled down everything that was running on the CHERL system."

Lucas and Dennison watched and listened as Dr. Josh Brodsky paced the length of the control room at Sway as he motioned to the giant wall-sized screen displaying the corrupted results. He explained Sway's AI system in detail before describing the roster of clients and businesses already exposed to CHERL's advice and recommendations.

"I can't believe Nicole worked here for almost a year," Brodsky groaned. "What kind of screening is our People Experience team doing? How did our security let a hacker operate right under our noses?"

"It's clear she had help, Dr. Brodsky," Dennison said. "Are you suspicious of anyone else?"

"Nicole pointed us at Agnes Nowak, but she's dead."

"How'd she die?" Dennison asked.

"She went home to Poland last May. We read that she was found in Warsaw with a bullet in her head. But my team has been scrubbing through everything Agnes touched. So far, her work looks clean. That," he went on, "will not be the case with the work performed by Nicole."

"How do you know?" Lucas asked.

Brodsky pointed at the giant screen. "Take a look at this," he said.

Lucas read Sway's analysis of the two CHERL clients that had entered into joint ventures with a Russian company run by former KGB officers. And a half-dozen other clients were under investigation by the Securities and Exchange Commission for potentially leaking information about six other business deals.

"It appears to be a Russian insider trading scheme, generating over three hundred million dollars in illicit gains," Brodsky explained.

"Do you think Ryder did something to leak information about these transactions?" Lucas asked.

Brodsky shook his head. "I wish we were dealing with a leak, but I'm afraid it's worse than that."

"What do you mean?" Lucas asked.

Brodsky waved his hand over a motion-activated system. The giant screen started streaming a string of alphanumeric characters. All were green except for several short bursts highlighted in red. Numbers and letters snaked across and down until they filled the entire wall.

"You are viewing a corrupted file that was being loaded into CHERL's version of Lee Iacocca. I found Nicole Ryder working on this in our Tower Ops room just yesterday. Luckily, I interrupted her before she executed the final load." Brodsky pointed to the screen as he continued. "We built strong edit controls, but we deal with millions upon millions of pieces of data. Even small changes like those in red would have altered CHERL's recommendations."

Brodsky blinked rapidly, as if calculating a math problem in his head. After a few moments he nodded at the screen and said, "Based on what I'm seeing with the Iacocca data, it's highly probable Nicole caused CHERL's experts to recommend those joint ventures and urge clients to execute specific business transactions." He rubbed his chin. "Whoever Nicole Ryder worked for knew exactly which stocks to buy, and how much they stood to gain once our clients followed CHERL's advice."

"But how would they know what data to change?" Lucas asked.

Brodsky shrugged. "They could have created a CHERL prototype. But only if they had gained access to the design specifications. But we have guardrails against that. Very few people have access."

"Did Nicole Ryder?" Dennison asked.

"Absolutely not," Brodsky said. "Alvarez's team was not on the approved list."

"How about Dan Barry?" Lucas asked.

Brodsky leaned over and punched keys on a laptop. After a few moments, he slowly straightened up and winced. "Barry was on our approved access list."

"We have him in custody," Dennison said. "We'll find out if Barry was part of her scheme."

Incredible, Lucas thought. Once news of this broke, he couldn't imagine future leaders trusting a piece of artificial intelligence produced by Sway.

"My team is in the next room," Brodsky said, his eyes glazed. "They're reviewing every piece of data Nicole worked on."

"We'll bring in our forensics team to assist," Dennison said.

"Understood." Brodsky dropped into a seat. "It's hard to believe she's the same hacker that planted ransomware onto CHERL last year." Dennison had called during the drive from Barry's apartment and told Brodsky of the connection to the hacker from the Horizon's coding school. "How did she know to target my system?" Brodsky asked.

"Most likely she got lucky," Lucas said. "She signed up for the same AI boot camp as your brother to help her build some type of AI search engine. I don't think she knew anything about you or your system until Donny started running his mouth off about his successful brothers. Somehow, the malware that planted the ransomware also transferred details about CHERL back to her handlers."

Brodsky looked away. After a few moments he slowly nodded, his expression pained. "I think I was working on a document about CHERL for the board of directors the night Donny's email arrived." He rubbed the back of his neck before adding, "Maybe ransomware wasn't the only thing she included."

"Sway obviously presented an enticing target," Dennison said.

A door at the top of the control room stairs opened and four men emerged in the gallery, one carrying a laptop, just as Lucas's cell phone vibrated with a message from Fernandez:

CALL ME! URGENT!

"Give me a minute," Lucas said to Dennison. He walked to the far end of the control room for privacy. As the man carrying the laptop descended the side stairs, Lucas dialed Fernandez. "What's up? I'm in the middle of—"

"Agent Foley," Fernandez interrupted. "I'm at the Waldorf Hotel. I just spoke to the older man watching the sugar baby in the surveillance tape. His name is John Dempsey."

"Can it wait? I'm—"

"You were right, Agent Foley. I showed him the footage, and he remembered her instantly."

"Who was she?" Lucas asked as he watched Dennison and Dr. Brodsky hovering over the laptop.

"Dempsey has worked at several Chicago area hotels over the past thirty-five years. Not just the Waldorf but also the Four Seasons, the Ritz-Carlton. But he started out at the Drake back in the nineties. Dempsey says our sugar baby is practically an identical twin of a woman who worked for him back when he was at the Drake. A woman named Diane Backus."

Lucas rubbed the back of his neck.

"He's seventy-two but sharp as a tack," Fernandez continued.

Dennison was scratching his head as he carried the laptop toward Lucas.

"What else did he remember?" Lucas asked Fernandez.

"He remembered the weekend twenty-five years ago

when Diane didn't show up for work. He said she simply vanished. The FBI came asking hotel staff about her. Dempsey said the agent who interviewed him never came right out and said it, but from the questions, Dempsey said it was clear that Diane Backus was suspected of being some type of foreign spy. A Russian spy."

Lucas tasted bile rising in the back of his throat. Diane Backus and Brianna Danis weren't twins. They couldn't be. They were at least twenty-five years apart in age. They had to be—

"Agent Foley." Dennison grabbed Lucas by the arm. "Dr. Brodsky's team discovered a program Ryder was secretly running before she left. You need to see this."

Lucas glanced down to read the laptop's screen. The heading at the top read AI SCOUT RESULTS. Eight names were listed, with the word *alive* or *deceased* next to each. Lucas didn't recognize the first seven names, but the final name, listed as alive, made Lucas's body freeze. It took only seconds for his mind to piece everything together.

"What do you think it means?" Dennison asked.

Lucas didn't respond. His mind, once again, was taken back to the surveillance footage of the sugar baby walking through the Drake, her eyes nervously darting around the lobby.

She *was* looking for someone!

"We don't have a lot of time," Lucas said to Fernandez. "I need you to dig into something for me."

When Lucas finished his instructions and disconnected with Fernandez, Dennison said, "I don't understand."

"I'm not sure I do either," Lucas replied. "But it's time we go see Assistant Director Gilroy."

CHAPTER SIXTY

ALINA RUBBED her wrists and ankles where the flex-cuffs had left angry red marks, but she could not erase the memory of the pain inflicted upon her body—and not, as it turned out, by the Americans, but by her fellow countrymen. But why? She was still waiting for answers as she sat in the otherwise empty airplane cabin staring at the lights coming from the hangar visible outside the window. She continued to check the exit door, which remained locked. There was nothing she could do but wait.

Wait for the woman who had claimed she, too, was Russian.

Alina took a bottle of water from a shelf between the cockpit and the cabin and took several long gulps. As she returned to her seat, she heard a single set of footsteps coming up the stairs leading to the plane. The door opened, and the blonde-haired woman returned. She said nothing as she slowly slid into the opposite seat, providing Alina with her first clear look at the person who had ended Franco's interrogation.

She was slim and attractive, her high cheekbones accented by a small beauty mark on the left side. A dark blue pantsuit and open-collared white blouse gave her a polished look, like one of Sway's CEO clients. Alina guessed she was probably in her mid to late fifties, her hair neatly styled in a side part. But her deep brown eyes were ringed with red, and what little makeup she wore was noticeably streaked. Still, she stared at Alina as if examining a newly encountered species. The woman shook her head, looked away, and said softly, "I am so sorry."

"Why would you do this?" Alina asked, barely controlling her anger. "You say you are Russian?"

The woman nodded.

"How do I know you are not lying?" Alina asked.

"I know I haven't given you a reason to trust me," the woman answered. "But you must."

"Trust you?" Alina held out her arms, bruised by the combination of restraints and electric shocks. "How can I trust you if you allowed this?"

"We did not know for sure who you were. And why you were here." The woman propped her right elbow on the armrest and rubbed her forehead. "I had little say in who the SVR hired to investigate."

Alina tilted her head. "I don't understand."

"Franco's methods are too unorthodox," she replied. "Yet his analysis showed almost everything you told him was true." The woman lowered her hand and peered at Alina. "That Alexi Romanoff was behind your entire mission." She said his name with an air of familiarity.

Alina squinted. "Wait. Do you know Alexi?"

"Let's just say I *knew* him. A long time ago. But I never trusted him. You were wrong to trust him, too. You should know," she went on, "that Russian intelligence claims you were never recruited to work for them. They know nothing of your coming to America."

"What?" Alina gripped the armrests. "How can that be?"

The woman shrugged. "And Romanoff insists he met with Alina Petrova at her father's request, but he found no use for her services."

"He is a liar!" Alina snapped, feeling the blood drain from her face. "The sugar daddy scheme. The ransomware attacks. Planting the data in the CHERL system. Ask Dmitri Fedorov!"

The woman shook her head and said, "I do not know this man."

"Romanoff told me I would be helping Mother Russia."

The woman took a deep breath, and her eyes remained locked with Alina's. After a long pause, she shook her head and said, "Alexi Romanoff is a fool. I am not surprised by his escapades. He has been allowed to run his own fiefdom with little oversight. As I said, I never trusted him." She paused again and added, "And Grigory should have known better than to trust him with…his daughter."

Alina locked eyes on the woman. "How do you know my father's name?"

The woman broke her gaze, and as she did, she seemed to sink into the leather chair. She squinted, as if being blinded by a bright light. "I will explain," she said. "But then I need you to tell me what you would not tell Franco." Alina froze as the woman peered back at her and added, "I need to know if *I* am safe."

Alina tilted her head, trying to decipher this last comment.

The woman wiped at the corner of her eye with the back of her hand. "You know," she sniffled, "you are more beautiful than I could have imagined."

These words made Alina's body flinch. The woman studied Alina's features, as if trying to memorize every facet, before clearing her throat. There was a long pause before she spoke again. "I never thought I wanted a family. I never had that…maternal urge." She smiled wistfully. "Not me. That was never going to be my future. I wanted my life to be one filled with adventure. A life of purpose." Her expression tightened as a tear ran down her right cheek. "But I never imagined I would live my life like this. Forever a spy."

Alina's shoulders started to quake. She opened her mouth but could not speak.

"Your father and I were so young," the woman continued. "Patriotic. Eager to help the new Russia emerge as a strong nation. Neither of us thought of our individual futures. As they say, we were living in the moment. I thought nothing could ever change that." The woman pulled a small case from her pocket. She leaned forward and removed what appeared to be a contact lens from her left eye and placed it in the case. She did the same with her right eye. She sat back, looked directly at Alina, and said, "But then I had you."

Alina's chest heaved as she gasped for air. She sat in stunned silence and gazed into the woman's eyes.

The same vibrant green eyes Alina had been staring at in the mirror her entire life.

"Oh my…God," Alina whispered.

The woman placed the case containing the color-changing contact lenses back in her pocket before looking away and saying, "You don't think anything will change your life. When the SVR requested a prop, I told myself having a child meant nothing." She paused, looking back at Alina, her eyes cloudy. Pleading. "But I was wrong. You meant everything to me."

Alina couldn't stop the tears, despite hearing these words—words she had longed to hear from a mother she never knew. Tears dripped onto her blouse as she finally managed to whisper, "They said you were…dead." Alina reached for the half-empty water bottle and took a sip, but the liquid struggled to pass the lump stuck in her throat. She tried to think of all the questions she had been prepared to ask about her parent's relationship. Why her mother had disappeared. The truth behind her mother's tactics with men. But Alina's mind was in disarray. No

words formed, until she weakly managed to ask, "How...
how did you...find *me*?"

Her mother leaned back. "I am in a position to review
images of anyone who attempts to infiltrate this country. I
only had to look at the passport photo captured by US
Customs the day you arrived to know it was either you or
someone made to look like you. Five months later, I
learned that your image was identical to the sugar baby
hacker in Chicago." The woman smiled. "And then I saw
your picture. From a hotel surveillance video. That's when
I thought it really could be you."

"So you've been watching me since Chicago? And you
only came for me now?"

Her mother leaned forward. "I did not know for
certain where you were. Or why you were in America.
And I did not know if it was you or someone disguised to
look like you. I had to be sure you weren't being used as
bait by someone trying to force me out into the open."

"Who?" Alina asked. "Who would do that?"

"Very few within the SVR know what became of
Valeriya Petrova twenty-five years ago. My success over
the years is the result of this secrecy." She looked down
and added, "But careers were destroyed when I...died.
Even after decades, I worried someone might be out to
settle some scores." When she raised her head, she again
peered into Alina's eyes. "So I need to ask. Did someone
send you here to look for me? Did Romanoff send you to
find me?"

Alina thought about this question. It had been *her*
idea, wanting to find her mother, hadn't it? *She* was the
one who had pushed to come to America. Yes, Romanoff
had the sugar daddy plan at the ready. He'd provided her
with all the resources she needed. The files on Valeriya
Petrova. But it had been Alina's idea to come to America
to search for her mother. Or had it been?

"Romanoff knew I wanted to find the truth," Alina
said. "Papa said you didn't die of cancer, that he didn't

know what happened to you. He knew you'd disappeared, that's all. He gave me hope. Hope that you were alive. I knew I could not go on with my life without knowing. That's why I put myself through all of this. Romanoff offered me an assignment to get me into the US. He gave me all the files he had on you. But nobody—"

"He gave you his files on me?" her mother asked.

Alina nodded.

"He gave you everything?"

"That's how I built the search engine that—"

"That's what you built at that Horizons coding school?"

Alina's mouth hung open for a few moments; then she said, "You really *have* been watching me."

"Did your program work?" Her mother leaned forward. "Did your search program…reveal my identity?"

"I…I'm not sure," Alina stammered. "I left it running. Back at Sway. They locked me out before I could go back and find the results." She shook her head and added, "I don't know if it worked or not."

Her mother looked off to the side. "Then we do not have much time, Alina. Perhaps it is now unsafe for both of us. A car is coming soon. It will bring you to a transport."

"Why can't I stay here? Why can't I stay in America? With you? If I'm captured by the Americans, won't they simply trade me for someone sitting in a Russian jail?"

"If the Americans arrest you, you will be charged with espionage. You will also be charged with murder."

Alina shot up. "What? Murder? I haven't killed anyone!"

"That's not what the Americans believe, Alina. And it may not be what the Rojas Cartel believes, either."

"I don't understand. What's the Rojas Cartel?"

"The Americans have evidence linking you to a murder in a Chicago safe house. A soldier in the Rojas Cartel named Guillermo Garcia."

"Garcia," Alina whispered. Suddenly the memories of that night came rushing back to Alina. The metal statue. The bag filled with stacks of money.

"Henry Garcia?" she asked, softly.

"Investigators said he used the name Tuxedo on his dating profile."

So *that's* who Franco had been referring to.

"He was going to hurt me," Alina said. "I hit him to get away…I didn't know I…killed him." Alina paused as she processed the news.

"There may not be any trade big enough for the Americans to release you, Alina. You will be sent to a maximum-security prison where the cartel will certainly pay to have you killed. You must leave on my transport at once."

Alina slumped back. "Where will it take me?"

"I have someone…not Franco. Someone I trust who will take you back to Russia. I will make sure you are protected."

Alina stared at her mother, her body vibrating like a tuning fork, her thoughts in disarray. She had come all this way. She had gone through so much to find her mother. And now, after only a few minutes, her time with the woman who had brought her into this world was coming to an abrupt end. Alina steadied herself.

"I'm not going anywhere till you answer one question," Alina said as she leaned forward. "Why did you leave?" She paused before repeating, "Why…did you leave…*me*?"

"There is no point, Alina. It is all history. It has nothing to do with your life now. The life you must go home and build."

"No!" Alina shouted, feeling the blood rushing through her neck. "I have a right to know!"

"It is dangerous for you to know."

Alina tried not to laugh. "More dangerous than what I've already been through?"

Her mother looked off, seemingly lost in thought. After a few moments, she finally whispered, "Perhaps it doesn't matter anymore." She locked eyes with Alina and said firmly, "If I tell you, you must promise me, when I am done, you will go on that transport. And never come back to America."

Alina could see her own intensity reflected in her mother's gaze. Slowly, Alina started to nod.

And then her mother told her.

"IT WAS A VERY heady time for me," her mother explained. "I was having great success gathering information and passing it back to our superiors. So much success that important people took notice of my skills." She smiled weakly. "I was an expert at what I did. It was exciting. Thrilling. And I felt I was doing important work." She paused. "But your father was always pining to return home. He desperately wanted to return to Russia. Especially after you were born. That's when the SVR's top director approached me. He brought a request from our president. He asked me to take on a...*lifetime commitment.* They had studied my background. Assessed my history, my experiences, and accomplishments. Even my personality traits. No one but our president and the head of the SVR would ever know about this new mission. A mission," she said, "to infiltrate America's FBI and work my way up to occupy one of their most senior law enforcement positions. A mission that would last until the end of my days."

"But you must have had a choice."

"I could not refuse."

"You had a family!" Alina said, her voice rising.

Her mother's eyes glistened. "If I refused, they said they would...take you."

"Take me? Take me where?"

"To be raised by a different set of...scouts. Some-where your father and I would never find you. Your father and I would be sent back to Russia, never to see you again."

Alina's entire body felt numb. "So, you left me...to *protect* me?"

Her mother took in a long breath. "As I said, I had no other choice." They sat in silence for a few moments before she continued. "In the eyes of the SVR, I was a soldier, asked to make what I considered the supreme sacrifice. But at least you would be home. *You* would lead a normal life." She waved her hands around and added, "I never wanted any of this for you."

Alina felt her shoulders shake as the tears returned. Her mother reached forward and clasped Alina's hands. "Don't you think I know what I gave up? But there was no escape for me." Her grip tightened. "I held out hope that —that someday, I would be able to come home. But the more successful I was here in America, the more impos-sible it became." She glanced away, her eyes moist. "It *is* impossible. I will never be allowed to return. I am too valuable for our government to bring me home. When—*if* —I am revealed, it will be too damaging and embar-rassing for the Americans to admit." She looked directly at Alina again and said firmly, "There'll be no trade of American spies for me, either, Alina. I'll never allow myself to be captured. I know what happens to enemy combatants. I will not spend my remaining days rotting in a cell." She paused and looked away. "There is only one way my mission will come to an end."

Alina shuddered. "What does *that* mean?"

Her mother did not answer.

Alina heard a car pull up alongside the plane. Her mother checked her watch but did not look up.

"Now it is time for you to go."

"I can stay too," Alina pleaded.

"I told you. Even if I could keep you safe, this is not

the life I want for you. A life of lies. Waking up in a cold sweat every day, thinking this is the day they find me out."

Alina dropped down on one knee next to her mother's seat and held her hands. "Then come with me," she said. "We'll find a new home. Someplace together."

Her mother kissed Alina's hands. "My fate was sealed twenty-five years ago, Alina."

Alina heard a car door open and looked out the window to see a young woman emerge from the sedan. Alina held her mother's grip as footsteps climbed the stairs.

"Maybe someday, my Alina," her mother said. She smiled weakly and wiped the last tears from Alina's cheeks. A figure appeared in the doorway. Her mother released Alina's hands and turned away.

"Maybe someday, *lyubov moya.*"

CHAPTER SIXTY-ONE

"AGENT FOLEY, the assistant director is getting ready to leave for a last-minute trip."

"I'm sorry," Lucas said to Sonia Gilroy's secretary. "But I took the red-eye to get here. It's urgent that I see her."

Sarah Lake glared at him. "We can schedule something for you when she returns."

"I know this is highly unusual," Lucas said. "But I won't take a lot of her time."

Lake rolled her eyes and went into Gilroy's office. She returned in less than a minute. "If you can wait, she'll be with you shortly."

Twenty-five minutes later, the door to Gilroy's office opened.

"Game time," Lucas whispered to himself.

Gilroy emerged and extended her hand. "Sorry to keep you waiting, Agent Foley, but I wasn't expecting you."

They shook hands. Lucas noticed her palms were sweaty. "I'm the one who should be sorry," he said. "I know how busy you are."

"I do have a flight to catch," she said.

"I'll be brief."

She showed him in, closed the door, and sat behind her desk. She motioned for Lucas to sit in one of the straight-backed chairs to the side. "You've got fifteen."

Gilroy's desk looked even more austere than it had during last year's videoconference. He noticed a shredder plugged in under the window as he placed his backpack next to the desk.

"I'll get right to it. Agent Dennison and I thought we had Brianna Danis cornered in San Francisco. We were about to take her into custody, but some people got to her first."

Gilroy shifted in her seat. "What people?"

"We're not sure. But she was living and working in Silicon Valley. She stole the identity of an AI engineer named Nicole Ryder and used her resume to get a job inside the Sway corporation." Lucas walked Gilroy through the story: what he'd learned about Buford Chambers from the Justice Department lawyer, the reviews of Aztec personnel's credit reports that led to the revelations of the real Nicole Ryder, and how close he and Dennison had come to making an arrest. He told her about the corrupted data loaded into Sway's CHERL AI program, Polynef Industries, and the CEOs who were persuaded to pursue deals lining the pockets of Russian stock traders.

"When did you learn all of this?" Gilroy asked, looking surprised.

"Everything came together in the last forty-eight hours," Lucas explained. "I apologize for not alerting you sooner, but as you can tell, events spun out of control quickly."

"Still, there was no need to fly all the way to DC," Gilroy said. "A phone call would have been quicker."

"I already had plans to be in DC," Lucas lied.

"So this entire operation came out of Russia."

"I'm sure of it," Lucas replied.

"You've done good work here." Gilroy smiled. "But you look like you've been through the ringer."

"It has been a bit of a whirlwind."

"Any leads on the men who took Brianna Danis from the apartment?" Gilroy asked.

"Her boyfriend said they looked like FBI agents."

"I assume you ruled out agents from the Frisco office," Gilroy said.

Lucas nodded.

"That leaves the Rojas Cartel," Gilroy said softly. She stood and glanced at her watch. "Now if you'll excuse me—"

"It could be the Russians," Lucas said.

"That would be a strange way to extract a spy from a mission," Gilroy said. "But I'll call my lead counterintelligence agent on my way to the airport. He'll assemble a team to get right on it."

Lucas took a deep breath and steadied himself. "Are you sure your team is not already *on it*?" he asked.

Gilroy's eyes narrowed quizzically as Lucas opened his backpack, pulled out a folder, and placed it on the desk. Gilroy flipped the cover and glanced inside. "What is this?"

Lucas thought he noticed the color draining from her face.

"Another surveillance screenshot," Lucas said.

"I can see that," she said.

"Buford Chambers and Brianna Danis had their encounter at the Waldorf in Chicago."

Gilroy's eyes remained glued to the photo on the desk.

"Agent Fernandez on my team spoke with a gentleman named John Dempsey. Mr. Dempsey works at the Waldorf. But twenty-five years ago, he started out at the Drake Hotel." Lucas pointed at the man in the photo. "That's Mr. Dempsey, watching Brianna Danis leaving the Waldorf the night of her rendezvous with Chambers. Dempsey swears Brianna Danis is the spitting image of a lady who worked for him at the Drake all those years ago. Right before the lady disappeared..." He paused. "And the FBI came asking questions."

Gilroy slowly lowered herself back into the chair, her expression void of any sign of emotion.

"Agent Fernandez dug into the FBI archives, and Dempsey was right. There's an entire file on the female suspect who worked at the Drake back then. The bureau never found her, but according to the case notes, agents believed a woman named Diane Backus was one of those Russian spies that lived among us in America. Living like normal citizens. Diane and her husband, Harold, even had a child." He paused. "Her name was Julie Backus."

Gilroy turned her head and looked out the window, her mouth open, as if suddenly marveling at the flight of a rare bird.

"Julie would now be twenty-eight years old, about the same age as our Brianna. The same as Nicole Ryder. And Diane Backus would be in her fifties now," Lucas continued. "That would make Dempsey's coworker...about your age."

Gilroy's gaze remained fixed on the scene outside her office window.

"Now, I've admired your work, Assistant Director." Lucas let out a forced laugh. "You've had an impressive career for someone who didn't arrive in America until you were, what, twenty-one years old? Agent Fernandez learned you were born in Canada. But here's the strange thing." Lucas pulled his chair closer to the desk. He wasn't sure Gilroy was still listening, but he continued. "When Fernandez dug in further, she found records of someone named Sonia Gilroy buried in Beechwood Cemetery outside Ottawa. *That* Sonia Gilroy died in a car accident a year before you came to America." Lucas raised an eyebrow. "She even has the same birthdate as you."

Gilroy finally spoke, saying flatly, "That's quite a coincidence."

"True enough," Lucas said. He kept his eyes on Gilroy

as he slowly reached into his backpack again and retrieved a single sheet of paper. "But it looks like I'm not the only one piecing everything together. Remember that search engine Ana Dafoe was building when she was attending the Horizons boot camp? Well, Dr. Brodsky's team at Sway was able to break into the laptop Nicole Ryder left behind. His team uncovered an extensive set of material fed into the search engine she created—everything there is to know about the Russian agent known as Diane Backus who worked undercover at the Drake Hotel twenty-five years ago." Lucas placed the paper on the desk.

Gilroy glanced at the list of names printed on it.

"Agent Dennison thought this might be some kind of Russian hit list." He paused. "But some of the names are marked as deceased, so that doesn't make much sense. It's possible the Russians are targeting a few of them." Lucas shook his head. "But you know what I think?" He took in a deep breath and withdrew his Glock from his holster. He pointed it at Gilroy and said, "While we were searching for Brianna Danis, *she* was searching, too. She was searching for...*you*."

Gilroy's eyes moved down the list that came from Nicole Ryder's search engine.

The list with Sonia Gilroy's name at the bottom.

"I need you to place your hands on the desk," Lucas said.

"There is no need for that, Agent Foley," she said softly.

"Where is she?"

"What makes you think I know?"

Lucas shifted his pistol. "The only person who knew that the FBI was about to arrest Nicole Ryder was Dennison's 'by the book' bureau chief." Lucas leaned forward. "I figure he felt compelled to let you know, giving you plenty of time to get your people into position before we arrived."

"The Frisco office chief is a good man," Gilroy said.

Lucas tightened his grip and asked again, "I just want to know where she is."

"Trust me," she said, her eyes now clear. "Someplace you will never find her." A small tear emerged from the corner of her right eye and ran down her cheek. Lucas heard the slight, almost imperceptible sound of a crack.

In an instant, foam started oozing from the side of Gilroy's mouth.

"Shit!" Lucas screamed. "Get in here!"

Gilroy's body convulsed violently and hit the desk before dropping to the floor. Lucas kneeled beside her as her legs jerked and spasmed. Dennison and the dozen FBI agents who had been waiting down the hall stormed in, guns raised. One radioed for an ambulance while another started administering chest compressions. In less than a minute, the seizures ceased, and Gilroy's eyes rolled back in her head. By the time paramedics and a swarm of additional FBI agents arrived, Gilroy lay motionless, unresponsive.

As the body was taken away, Lucas removed the miniature microphone and camera he had concealed in the collar of his shirt. He picked up the surveillance photo that had fallen next to the desk and studied the image one last time as the realization set in.

Brianna Danis, Ana Dafoe, Nicole Ryder—the sugar baby hacker and Sway infiltrator—was probably out of their reach forever.

CHAPTER
SIXTY-TWO

SIX MONTHS LATER...

ALEXI ROMANOFF CLIMBED up the steps leading from the rocky shoreline and turned to admire the stunning view of the sun setting over the Adriatic Sea. He inhaled and slowly let the salty air escape from his lungs. And then he smiled.

He was on top of the world.

It had been six months since he and his brother, Ilya, fled Russia. His business-connected brother worked with a clandestine network of lawyers and money launderers to funnel the proceeds from their insider trading scam into shell companies and bank accounts around the globe. The equivalent of almost $400 million in US currency had been sprinkled across safe havens like Luxembourg, Cyprus, and the Cayman Islands. Romanoff felt secure that their fortune was safe.

Yet he accepted that for the rest of his life he would need to avoid potential informers and the vast network of Russian spies who roamed throughout the European continent. He worried more for Ilya, who insisted on making his home in a major city like Paris. Romanoff preferred the quiet seclusion and safety of a small town. And a life near the sea.

But after a cold winter in a rented villa on the Amalfi Coast, Romanoff opted for the more inconspicuous country of Montenegro. Ulcinj was exquisite, especially in the spring and summer. And, in Romanoff's view, far safer than the usual playgrounds of the Russian oligarchs. Here, residents and tourists keep to themselves. Still, while Romanoff had plenty of money to indulge himself in anything the town had to offer, he made sure to maintain a low profile. Up to this point, no one seemed to notice the former KGB officer strolling the town's beaches and streets. So after several months of seclusion, Romanoff now felt secure enough to venture out for dinner. While he would eat alone yet again, he would enjoy his meal at Sapore di Mare, one of Ulcinj's finest seafood establishments.

The restaurant was perched atop the rocks over-looking the beach—and the scantily clad sunbathers who remained to have a drink and watch the sunset. Over the next two hours, Romanoff chewed slowly, relishing a scrumptious meal of fish soup, Caprese salad, and pan-seared sea bass. Paired, of course, with a fine Vouvray from the Loire Valley.

By the third glass of wine, a calmness fell over him. Perhaps tomorrow he would hire one of those private fishing charters he'd seen advertised at the local marina. He felt satiated from his dinner but still surveyed the dessert menu as he asked the waiter for a double espresso. When the coffee arrived, Romanoff took a sip. Without looking up, he said, "I'll have the baklava." But he sensed the waiter still standing at his side. And then Romanoff glanced up.

At first he didn't recognize the attractive redheaded woman wearing oversized glasses. Before Romanoff could say a word, the woman swiped the side of his face with a white napkin.

"That's for Valeriya Petrova," she said as she removed her glasses, revealing a pair of bright green eyes blazing with fury.

And then Romanoff knew. He tried to stand but couldn't find his balance. He fell back into the chair as his vision blurred. He tried to grab her arm, but his hands wouldn't respond. His heart rate accelerated but his breath slowed, and he gasped for air. He fell sideways onto the ground, his lungs refusing to respond, unable to draw in another breath. He managed to look up and saw his assailant drop the napkin to the ground.

The napkin that he now knew had been used to deliver a lethal dose of the SVR's latest nerve agent. And as Romanoff slowly suffocated to death, he watched her hurry past the shocked patrons and disappear into the Montenegrin night.

———

ALINA RECLINED IN HER SEAT. The Turkish Airlines flight from Montenegro's Tivat Airport to her final destination would be less than three hours, but she would try to get some sleep.

Her *real* career was about to begin.

She was on her way to Istanbul—to a position as an AI engineer with a high-tech software company.

A company specializing in artificial intelligence.

Thanks to a well-placed phone call from the Kremlin to Turkey's presidential palace, executives with the software company had welcomed her with open arms—at a starting salary that was thirty percent higher than the positions she had been offered immediately after graduate school.

The SVR had delivered on its end of the bargain.

Her final mission for the Russian government began upon Alina's return from America six months earlier, when she had been escorted by her mother's private security agent to a safe house in the Russian countryside. There she spent three days debriefing the SVR's two most senior officers, Anton Kuznetsov and Viktor Mikhaylov—officials who claimed they and the Russian president were the only three people in Russia who knew of Valeriya Petrova's existence as FBI assistant director Sonia Gilroy. Kuznetsov and Mikhaylov admitted they sent Franco to find out Alina's true identity and see whether she posed a threat to their longtime asset. They reviewed Franco's notes from Alina's interrogation and knew what Alina had divulged about Alexi Romanoff's operation. Yet they wanted to hear Alina's firsthand account of her ransomware attacks on American businessmen, including her physical encounter with Garcia. Kuznetsov repeatedly questioned her about her infiltration of the Sway corporation as Nicole Ryder and how she managed to load Romanoff's alternative data into Sway's CHERL system. He probed into how Alina discovered she had been duped —that instead of helping her country, the data she loaded had caused Sway's AI to recommend transactions generating hundreds of millions in stock market gains for Romanoff and his brother.

And at the end of the second day of questioning, Kuznetsov revealed what they learned about her mother.

"I'm afraid Valeriya Petrova is dead."

Alina's mother had taken her own life when confronted by an FBI agent. Kuznetsov said, "The most successful undercover operation in Russian history has come to an end."

The news left Alina numb but not surprised. She remembered her mother's vow at the end of their short reunion on that tarmac in America: *"I'll never allow myself to be captured...There is only one way my mission will come to an end."*

Still, Alina wondered. Was this just another story, no different than the ruse her mother and the SVR created over twenty-five years ago? Was her mother really dead?

Or had Valeriya Petrova moved on to her next clandestine mission for Mother Russia?

Alina might never know for sure.

The SVR officers left Alina alone for several days to process the news. But later that week, Mikhaylov returned and questioned Alina for hours about the AI scout she had built to search for her mother. The program she left behind at Sway's headquarters. Eventually Mikhaylov identified the reason for his latest queries.

"Alexi Romanoff has fled the country," Mikhaylov said. "Do you think your approach can help us locate him?" Before Alina could respond, he added, "We consider his operation an act of treason. In fact, we believe your mother would still be alive if not for his deception. If you help us, we will give you anything you want."

Alina did not hesitate.

She asked for every piece of historical information the SVR and former KGB had about Alexi Romanoff. It took several months to train her algorithms with the voluminous data. Yet it was one final, simple piece of information that helped her newest AI scout narrow the list of Romanoff's potential destinations from over one hundred to fewer than twenty. Information she remembered from her first meeting with Romanoff at the former KGB bunker.

She remembered he liked to fish.

Informants positioned in each of the targeted coastal communities had been provided with Romanoff's description and tendencies. Two weeks later, their quarry had been spotted.

Once Romanoff's whereabouts were verified, Alina insisted on flying to Montenegro to deliver her final blow.

A LOOK AT BOOK THREE:
PARALLEL MINDS

A heart-pounding thriller that blurs the lines between technology and morality.

Three years ago, Dan Barry's high-tech life in Silicon Valley was shattered when he learned his lover, Nicole Ryder, was a Russian hacker named Alina Petrova. Now, after taking a job in New York so he could care for his ailing father, Dan is ensnared in "Operation Turncoat", a high-stakes game of cat and mouse orchestrated by the FBI.

Special Agent Lucas Foley is so repulsed by the bureau's gut-churning tactics against Dan, he provides confidential documents to Dr. Josh Brodsky's latest CHERL recreation, hoping AI can short-circuit the FBI's mission by tracking down Alina.

But with his father's life hanging in the balance, Dan must navigate a labyrinth of deceit and high-tech counter espionage to unravel the truth. Has his own AI effort been manipulated by a powerful CEO? Or are unknown forces behind the fraudulent scheme? When the FBI finally offers a way out, Dan must choose between a dangerous mission or spending the rest of his life behind bars.

Will Dan Barry uncover the real mastermind behind the conspiracy, or will he become the ultimate pawn in a deadly game?

Follow his gripping journey of survival and justice—where every move could be his last. Order your copy now and join the chase!

AVAILABLE SEPTEMBER 2024

ACKNOWLEDGMENTS

I want to thank my development editor Chris Belden, my copy editor Lorraine Burton, and, of course, all my friends and fellow writers at the Westport Writers Workshop.

Several individuals provided technical guidance on everything from cyber security, artificial intelligence, FBI processes, tracing individuals through their credit bureau activity, and of course, roofies like GHB. So big shout out to Mike Rothman, Tony Wolf, Max Blumenthal, Val Sagitov, Brianna Yellen, Gurvais Grigg, Dmitri Alperovitch and Kevin Clark.

I'd also like to thank the team at Rough Edges Press, led by Rachel Del Grosso. Thank you to all my beta readers who took the time to provide their thoughtful feedback pre-publication. These include Rob Laub, Val Sagitov, Lloyd Wirshba, Sheldon Goldfarb, Glen Marino, Katy Fraser, Robert Schanilac and of course, my family (Hildy, Noah, Perri, Steve and Marsha)!

If you're interested in learning more about the Russian spies that lived undercover in America, a great book on the subject is Russians Among Us, by Gordon Correa. There's also been a lot written on artificial intelligence but one interesting source I found helpful was The Age of AI: And Our Human Future, by Daniel P. Huttenlocher, Eric Schmidt, and Henry Kissinger. And for a great source on cyber security and the increasing threat, check out, *This is How They Tell Me The World Ends*, by Nicole Perlroth.

And, of course, if you have any more questions, you can always ask Chatgpt…

Marc Sheinbaum grew up in Sheepshead Bay, Brooklyn. He set out to be a writer from a very young age, but like the characters in his stories, life doesn't always turn out as planned. Instead, Marc spent over thirty-five years in business, working for a variety of American companies. Now retired, he spends his time writing and serving on public and non-profit boards. He and his wife, Hildy, split their time between Westchester County and Westport.